*Hot
Showing
Supper
Tub*

Diamondz IN A
ROUGH

Diamondz in a Rough
life's no fairytale

❦ T M D ❦

TMD Publishing

ISBN 978-0-9835935-0-8 [perfect bound]

First printing 2011.

Acknowledgments

◇◇◇

*I*WOULD LIKE TO FIRST THANK GOD FOR *delivering me in my gift and revealing my purpose. Special thanks to my editor, Taifa Peaks. Thank you for all your help in making this novel the best that it can be. Much thanks goes to my wonderful artist, Douglas Draper Jr. I appreciate you bringing my vision to life. I have been blessed with many angels here on earth: Shanna Hughes, Belma Golden, Ivan Forney, Ronel Mcclain, Anthony Downer, Latonya Downer, Kyshia Harlee, Sharon Hill, Lorriane Miller, Carolyn Owens, Jennifer Bruce, Kyra Burman, Shaivonne Thompson, Candes Daniels, Shena Conroy, Angela Frierson, Kevin Howard, Amir Downer, Shetia Lee, Latora Hawkins, Omitayo, and for anyone who has ever supported my dream that I may have missed. Thank you! Last but not least, I would like to give special acknowledgement to anyone who has said that you can never accomplish your dreams. We can turn all negative things into positive things, if we just believe. We are all Diamondz In A Rough, with the ability to shine!*

~ *TMD*

IN LOVING MEMORY OF:
  —*Chanel Holmes*
  —*Jackie Mitchell*
  —*Felicia Carroll*

All Diamondz In A Rough gone too soon

Contents

◇◇

Chapter One: In the Beginning

<<<<<<<<<<<<<<<<<<<<<<<<<<<<<<<<<<<<<<<<<<<<<<<<<<<<<<<<>>>>>>>

RADIANCE LAY IN HER BED STARING AT THE ceiling, frustrated about her life and wondering to herself, *Why do bad things happen to good people?* As she lay there, she began to see shadows of herself on the walls from the flickering of the candles. Radiance was 16-years-old and already a free spirit. Her skin was a honey-toned complexion. She had the measurements of thirty-six, thirty, thirty-eight; her hair was sandy brown and shoulder length. She wore it in a straight wrap to frame a face that displayed one deep dimple on the right side of her cheek. Her smile was bright enough to light up the darkest room. Her eyes were hazel and if you looked deep inside them you could see that they were full of dreams.

Radiance was the middle child and had two other siblings, Walter and Miguel, from her mother. Her mother was a single parent who worked as a nurse's assistant. Radiance's mom often worked many long hours which caused Radiance to have to take care of her younger sibling, Walter. This did not leave her with much of a chance to be a teenager. She often had to play the role of a young mother. She even worked two jobs to support herself and contribute to her family's household. Radiance hated having to care for her brother because she could never hang out with her closest friends. But, she realized that sometimes in life you have to do what you have to do in order to keep peace in your home and survive.

Radiance made a promise to herself, as she drifted off to sleep, that when she came of age, she would leave and do whatever her heart desired.

It was a long day and she knew that morning would soon come. "RA-
DIANCE, RADIANCE, RADIANCE, WAKE UP! I SAID WAKE
UP!" As Radiance heard loud echoes, she slowly opened her eyes and
rubbed them profusely. "Girl! Do you have any idea what time it is? I
will tell you. It's 7:15 a.m. and your ass is not up yet! I have been working
all night long and your brother has not yet eaten his breakfast or gotten
himself ready for school. *And* neither have you! I suggest that you get
yourself and your brother together quickly, and don't forget to take out
the damn trash!"

"Mom! Where is Miguel? I hope he is in fucking skin."

"Quit asking questions about him and do as I say right now."

Radiance rolled her eyes up in her head and thought to herself, *I am
tired of this shit! I can't wait to turn eighteen and move the hell out of this
place*! Her mother walked out of the door and said, "Don't be rolling
your eyes at me, either."

Damn, how does she do that all of the time?

As Radiance walked into Walter's bedroom, she found him wide
awake playing his Playstation in his underwear. "Boy, get up! You know
you have to go to school! Besides, Mom is tripping again and quite frank-
ly, I don't want to hear it. It's way too early for that."

"Wait one second! I am about to go to the next round, boy!"

"That Mortal Kombat game ain't going nowhere!" she said, as she
leaned over to unplug the game system.

"Damn! Radiance, what did you do that for?"

"Come on, boy."

As Walter pouted, he began to get dressed.

"Don't forget to wash up and brush your teeth! Hurry up, your bus
will be here in twenty minutes."

"A'ight!" replied Walter.

As Radiance opened her closet door, she grabbed the first thing she
saw, a pair of fitted jeans and a pink shirt. She reached underneath her
bed to grab her sneakers. She placed her shoes on her feet and tied them.

Then, she stood up to look at herself in the mirror and combed out her hair. She began to think to herself, *I need a new look.*

As Radiance rushed downstairs and ran to the kitchen, she noticed her brother Miguel was sitting at the table eating what he called doughnuts that he fried from Pillsbury biscuit dough. He poured syrup on top (he often did things like that for Radiance and Walter) to cover up the fact that there was no food to eat. He was the oldest of the three. He was 6'4", one hundred and seventy pounds, with jet black hair and dark features. He was loved by many women. "What's up?" he asked, as he placed plates on the table with his creation of Pillsbury Doughnuts. Radiance then responded by saying "Good morning, Miguel!" He then instructed her to grab breakfast.

"No thanks! I'm running late and I still have to get Walter to the bus."

Walter ran downstairs and proceeded to the doughnuts.

"Aw man, these are my favorite!" Walter laughed, as he stood there. He was brown-skinned with dark hair and a beautiful smile. His eyes were the color of chestnuts.

"Grab it to go, were late."

"Okay," Walter replied.

"Where is mom?"

"Upstairs with Thomas's sorry ass. Let's go, Walter. See you later on, Miguel."

As Radiance walked Walter to the bus stop, she started to wonder what it was going to be like in school today. She was beefing with a girl name Jewel over a dude that she wasn't even talking to, but Jewel assumed that she was. As Radiance walked, she heard her name being called. As she turned around, she saw Constance.

"Hey, C, what's good?"

"Nothing much," Constance said, laughing. "I heard your moms earlier yelling at Miguel about taking the trash out."

"Damn! I forgot to take it out. You know her ass is going to trip as soon as I get home."

Constance just chuckled. Radiance then asked, "You walking with me to school?"

"No, girl, I have to go and meet Damon. His ass is home alone. He lied to his mother and said that he was sick. So I have to go and meet him, so we can get it in."

"Girl, your ass is crazy. Your mom is going to go ballistic when she finds out!"

"She has to catch me first! I will call you later," she said as she walked away swiftly, waving her hand. Radiance walked away shaking her head. She then began to think to herself, realizing that it was already 8:15 a.m. *I am running late as hell.* She started to pick up her pace. It wasn't easy carrying heavy-ass bags weighing at least twenty pounds! Radiance entered the school just before the bell rang. *Nice!* she thought to herself. *Today might be an okay day!* As she walked to homeroom, she began looking down at the tan tiles. She then began to pick up her head slowly, looking over to the right. She saw that the clock was showing that it was already 8:35 a.m. *Damn! Ms. Dooley is going to trip.*

As she entered the classroom, Ms. Dooley felt the need to welcome her, "Nice to see you made it, RADIANCE."

"Yeah, whatever!"

"Aren't we quite spicy today, Radiance?"

"Ms. Dooley, I'm really not in the best mood today. Please, just let me be."

As everyone stared at her, she sat down. The only nice thing about homeroom was Jermaine, with his sexy ass. He was the pretty-ass thug that all of the women lusted over. He was about 5' 10", one hundred ninety-five pounds, all solid muscle. He was active in all sports, so his physique was always tight. He stayed in the flyest shit--Polo, Gucci, Prada, Louis. Anything you named, that nigga had it. He walked with confidence and knew that he was the shit!

As Constance walked in Damon's house, she heard New Edition playing on the radio. She began to think to herself, *This muthafucka is in for a treat!* He lay down in the bed, butt-ass naked, with his black, 10-inch dick slinging just a little to the left. Constance began to think to herself, *This man looks delicious to me.* As she was humming to the music, she started taking her clothes off, giving Damon a strip tease act.

"Is that all for me, baby?" Damon asked in a seductive voice.

"Everything that I do is all for you, sweetheart," replied a very smiling Constance. Damon loved the way that Constance made him feel. He thought that she was beautiful inside and out. He had been with many women, but there was something about Constance that was different. He lied to Constance and told her that he was a virgin. He wanted her to take full control the first time they made love. He promised himself that he would one day tell her the truth, but no time soon.

As he watched Constance undress, he found himself wanting her more and more. He loved the fact that she wasn't a petite lady. He loved a large woman. Constance was a perfect size 20 with hair to the middle of her back. Her skin was the color of cinnamon and even though she was larger than the average woman, she was still very well proportioned. She crawled towards Damon, while stopping at every part of his body to explore it with her tongue. His dick began to expand and Constance then asked, "Are you that happy to see me?" All Damon could do was shake his head, nodding "yes." He was totally and completely speechless. Constance then replied, "I know this is your first time, but Momma is going to be real careful with you," with a devilish grin on her face.

As the clock struck 12 p.m., everyone proceeded to the lunch room. Radiance went to sit at the bench by herself. She did that often since lunch was her time of peace and quiet. She always considered herself to be a loner and kept herself very isolated. Her circle of friends was slim and she did not trust many folks. As she sat down, she began to giggle to herself wondering what kind of foolishness Constance's crazy ass was up to. She then heard a voice from behind her. "Excuse me, is anybody sitting here?" As she looked up, she realized that it was Jermaine's sexy ass. Radiance began to think to herself, *Is this happening right now?*

"No, please, by all means take a seat."

"Listen, Radiance. I have been checking you out for a while now and I like what I see. I was just wondering if you were feeling me too."

"You are okay, I guess," she replied with the biggest smile on her face. Jermaine just laughed and licked his lips. Radiance often wondered what they would feel like. They appeared to be as soft as satin and as moist as her pussy was at that very moment. Jermaine didn't have to do much to turn her on. He had unusual thug appeal and even the way he walked turned her on.

"So Radiance, is it possible for me to take you out and get to know you a little better?"

"Well, J, anything is possible. What did you have in mind?"

"Maybe we can check out a movie or something."

"Okay!" Radiance did not wait one minute to accept the invitation.

"So, can I get the digits so that I can hit you up later?"

Radiance paused when he asked her for her number. She thought to herself, *No way is this possible.* Her mom was strict as hell and there was no way she was going to have any nigga calling her phone. She then thought that she had to think fast! "Um, I am sorry, J, but I don't have a phone. Is it possible that you can give me yours and I will hit you up later from my homegirl's house?"

"Sure, it's 410-555-1111. We are going to have to fix that situation and get you a cell phone."

As he walked away, he winked his eye at Radiance and told her to call him later. As she waved goodbye to him, she smiled and thought to herself, *This day is turning out to be okay after all!* As she turned around and saw Jewel walking in her direction, she stated "DAMN! I spoke too soon!"

"There you go again, trying to talk to somebody else's man."

"Listen, Jewel, it's been a long day and I'm not in the mood for this shit! Besides, Jermaine is single and available. I don't even know which dude of yours that you think that I am interested in, but I can assure you that I am not. As a matter of fact, I don't even know who he is."

"Oh, BITCH! You know who he is."

"Oh, HELL NO! You must have lost your mind. I ain't nobody's bitch. I suggest that you walk the fuck away before I floor your ass."

Jewel then knocked Radiance's lunch tray on the floor and swung at her, missing her face by only a centimeter.

"OH, NO THIS BITCH DIDN'T!" Radiance rose out of her seat and banged Jewel straight in the face, causing her to hit the lunch table. Then, Jewel began swinging in a circular motion. Radiance grabbed her keys on the bench and began to hit her in the face continuously with them. The other students then began to yell "fight" in the background. As the students watched, the janitor, Mr. White broke up the fight, but not before Radiance pulled out Jewel's extensions that she wore in her ponytail. After the fight was broken up, Radiance thought, *This day couldn't possibly get any worse.* She knew that her mother was going to kill her. As the girls were escorted to the principal's office by Mr. White, they just looked at each other with evil glares in their eyes.

Ms. Roscoe then entered the room and asked the ladies to close the door to the office.

She then thanked Mr. White for bringing the ladies to the office. "Well girls, you have a lot of explaining to do." Ms. Roscoe was a very attractive slender woman. She was mixed with Spanish and black. She wore her hair in a neat bun and had one tantalizing curl that often dangled in front of her glasses that were placed on the tip of her nose. She stayed in the latest designer clothes and on this particular day she chose to wear an all-black Chanel suit that gave her a look of sophistication. The skirt was a pencil skirt with a bow just below her ass. Even though Ms. Roscoe was very slender, she still had a nice shape that often caused men to stare at her every time she walked by. Her fragrance was a very light scent, kind of like a lily flower on a bright summer's day. "Radiance, why are you in my office yet again? This is the second time this week." Radiance had gotten into trouble earlier in the week for smacking her classmate, Justin, for touching her ass.

"I..."

Ms. Roscoe immediately interrupted to say, "I'm tired of this and I don't want to hear it. I see that you brought company this time. Jewel, explain yourself."

"Well, Ms. Roscoe, I was sitting..."

Ms. Roscoe interrupted again and said, "Just save it! I really am not prepared to sit here and listen to this right now. You are a straight-A student with the potential to be anything that you want to be and you choose to jeopardize that over foolishness. Your mom serves on the PTA committee. This is unacceptable for a young lady of your caliber. I will have to talk to your mom and send you to detention this afternoon. You are dismissed for now."

As Ms. Roscoe reached below, looking through the files in her cabinet, Jewel walked off and whispered to Radiance, "Bitch! This is far from over." She blew a kiss at her and stormed out of the door.

"I've got it," Ms. Roscoe replied, as she placed Radiance's file on the table. "Radiance, looking at your file, you have been suspended three times this year for fighting. Consider this your very last warning. Such behavior will not be tolerated here. I will need to meet with your mother in the morning. I will have to call to confirm this."

Oh, shit ! Radiance thought to herself. *I have to beat Miguel home to answer the phone this evening, but I have detention this evening right in homeroom!*

"Radiance, you are dismissed. You..."

"Yeah, I know, Ms. Roscoe. I have detention this afternoon in homeroom." Ms. Roscoe then responded, "Never cut an adult off when she's speaking."

"Yes, Ms. Roscoe."

As Constance finished washing and putting her clothes on, she gently ran her hands through her hair, fixing the strands that stood straight up on her head. Damon was still fast asleep in bed. Constance had to head home before her mom, Pauline, arrived. She went home every day to catch 'As the World Turns' on her lunch break. Constance was a part of a work-study program at school. She was a year older than Radiance and had enough credits to graduate early. Constance was a great student when she applied herself. She worked as a shampoo technician through work-study and she was an intern in the cosmetology program offered at the school. She would be a licensed beautician after she took her state board exam.

As Constance tip-toed down the stairs quietly, she began to think about how displeased she was with Damon's sexual performance. She remembered that it was his first time and was looking forward to teaching him how to please a woman. She thought to herself, *This nigga might need a manual.* Constance was way more experienced. She had lost her virginity at the age of twelve and she was raped by her stepfather on more than one occasion. She tried to block it from her mind, as it was a very painful memory. When she went to her mother about it, she called her a lying bitch, a home-wrecker, and a Jezebel, so Constance kept it to herself. The only other person who knew was Radiance.

Radiance often tried to get Constance to seek counseling, but Constance just ignored her comments and maintained a nonchalant attitude. *Besides,* she thought to herself, *it had been many years since it happened.* The last time was about four years ago when Constance's mom was working overnight. She had just finished taking a shower and was sitting on her bed putting lotion on her body. Her stepfather busted in her room drunk and forced himself upon her. She tried to fight him off but he was way too strong. She screamed, kicked, and cried for help, but no one could hear her. All that she could do was wait until he reached his climax. In trying to defend herself, all she managed to do was apply scratches to his face. He eventually stopped and went to his room. She cried on the bed until she fell asleep.

The following day, she woke up traumatized about what happened the night before. She then went to Damon asking him for his "six shooter." Constance told him that she needed it for protection for when she worked long hours in the hair salon and had to walk home alone. Damon adored Constance and was often overprotective when it came to her, so he agreed and gave it to her. He had no idea what she had planned in her head or what she went through the night before. As Constance retrieved the gun, she rushed home and went into the living room. She saw her stepfather sitting on the couch. She then pointed the gun straight at his head and called his name with tears pouring down her face. She told him that if he ever touched her again, she would kill him and that he would never touch anyone else.

Constance snapped back to reality after hearing the sirens of police cars riding down Damon's street. As she left Damon's house, she gently closed his door. While walking home, she noticed Eric on the other side. She waved at him as he rode by in his cherry red Navigator. Eric lived directly across the street from Constance and Radiance. She instantly thought of Radiance because she had the biggest crush on Eric. Constance for the life of her never understood why! All she knew was that whenever Radiance saw Eric, she had the biggest smile on her face. She had once told Constance that she felt butterflies in her stomach whenever he came around and Constance thought that it was the silliest thing ever. As Constance walked up the stairs, she began to search in her purse for the keys. She carried large purses, therefore it was easy to lose things in them. As she walked in the house and proceeded to the kitchen, she stopped at the refrigerator to get something cold to drink. It was ninety degrees outside and she had to cool off. She was exhausted from the events that had taken place earlier in the day.

Radiance hated the fact that she had detention and she sat at her desk creating spit balls and throwing them at the ceiling when Ms. Dooley wasn't looking. She was the only one in detention and she impatiently watched the clock as it showed exactly 3:45 p.m. Ms. Dooley sat at the desk, tapping her pen on the shelf used for her folders. She looked at her watch and said, "Radiance, you are dismissed."

"Damn, I thought this day would never end," she whispered to herself.

She raced home trying to beat Miguel to answer the phone before Ms. Roscoe had a chance to call her house. She had to meet Walter at the bus stop and she was already thirty minutes late. As she looked straight ahead, she saw Walter standing on the corner of the bus stop. As she called his name, he turned around. She smacked him on his head and started to run. Walter began to chase her as he screamed, "I'm going to get you!" They lived two blocks away so it wouldn't be long before they would make it home. Radiance was nervous and hoped that Ms. Roscoe hadn't called yet. Radiance slowed down and Walter continued to run. He suddenly passed his sister, but not before reaching out and hitting her, laughing the whole time. Radiance slowly climbed the six steps to her house and was glad to see Walter opening the door with the key on a shoestring tied around his neck. He opened the door slowly. *Great, nobody's here*, thought Radiance. *Let me go in the room and check the answering machine and wait for the phone call.* As she looked at the answering machine, she noticed that there were no messages. Less than ten minutes passed and the phone rang. She nervously picked up the phone.

"Hello..."

"Bitch! What are you doing?" Radiance felt relieved when she heard Constance on the other end.

"Girl, it's good to hear your voice!"

"Why, what's wrong with you?"

"Girl, me and that bitch Jewel got into a fight today."

"What in the hell happened?"

"Well, you know that she was tripping about me talking to some dude named, Howard. I don't even know who the hell that is!" Suddenly a beep interrupted.

"Shit, C, that's the school on the Caller ID, hold on. Armstrong's residence," she said in a professional voice.

"Is Ms. Armstrong available?"

"This is she, how can I help you?"

"Ms. Armstrong, this is Ms. Roscoe. I'm calling about your daughter, Radiance. She is quite the star pupil and she really does do well when she applies herself, but lately I have noticed a change in her behavior. She got into a fist fight with another student today and it was quite disturbing. This is her third altercation this school year and this type of behavior will not be tolerated in this school."

"I understand. Was my child just trying to defend herself, possibly?"

"I'm not sure, but it can't happen again. I would like to see you in the morning; otherwise Radiance will not be permitted on the school grounds."

"I understand that just fine. I will be there in the morning."

Shit, I really fucked up, Radiance thought to herself. She clicked over.

"Girl, that was Ms Roscoe. I had to act like my mother. She told me that I will not be accepted back on school grounds until she brings me back."

"Shit! Girl, what are you going to do?!" yelled Constance.

"I don't know. I'm thinking now."

There were three minutes of silence on the phone. "I got it!" Constance yelled. "Come over right now before Miguel gets home and bring some cash."

"Cash? Girl, what do I need money for?"

"Bitch, just trust me. Stop being tight with your money. I know you have some."

"Only the money from tips from the diner I worked last week."

"Well, bring your ass. You are wasting time talking to me on this phone."

Radiance jumped off her bed and told Walter to complete his homework. She told him that she had to go next door for a second and for him not to touch anything. As she ran outside, Constance was already on the porch of her house walking downstairs heading towards Radiance.

"Okay, Constance, what did you come up with?"

"We are going to get Lisa to take you to school..."

"Enough with the jokes, C, this is serious..."

"I'm serious, Radiance. We can get Lisa to take you back to school."

"What are you talking about, Constance?"

"You heard me. We are going to have Lisa take you back to school in the morning."

Lisa was a dopehead who lived about a block from where Radiance and Constance resided. She often walked the streets as a lady of the night, offering herself to various men in exchange for money. Although Lisa was a dopehead, she didn't appear that way. She still managed to keep up her appearance. She wore some of the baddest knock-offs that money could buy.

"Let's go, I saw her earlier at Joe's sub shop."

"Constance, Walter is in the house alone and I can't leave him there."

"Girl, come on, we will be right back."

"Shit, I certainly hope so. We have to be as quick as possible."

Constance and Radiance headed up the street. They couldn't help but notice Eric sitting down on the porch of his home across the street talking to his friends, all local thugs from the neighborhood. Radiance's mind traveled to another place as she looked across the street and saw Eric. He was fine! 5' 10", his skin was light and he was very easy on the eyes. Neither one of them really knew anything about the other, but you could still see that they were both curious about one another. Their eyes only met in passing and he first introduced himself when Radiance and her family moved into the neighborhood two years ago. Constance kept talking, but Radiance heard nothing as she looked across the street. She began to enter a fantasy world, wondering would it would be like to kiss Eric's lips and be embraced by his strong arms, followed by being lead to his bedroom; being thrown on his bed and slowly having him undress her using nothing but his teeth. She was envisioning him behind her and biting her perfectly round ass while taking his tongue and licking the crack of her ass in circular motions. Then, being instructed to lie down and spread her legs apart as he visited her tropical place. Licking and nibbling at her clit, the taste as sweet as butterscotch.

"RADIANCE, RADIANCE! Bitch, do you hear me talking to you?"

"I'm sorry, Constance, what did you say?"

"Girl, are you walking while daydreaming again? What, are you thinking about that nigga, Eric, again?" I don't see why you won't just give him some pussy. It's about time you let somebody break your ass in, anyway. Sixteen and still a virgin ain't cool. Hell, I commend you. Anyway, as I was saying, there is Lisa."

"Constance, how do you suppose this will work?"

"Give me the money and leave it to me. Stay right here."

Constance headed across the street to where Lisa was. She had just gotten dropped back off at the corner of the sub shop. As she stepped out of the black car and went back to the corner waiting on her next customer, Constance yelled out, "LISA!"

Lisa turned her head, looking around to see who called out her name. She noticed that it was Constance.

"Hey, diva," said Lisa, "this is no place for a young lady." Although Lisa was a drug user and slept with various men for money, she displayed a very nurturing spirit and often tried to keep the young women from the neighborhood informed about what was out there in the streets. She feared what could happen to them at such a young age. She remembered being young and full of dreams that never came true. She was in college studying fashion and had dreams of becoming a big-time designer in the industry, but never fulfilled them. She met a brother in college and fell in love. He exposed her to money and all things that were considered fabulous. They traveled to exotic places and he gave her whatever her heart desired. He also gave her drugs for the first time and that one experience gave her such a feeling of escape from reality that it was impossible in her mind to never travel there again.

"Lisa, I need you to do a major favor for my friend Radiance. She got in a bit of trouble in school today and needs to go back tomorrow. She is not allowed back on the premises until she is escorted back. I need you to take her back for me."

"Constance, I don't think that is something that I should be involved in. Your friend should go to her mother with this. I can't do it."

"You don't understand, her mother is going to overreact. Besides, we can compensate you."

"I don't know about that, sugar."

"Come on, Lisa. I will make it worth your while." Constance then pulled out five crisp twenty dollar bills. She thought to herself, *I hope this works.* She couldn't let her girl go out like that. Besides, if Radiance's mother ever found out about the fight, it would be ugly and she might not see her friend for a very long time.

"Well... okay Constance, I will do it," Lisa replied, as she extended her hand out for the money.

"Not so fast, Lisa. I will give you fifty now and you will get the other half in the morning when you meet Radiance in front of the bus stop, okay?"

"Constance, just remember that money talks and bullshit walks."

"Don't worry, I got you, Lisa. Just wear something nice in the morning. Maybe a skirt or dress, or something."

Constance handed her the money and walked away quickly. Radiance was standing at the same corner where Constance left her and she was shaking nervously.

"Girl, stop shaking like you got a serious nervous condition!" laughed Constance. "I told you that I had you. Lisa will meet you in the morning."

" Thank, God!" Radiance screamed out as loud as she could. "Shit! C you came through once again. I have to get my ass home. Walter's in the house alone and has been for forty-five minutes."

"Let's go. We can take the shortcut through the alley. We can be there in like ten minutes."

As Radiance and Constance rushed through the alley trying to get back home to Walter, they both heard their names being called and neither knew which direction it was coming from. They turned all around and then they both looked straight ahead and noticed their girlfriend from the neighborhood, Unique. It was so surprising seeing her. She moved away last year to go and live with her father.

"Radiance and Constance, is it really you two? Oh, shit!" She ran towards them and then opened her arms to hug them at the same time. They all screamed out together, "It has been too long since we seen each other!"

Constance then asked Unique, "What the hell are you doing back here, girl?"

"I went to ATL to stay with pops but his fiancée and I didn't see eye-to-eye on things. We were doing fine until her ass came around acting like she was running shit! We got into a fight and I kicked her ass," laughed Unique, "so she pressed charges against me. To prevent me from going to jail, my father thought it would be better sending me back here with my grandmother. I missed you bitches, though. What's been good in the hood since I have been away?"

"Girl, way too much," Radiance replied. "My moms is still crazy as hell and Constance has just been herself as always."

"How are your brothers?" Unique asked.

"They're good. Shit, girl, speaking about my brothers, I have to get back home to Walter right now as we speak. Give C your number. I will call you later."

As Unique wrote her number down for Constance, Radiance ran off fast. She didn't want to look at her watch. She already knew she was late as hell.

"Here, C, make sure you call me."

"Don't worry. I will hit you up later." Constance then yelled out Radiance's name, telling her to wait up. "Stop running, you know my ass is too big to catch up with you."

"Well, try to," screamed Radiance, almost halfway up the street. As they finally got home, they couldn't help but notice the local neighborhood thugs running in and out of Radiance's house.

"What the fuck is going on in there?" Constance asked.

"I don't know, let's find out."

As they walked in the house, they noticed Miguel and his friends going in different areas of the house.

"What the fuck is this?" Radiance asked Miguel.

"Don't worry about what the fuck is going on in here. Where the hell did you go for the past hour, leaving Walter alone in this house? I told you about that shit, Radiance. I'm going to talk to you later about that bullshit!"

"Yeah, whatever, Miguel," she said as she looked at him and rolled her eyes. She couldn't help but notice the passion marks on his neck, appearing to be as bright as candy red apples.

Constance came from behind her and told her about the girls that were in Miguel's room. She described them as beastly and as dark as midnight. She said that they looked related, maybe sisters or something. One was at least two hundred and fifty pounds and the other was petite and had a face resembling what death should look like.

"Girl, you also have a bitch in your room with like six niggas waiting in line to stick their dicks in her. The other strays are in Miguel's room."

"What the hell do you mean, they're in my room? Oh, hell no!" Radiance rushed back to her bedroom to find the door locked and she heard nothing but moans coming from her room through the door. She immediately began knocking and banging at the door, just to get no answer. She went across the hall to Walter's room to find him playing Mortal Kombat with two dudes that she had never seen before. She then started yelling at the two of them, "Who the hell are you and what the fuck are you doing in my brother's room?"

"Bitch! What the fuck does it look like? We are playing the game, obviously, now leave us the fuck alone. Bitch!"

"Oh, I got your bitch!"

The closet door suddenly flew open and she reached for the metal bat in the closet. She walked over to them and began swinging the bat around, hitting one and trying to hit the friend that was with him. The two men both stood up like they were ready to attack her like two vicious dogs. Walter then paused his game, went under his mattress, and pulled out a sharp pocket knife. He told both of the males, "If you touch my sister, I will kill you both, just try me." The two men just looked at each other and said, "This little nigga got heart!" Radiance couldn't seem to get any words out, her mouth just dropped wide open.

"Lil' man, we don't want any trouble, we are leaving now." They respected the fact that Walter was so young, but was ready to go to war like a little soldier. Radiance finally managed to get her words together after being so shocked, you would have thought she had seen a ghost.

"Where in the hell did you get that knife?"

"I got it from school, don't trip."

"Give it to me right now," she demanded. "Why would you need this?"

"It's for protection."

"Give it to me, right now. I never want to see you with this ever, do you understand?"

Walter said nothing

"I asked you a question. Do you understand me?"

"Okay, I hear you."

"Good, where is the cordless?"

"It's on the bed."

She picked up the phone and called her mother. The phone just continued to ring. She thought, *It is so typical for her not to pick up the phone. I'm tired of this shit.* The phone rang five minutes later and Radiance answered it. It was her mother on the other end.

"What the hell did you call me for? This better be a fucking emergency. You know that I'm out with Thomas, trying to enjoy myself and take a break from you all plucking my fucking nerves."

Thomas was one of her mother's many boyfriends over the past few years. She made poor choices when it came to men. Radiance and her siblings all had different fathers, which sometimes reflected in their personalities. Thomas was the latest love interest. He stayed in and out of prison for credit card scams and petty thefts. He positioned himself as a playboy and everything about him was fake. There were rumors around the neighborhood that he was getting high.

"Mom I'm sorry to bother you, but there are at least twenty people in your house indulging in Lord knows what. I'm locked out of my room right now and Miguel's room is locked, too. You might want to get home."

"Where is Miguel?"

"I don't know. I believe he has locked himself in the room."

"I'm on my way home. If you know what's good for you, it would be wise to clear those muthafuckers out of my house before I arrive there."

"Why me? I didn't bring these people in the house."

"I don't care, but you better damn well get those bastards out before I kick your ass when I get there."

Radiance slammed the phone down.

"I hate this shit so much. It's always something crazy going on in this house. I need to get out of here before I lose it."

Constance appeared in Walter's doorway. "I see you called your mom dukes."

"Yeah, I did. She is yelling at me like this is my shit!"

"What the fuck did you expect coming from your mother? You know she is crazy."

"She told me to get everyone out before she arrives."

"GOOD LUCK with that shit!" Constance stated before she walked away.

"Where the fuck are you going, C?"

"I'm getting out of here before Crazy gets home."

"Help me get these people out of here, C, before you go."

"Girl, you are on your own! I came through once for you today already. I'm done."

"Real nice, C, real nice."

"Yeah, I know, boo. Love you and good luck. I will call you later."

The dumbest shit always happens to me, Radiance thought to herself. "Walter, stay in this room and lock the door. Don't let anyone in here!" She stomped out the room.

After running through the hallway, she ran in the living room, turned down the radio and yelled from the top of her lungs. "Get the fuck out of here now! My mom is on her way home!" Everyone continued doing what they were doing. Radiance then stood on the couch.

"I don't think everyone heard me. My mom is on her way home, so get the FUCK out!" She instantly gained the attention of many this time and individuals started flying out of both the front and back door entrances. Everyone scattered like roaches when the lights turned on. The phone then rang and it was Constance on the other end. She was calling from her porch, laughing as she watched individuals run from all directions leaving Radiance's house.

"Girl, I just saw your mother pull up," she chuckled, "and she doesn't look happy."

"That's just great, just fucking great. Thanks, C."

Radiance heard the door slam and she knew right away who it was. She heard her mouth before she saw her.

"What the fuck is going on in here? Where is Miguel? He is still in the room? We will just see about that," as she walked back yelling and clearing out the hallways of the few remaining people still there. It was easy because most had already cleared base. She finally reached Miguel's room to find the door opened with both females there in awkward positions. One of the girls was on a chair positioned in a doggie style she had learned. One of the thugs in the neighborhood was inside her, smacking her big black ass and she appeared to love it. Her breasts were exposed, jiggling as loose as jelly. They bounced up and down. Her sister was on the opposite side of her in missionary style. Her legs were gapped as if she was participating in a Pilates class and there was a line of men standing behind each other, waiting impatiently for their chance to enter her pussy.

It was there that Radiance's mom found Miguel, completely exposed.

"Miguel, what the fuck is going on?" She told everyone, "Get the fuck out of here!" as she waved the broom, pointing it at everyone, threatening to hit everyone with it. "Miguel, what do you think that we are running here, a whorehouse? You don't pay any bills here, therefore you don't run this shit. I do. That means no sexcapade games take place here. Look at you! Pull your pants up, with your dick slinging everywhere. Have some fucking class, sticking your dick in these dirty-ass little girls. Keep it up and they are going to land your ass straight in the hospital. Get these bitches dressed and out of my fucking house before I whip their ass!'

"What respectable woman allows multiple men to hump on them all at one time?"

"You are tripping woman, I am a grown-ass man."

"Well, if you're a grown man, then get the fuck out of my house and get your own. How do you feel about that? Exactly what I thought. Put some clothes on and get those sluts out of here. This is the last time that I will repeat myself. Radiance, what the fuck do you have going on here?

I don't have time to deal with this shit. You should be on top of your game!"

"How am I supposed to do that?"

"By watching over this house and by watching your tone when speaking to me. The next time I'm going to smack your ass. Just do and listen to what I say. Go in, check on Walter, and get ready for school. Make sure you change your sheets and clean up your room with disinfecting spray. Lord knows what has been in your bed."

Radiance hesitantly walked up the stairs and made her way to Walter's room. "Turn off the television and take a shower. Make sure you lay your clothes out."

"Okay, I' m going to do it now," Walter replied.

Radiance then went in her room and closed the door. She heard her mother and Miguel argue back and forth about what had just taken place. Her mother yelled upstairs, "Radiance, I'm going to drop these girls off to their parents and then I will be right back. Call me when Miguel gets back." She slammed the door and left out.

"Okay," Radiance replied to the silence. She then thought, *Finally some peace and quiet.* She knocked on the bathroom door. "Walter, after you get out of the shower, go to bed."

She went to her room and dived in her bed, landing on her book bag. She took the time to think about all that had happened throughout the day and was glad that it was ending. "This day has been crazy," she said to herself, "way too much going on for one person." She then remembered taking Jermaine's phone number and debated calling him. She decided against it at first, and then she thought, *Why not call him after all the dumb things that have taken place today?* She needed to smile about something and who was best to do the job other than Jermaine? She reached for the phone, took a deep breath, and went into her notebook. She got the number, blocked her number out, and dialed the phone. It rang three times before a deep voice answered the phone. "Hello, is Jermaine available?"

"This is he."

"Hey, J, it's Radiance. What are you doing?"

"I was sitting here waiting for your sexy ass to call." Actually, she could hear the laughter on the other end.

"Yeah, right, Negro. You were not waiting on me."

"Okay, maybe you're right," he chuckled. I just got finished taking a shower and now I'm laid out across my bed."

"You might want to put some clothes on, J, you may catch a draft."

"I enjoy being naked," Jermaine responded. "If I catch a draft, will you come over and keep me warm?"

Radiance was mute on the other end. Her pussy became wet instantly and you would have thought she just had an orgasm. She envisioned Jermaine naked and wondered what size his unit was. She thought about his bulging muscles and his eight-pack abs. His voice was soothing on the other end.

"So, Radiance, I asked you a question. Would you keep me warm if I caught a draft?"

"I just might."

"Suddenly I'm freezing. Why don't you come and keep me warm?"

"Don't worry, I will in due time, trust me."

"That sounds promising to me," Jermaine replied. "So when can I take you out, beautiful? I told you that I was feeling you and have been for some time now. So can we go out Saturday?"

"I am digging on you a little, J, so yes, we can go out. It has to be when I get off around four. What do you have in mind?"

"Let me surprise you. Don't worry, I got you," he replied.

"Okay, J, I'm going to let you make the call. Don't let me down," she then smiled on the other end of the phone. "I have to go now, Jermaine, I have a long day ahead of me."

"Okay, beautiful, it was good hearing your voice again. It really made my evening."

"The feeling is mutual."

As she hung up the phone, she continued to smile from ear to ear. She was really feeling Jermaine and had been for a couple of years, but she didn't want to show that. "No girl should appear to be pressed" was her motto. Now, *how in the hell was she going to pull it off?* was the question. Her mom was beyond strict and made her responsibilities her child's, especially when it came to raising Walter. There was no way in Sam's hell that she was going to miss the opportunity to go out with Jermaine. Radiance began to think to herself, "I have dreamed of this. Something is going to have to give." She then started to strategize a plan to make this date with Jermaine a reality, and she went back and forth in her head about how she was going to go on this date successfully. She heard the door slam and saw that it was Miguel coming inside. He had boxes and trash bags in his hands. Radiance went downstairs.

"What's up with all of the boxes and trash bags, Miguel?"

"Not right now!" Miguel yelled. "I'm trying to gather a few items. I have to go away for a while. Don't worry, I will be back soon. I have to make some moves and stack up on some paper."

"Where are you going?"

"What's up with the interrogation? It's not important where I'm going, just make sure that you look out for Walter. He needs you to be there for him; he loves you."

"Okay, Miguel, you are sounding like this is the last time that we are going to see you or something. You're starting to concern me. Do you mind telling me what the hell is going on?"

"Girl, you better watch your damn mouth and respect me. You are always cracking slick out of your mouth."

Miguel then continued to pack his bags which became filled up and his arms became full. He then said, "I will be back later for the rest of my things. Hold shit down in here while I'm away. Tell Walter I love him!"

He then began walking to the front door.

"Wait, Miguel, you still have not told me where the hell you are going!" She followed behind him, but he just ignored her and continued to walk out of the door. Radiance noticed a vehicle sitting outside and a lady that she had never seen before.

What the hell was going on, and why was Miguel taking all of his things? And who the hell was this woman?

Radiance continued to yell Miguel's name from the doorway. He didn't even look back once he entered the vehicle, and she watched them pull off. She closed the door and began shaking her head. "This shit is way too confusing to me," she whispered to herself as she closed the door and proceeded to go to the living room. She sat down on the couch and lay back. She turned on the radio and began to listen to her slow jams mix CD. This was a good way to relieve stress. She noticed her composition book on the table and began reading through it. Each page took her to another place in her life. The book was full of memories from her past. It was her personal journal for poetry. Radiance had a lot of painful memories, so when she wrote, it was therapy for her. As she picked up a pen and paper and began to write, she remembered speaking with Jermaine earlier in the evening and then remembered daydreaming about him coming to her rescue. As she started writing and thinking, the first thing that came to her was:

I'm sitting here waiting for you to rescue me. Waiting for you to help me! Live out all my fantasies. Alone waiting and desiring your touch. Wanting to feel the softness of your lips and the compassion of your kiss. Rescue me! As your face is implanted in my mind, the very thought of your smile melts my heart. Rescue me! Protect me from all danger, surround me with your love. Let's travel to a land where all dreams come true. Your touch is so reassuring. Rescue me! From all of the evil that exists in the real world, become my knight in shining armor. Allow me to be rescued. You're my prince coming to claim his princess. Rescue me! Hold me in your arms tightly making me feel secure in your arms. I am waiting, willing, and able. Rescue me! Show me how to become a prayer warrior. You're a God-fearing man, enlighten me in the spiritual world. Rescue me! Keep me motivated and remind me that there is no other for you. Rescue me! Protect me from living in a world that has no morals. Rescue me! Take me to a place where the sun always shines, but rain storms still make cameo appearances. Rescue me! Take me to a place where flowers always blossom and trees sway in the wind. Rescue me! I'm waiting on you to make your appearance. Embrace me with all of the love that you had stored away for so long. I need you right now. I feel that you are near. Rescue me! Let's travel to far places and explore new and exciting things together, ready to conquer the world. I have been waiting on you for so long. Hear my cries, Rescue me! Where are you? I am beginning to worry, but faith still exists in my heart. I know that you are coming, so until then, I'm waiting patiently. Remember that I'm willing, able and capable of being rescued. Rescue me! Rescue me, hear my request. I will be waiting.

As Radiance closed her eyes after writing in her journal, she really prayed that someone would come and rescue her from the life that she was living. Everything was in complete chaos and now Miguel was gone. She hugged the pillow on the couch tightly. While still keeping her eyes closed, she began praying that God would reveal some answers soon. No way was she able to continue living this way.

Chapter Two: After the Storm

◇◇

*I*T WAS LIGHT OUT BEFORE RADIANCE REAL-
ized that she had dozed off on the couch. She was awakened by
the sun that was beaming on the back of her neck. The journal was still in
her hand. Although she was awake physically, her mind, body, and spirit
were still exhausted. Radiance had to gather her thoughts and started to
get herself and Walter together, so that they could proceed with the day.
Radiance dropped Walter off at the bus stop as she usually did and to
her surprise, up at the corner stood Lisa waiting for her. Lisa was dressed
conservatively. Her hair was pulled back in a ponytail, light makeup was
applied to her face, the suit that she was wearing was navy blue, and she
had a pair of black pumps on. She looked amazing.

"Lisa, you clean up well!"

"Do I really, baby?" Lisa giggled. "Sugar plum, I try."

"I was worried that you wouldn't show up."

"Honey, I try to keep my word because your word is all that you got
sometimes. I was taught at a young age if you don't have your word, you
have nothing. I must admit, young lady, I don't agree with the way that
you are doing this, but I understand. However, I want you to know something and please don't judge me for it...I am not exactly the person that
can lead by example. Your character and image are everything, especially
in being a woman. There are certain expectations that you should require
from yourself like: demand respect, always realize your self-worth, and
never feel like you're unable to reach your goals and achieve your dreams.

Remember, baby, to think with your mind and don't always give in to your emotions. Keep your friends close and your enemies even closer, and most importantly, remember that even through all the darkness you still have the ability to shine. Even in some of the dullest, most tainted rocks lay a few diamonds in the rough with the ability to shine. You just have to polish them up and handle them with care."

Radiance just listened and told Lisa that she understood. She was in no mood to be lectured and didn't want to be disrespectful. Lisa then made another comment and said, "If you don't remember anything else in life I ever said, please remember that," as they walked inside of the school and headed to Ms. Roscoe's office.

Radiance instantly became nervous. Lisa glanced over and told her, "Don't be nervous, sugar. I'm going to get this all taken care of." Lisa then tugged her skirt down, brushed her hair back, and applied gloss to her lips. She took a seat on the chair and demanded Radiance do the same. For a moment there was complete silence. Five minutes passed and suddenly they heard the sound of stiletto heels as Lisa turned around and saw Ms. Roscoe walk in.

"Morning, ladies, I'm glad that you could make it in today. Ms. Armstrong, the reason that I invited you in today is because I have some concerns when it comes to your daughter. She has been in three fights just this year alone, not to mention the altercations with her teachers. Please advise me why this is happening. Are you having problems at home?"

"Ms. Roscoe, I can assure you everything is fine at home. I have taught my child to stand up for herself in the event that she ever needed to. Have you ever taken the time out to ask what happened?"

"Well of course I have." Ms. Roscoe took her glasses off and placed them on her desk. "The bottom line is, I will not tolerate disrespect in this learning establishment, especially when it comes to disrespecting my faculty members. The next time that it happens, Radiance will be expelled, no questions asked."

"I will deal with my daughter, don't worry about that. As for your staff, please don't have them talk to my child in any kind of way. She has a parent and that's me. Please remind them of that. As for the young lady she was fighting, please make it known to her parents that if their child attempts to lay any hands on Radiance, that proper measures will take place."

"Will do, Ms. Armstrong. I will meet with Jewel's parents. Also, there are no favorites here, but please don't take anything that I say lightly. As your daughter is concerned, the next time she gets into trouble, she *will* be expelled. I will allow Radiance back into school today, but I need to know if you understand what was just said."

"Yes, Ms. Roscoe, I understand just fine. Thanks for allowing me to come back to school," Radiance responded.

"Well, okay honey, let's go walk you back to class," Lisa said as they walked out of the office and into the hallway heading towards the main entrance door. Radiance responded, "Damn! Lisa, you had that mother thing down pat. I was starting to believe that you really were a parent! Thanks so much! I'm going to have to remember that for next time in case I have to dust you off and use you again."

"Next time, Radiance? You clearly have to be mistaken. There can never be a next time," Lisa replied. "Did you hear what Ms. Roscoe was saying in there? If you get into trouble again, you will be expelled no questions asked. Don't fuck up your life. Look at me, I'm what a fuck-up looks like. Do you want to end up like me?"

Radiance just looked at her with a blank stare.

"Exactly. I know you don't want to be like me. You're so much smarter than that, but baby, if you keep playing with fire you will eventually get burned and princess you're way too precious to end up burned all up," Lisa said smiling. She then looked at her and said, "I only want the best for you, sugar." She then extended her arms and gave her the biggest hug ever. "I have to go, baby girl." Lisa then walked away slowly and looked at Radiance. "Now dear, go on and get to class, and learn something for me.

I don't know what it is about you but you have an unusual shine today, just like a gem; a princess-cut diamond to be exact!" Lisa winked at Radiance and left out the school's main entry door.

Radiance waved goodbye. "What the hell was that long lecture all about? I'm so tired of muthafuckers! Thinking that they know what's best for me and my future. Lisa is a crackhead for Christ's sake." Radiance thought out loud. "I can't wait to get away from this fucking neighborhood and get my own shit!" As she walked towards her locker and began to open it, she suddenly heard the sound of a very deep voice on the other side of her locker door.

"Glad that you made it back, baby! I have missed your sexy ass."

As Radiance closed the locker door, she noticed that it was Jermaine. He looked like a tasty treat, as she looked at his black label tee shirt and how it complimented his bulging muscles.

"Damn! Baby, you look great," Jermaine responded, while biting his lower lip. "Come show me some love, Radiance. I know it has only been a day, but it seems like it was a year." As he extended his arms and hugged her, Radiance started to become nervous and completely turned on all at the same time. Her heart began to race and her pussy became moist as he let her go. Radiance had to catch her breath and suddenly she felt speechless.

"So, baby, are you ready for Saturday?"

"Well, yes I am. I hope you made some good plans for us."

"Don't worry, sexy, I told you that I got you." He then smiled, showing his sparkling white teeth.

Damn, he's fine, Radiance thought as she leaned on her locker.

"Well, sexy, I can't wait." He then started to get closer and extended his arm blocking Radiance from moving. He took his other hand and moved her hair from her face to behind her ear. He began whispering in her ear, "Do I make you nervous when I do this?" As Radiance's eyes closed and she began breathing heavy, Jermaine kissed her on the side of her neck gently, and started to nibble on her ear. He then started to take his hand and rub in between her inner thighs. He could feel the moistness of her pussy through her black stretch pants. He then pulled her close and tilted her head back while sticking his tongue down her throat. Radiance could feel the hardness of his dick in between her legs. Although she had never experienced what it was like to have a dick inside of her, she felt as though she was ready at this very moment. The bell then rang, and Radiance and Jermaine suddenly remembered where they were.

"Let's slow down."

"Baby there is much more excitement to come on Saturday," Jermaine replied. "Until then!" He kissed her on the forehead and took a second to get himself together and walked away. Radiance had to take time to get her mind right.

"What the hell just happened here?" She was confused and her pussy was wet as her liquids poured down on the side of her leg. "Damn, I have to go home and get myself together," she said, as he headed to the door.

As she walked, she had visions of what had just happened and was totally and completely at a loss for words. *What is it about Jermaine that has me so attracted to him? Everything about him is so amazing. Even the way that he smells puts me in a trance.* As she got home, she rushed upstairs to the shower to cool down. As she undressed, she started to touch on herself, first starting off with grabbing her breast and then taking her fingers and inserting them in her pussy. As she finger-popped herself, she imagined that it was Jermaine's dick inside her, throbbing in and out of her.

She envisioned him pulling her hair and then having him pick her up in the shower with her back against the wall, as he placed his mouth on her breasts sucking them as if his life depended on it. As she moaned over and over again, her eyes began to travel behind her head. As she held her arms around his neck trying to assist him in holding her, her grip became stronger and he pumped harder and harder, bringing tears of joy to her eyes. The water was pouring on his back, making him shine all over. He was also becoming too slippery to hold on to and she then instructed him to put her down. He continued to fuck her while putting her down slowly. She then got down on her knees with water still pouring in her face. She grabbed his dick and inserted it into her mouth, sucking his dick as if it was a blow pop and she was trying to get to the gum under the tasty, hard surface. He then opened his mouth, roaring as if he were a lion in a jungle. As the cum squirted in her face, she caught the remains with her tongue. Banging then started at the bathroom door and yelling followed: "Open up this door, girl. I have to use the bathroom." It was Walter.

"Okay, give me a minute. I have to dry off." She removed her fingers from her pussy and held her hand underneath the shower head to wash them. She gently turned the knob to turn the water off and grabbed a towel to dry off. She reached for her robe, placed it on, and left the bathroom.

"It's about time, girl. What where you doing in there? I have been trying to use the bathroom for a half hour. Mom's downstairs and she wants you to come down. Maybe you should get dressed first."

"Okay, I will be down in a minute." After she got dressed, she traveled downstairs to see what her mother wanted. She found her in the living room. "Mom, you wanted me?"

"Sit down, girl, and let me talk to you for a while, okay?"

"Are you okay? You never want to talk."

"I can assure you that I am fine."

"Have you heard from Miguel?"

"No, I haven't. He did not mention where he was traveling to when he left. He left with a girl that I never seen before."

"Well, let me know if you hear from him. I'm a little concerned about him. I have to go. Thomas is waiting on me."

"Mom, why do you waste so much time with this man? He is a loser."

"Excuse me, little girl. What do you know about life, much less love? You have so much to learn about life and all that it has to offer."

"I may not know much, but I know that you don't spend enough time with your kids and that Thomas is a jerk!"

"Watch your damn tone when you're talking to me."

"I'm sorry."

"That's more like it."

"What does he have over you that keeps you running back to him? I noticed the marks on you. Is he hitting you?"

"Stay in a child's place and out of grown folks' business. Things will make sense to you later on in life."

"Will they really? I'm not going to have any man mistreating me that's for sure."

"Never say never. You will be surprised; shit happens."

"Well it's not going to happen to me."

"I will be here waiting on you when it does. Go tend to your brother. I'm out of here, see you later."

As her mom walked out of the door, Radiance had an epiphany. *I'm tired of everybody having so many demands on me and expecting shit from me. From this day on, I am going to do what the hell I want to do, when I feel like doing it.* As she watched her mother leave, Radiance went into the kitchen, out the back door, and to Constance's house. She started ringing the bell...

"Damn, who the hell is ringing my bell like this?" Constance lifted up the shades and saw who it was. "Bitch, have you lost your fucking mind ringing on my bell like that?"

"C, just open the door."

"What the hell has got you so hyped up?"

"I just decided that from now on, I am going to take control of my life and do as I wish. I'm turning seventeen in a month."

"Exactly! Radiance you are just turning seventeen not eighteen, so you have to stay focused until then. Just be mindful of that."

"Bitch, please! I can still do what I want."

"Well I hope you getting some dick in that plan," Constance laughed. "Where is your brother?"

"Oh, he's in his room, sleeping."

"Put some fucking clothes on. It's Friday and everybody's missing in action, so let's go to that party Damon was talking about."

"My moms is not coming home tonight."

"Bitch, you not saying nothing but a word."

Radiance replied, "Let me call Unique's ass back and see if she is trying to go."

"I know that Destiny said that she was going to go."

" Destiny. Now that's a name that I haven't heard in a while. She's been missing in action for a little minute now. Where the hell has she been?"

"She thought she was in love with that nigga Steven and realized he wasn't shit. Now she is back on the scene."

"Well, it's about got damn time! Let me go home and get dressed. C, I will meet you back over here in about thirty minutes."

As Radiance left out of the door and traveled home, she went upstairs and went in her room. She put on a Beyoncé CD and began rambling in her closet. *Now what should I wear*, she thought to herself. *Damn! I have nothing to put on.* As she danced to the music, she looked in her drawers and still found nothing. *When in doubt, always go for the little black dress,* she thought to herself as she went to the closet and grabbed her dress. She put it on and began admiring how it showed off all of her curves in all the right places. *Bingo, I think I found a winner!* She then grabbed her accessories, put them on, combed her hair down, and went to the closet and grabbed her strappy shoes. *I think I'm ready.* She tip-toed out of her room and went across the hall. She cracked the door to Walter's room to find him fast asleep. She turned around, went back in her room, and locked the door. She went out of her window and ran over to Constance's house. As she opened the entrance door to Constance's house, she walked straight back to the living room to find Constance walking out of the bathroom with her leggings, white collared shirt, and some multi-colored pumps. Her hair was bouncy and appeared to be as light as a feather.

"Damn! Bitch, that's how you feel!"

Constance jumped. "Girl, don't yell like that. You scared me."

"Where the hell are you going looking like that?"

"Shit, girl," Constance replied, "you know Damon is going to be there, therefore I have to be on top of my game. Let me get my purse and we can head out of here and go and pick up Unique and Destiny."

"Now how do you suggest we do that? The cab is going to be expensive enough, C, with just you and me in it."

"Oh, I forgot to mention that we are not going to catch a cab."

"Well how do you suggest we get there? Is Damon taking us?"

"No, lady, I'm going to drive."

"Wait a second now, drive... what car are you plan on driving?"

"I'm going to drive my mom's car. You know she is down South until Sunday."

"Constance, you don't even have a license."

"Girl, relax! Did anyone ever tell you that you talk too much and ask way too many questions? I have a permit. That is just as good as a license. Let's go."

Radiance just looked at her and shook her head. "I don't know about this shit, C, but you are my girl, therefore I'm going to roll with you." She then began to pray to herself, "Lord, please look after us tonight. We are going to need it." As they left out of the door and got into the car, they turned the music up and pulled off.

"Let's get it!" Constance yelled out loud. "I gotta feeling that tonight is going to be a good night, chick, let's make the most of it. As they pulled up to Unique's house, they started to beep the horn.

"Damn, what's taking them so long?

"C, relax. It's only 9:30."

"I know what time it is. I'm trying to get there before 10:30. It's free before 11:00 p.m. for ladies and I don't plan on paying extra."

Radiance just laughed. "Girl, you are as crazy as it gets, but I feel you. I'm not trying to pay either." She then reached over and honked the horn again. They then saw Unique and Destiny walk out in their short, fitted dresses.

"I know you all better stop honking the horn like the police. I have neighbors," Unique said, while chewing and popping gum.

"Girl, get your ass in the car and let's get to this club before 11:00. I don't plan on paying to get in tonight," said Constance.

Destiny just laughed at Unique.

"Where the hell have you been?" Constance and Radiance yelled at the same time.

"Hey girls, I have just been laying low and taking it easy with Steven's no-good ass. I'm back, though.

"Well, you look great," Radiance replied.

"Well, you look good too, girl, but why is your face not made up? I'm going to have to beat your face up right quick. Let me get my makeup bag out of my purse."

"That's okay, Destiny, I'm good, really I am.

"Umm, no you're not. There is going to be money in this place and you might luck up and meet a baller. I'm trying to school your ass on what's really good. Now sit in this backseat and let me do your eyes."

"Whatever, Destiny. I'm going to let you do your thing," Radiance responded. "Just go on and make me beautiful. That shouldn't take long, I'm already stunning." She began to giggle. Destiny just looked at her, shook her head, and began laughing as she started doing her makeup. Constance pulled off while Unique was in the passenger seat.

"Man, it's too quiet in here," Constance said out loud. She reached over, turned on the radio, pressed play on the CD player, and pumped up the volume. "Oh man, this is my shit! I'm rapping in my Lauryn Hill voice. 'It's funny how money change a situation; miscommunication leads to complication.'" She danced in the car, moving her head. All of the girls started singing, "You might win some, but just lost one." Everyone started laughing.

"What do you know about this 'Miseducation of Lauryn Hill' CD, bitch!"

"Only that it is a classic," Destiny replied. "Girl, Lauryn helped me get through some things with her CD. I appreciate it."

Radiance responded, "Girl, you haven't been through anything."

Destiny interrupted, "You really have no idea. One day I will tell you a story that is real and based on facts."

"Well, I can't wait to hear about it," Radiance said, as she turned around in the seat and smiled at Destiny.

"You girls are too funny," Unique responded, while laughing with a stream of tears running down her eyes. "I can't take you crazy bitches."

"Constance, you are going like eighty on this highway. You need to slow down before the police stop your no-having-a-license ass," Radiance yelled from the backseat.

Constance responded, "Girl, I got this. I told your scared ass that already. I hate a backseat driver. Sometimes it's best just to remain silent, damn!"

"Enough of that shit," Destiny said. "Isn't that the exit that we need to take?"

"It damn sure is," Constance said. "Let me get over and off at this exit before I pass it. As they got off at the exit, they noticed the large crowd.

"This must be the spot. What's the address again?" Unique asked.

"This is it, lady, Club Envy. See, there is the sign right there." Constance then pointed at the flashing neon lights. "Let me find a parking space. . .there's a space right in front. Today is our lucky day." Constance said, "Let's go inside and get our party on. I need to go to the restroom to touch up my hair and makeup. I have to be fly. Damon is up in here and I have to represent him well. You know he has groupies and shit! I still just don't understand how regular niggas have groupies. Hell, his ass don't even play a sport."

"I hear that shit," Destiny replied, as they walked in the line.

Constance reached in her purse, pulled out fake ID's, and handed them to her girls quickly.

"What the fuck? Where did you?"

"Don't start your shit, Radiance," Constance quickly interrupted, not giving Radiance the opportunity to finish talking. "Don't ask questions, just smile, and be cute. Ask questions at the end of the night."

The bouncer checked their ID's and he granted entrance to all of the girls. As they walked in, the music was blasting and all eyes were on them.

"Damn! I hate it when women stare and roll their eyes," Unique commented.

"Well, honey, if they didn't look, you would have no indication on how fabulous you truly are," Destiny responded. "Now walk this hall as if you were on the runway, simply smile, and give them a wink."

"Lord, you two need Jesus," Radiance responded.

"Girl, please, I'm telling you some good shit!"

"Tell her again, Destiny. I have been trying to teach her that for a very long time now, but everything goes in one ear and out the other. It's just pointless," said Constance.

"Hello! Constance, I am right here.

"You know I'm aware that you're here. Radiance, maybe this time you will listen." Constance just blew a kiss at Radiance, laughed, and went into the restroom.

"These bathrooms are nasty as hell," Radiance said. "I don't know how anyone could use them unless they were getting ready to piss on themselves."

"You can say that again," a lady said, while reaching for some paper towels. "My name is Virtue. What are your names, ladies?"

"I'm Radiance, that one there is Constance, that's Destiny, and the one that just walked in is my girl, Unique."

"Well, it's nice to meet you divas. I'm new to the area. I just moved down here from New York and I don't know anyone outside of my brother."

"Well, welcome," Destiny replied, "but why would you come here from New York, honey? It's such a great place."

"Well, my mom passed last month and my brother just got a job out here, so we decided to pick up and start all over again."

"Damn! Virtue, I'm sorry to hear that," Unique responded.

'Thanks," Virtue replied, "but she lived a good life and it was time for her to leave this place. She suffered from cancer long enough."

Constance just looked over at her and turned back to grab her purse. "Well, ladies, I'm all done in here. Let's roll." She looked at Virtue and rolled her eyes.

"Well, it was such a pleasure meeting you," all the girls responded in unity, with the exception of Constance.

"Maybe I will see you around," Radiance responded as she opened the door and walked out.

"I hope so," Virtue said, as the ladies left the bathroom and walked around the club to feel out the atmosphere.

Radiance asked Constance, "Why were you so rude to Virtue?"

"Girl, please," Constance responded. "I don't do bitches and she strikes me as the type of woman that is not capable of being trusted."

"C, how can you determine that in a matter of ten minutes?"

"Sometimes you just know."

"I guess," Radiance responded, with attitude in her voice.

Unique interrupted, "Isn't that your boy, Damon, over there in VIP, Constance? And who is that lady that he is all on like that? They seem real familiar with one another."

"I don't know, but I'm about to damn sure find out." Constance stomped over to VIP, only to be stopped by the bouncer guarding the area. "Excuse me, sir, but I need to get in there," Constance responded.

"I'm sorry, miss, but you have to have a band on in order to get in here."

"I don't think you understand, sir. I'm not requesting that I get in there. I am telling you that I am. My man is right there and I need to speak with him."

"I'm sorry, miss, but I can't let you in here and that is what I am telling *you*. If you keep it up, I will have you escorted out of this club."

"Man, fuck you!" Constance said, as she turned around and stomped away.

"Honey, fix your face. It's not very becoming of you," Destiny responded, as she walked over to Constance. "Stay right here and I will be right back." Destiny switched over to the bouncer while every nigga she passed had his eyes on her. She walked over to the bouncer, smiled at him, and began talking to him. "Hey, sexy, are you working hard or hardly working?"

The bouncer just looked at Destiny and immediately drew his attention to her breasts. As he looked up he said, "I am hardly working at the moment, precious."

"Well, I was just admiring you from afar and you are quite strikingly handsome." A smile appeared on the bouncer's face.

"So you do smile sometimes?" Destiny asked.

"Sure I do, if there is something to smile about."

"Are you telling me that I make you smile, sir?"

"Maybe I am," the bouncer responded. "How are you on this evening, fair lady?"

"I'm doing just fine, but my feet are killing me. There's nowhere for me and my friends to sit and catch our breath for a second.

"How many are there including you, Miss Lady?"

"There are only four of us."

"Well, go get them and I will let you guys sit in VIP."

"You would do that for little ole me, sexy?" Destiny asked.

"Sure I will. You made me smile tonight."

"Well, okay, let me go and get them."

As she walked over to get her friends, the bouncer just smiled at her ass. "Come on, ladies," Destiny yelled out, as she found them in the center of the floor getting their dance on. No one heard her. She then tapped them on the shoulders and told them to come on. As they walked back over to the bouncer, he let everyone in VIP with the exception of Constance. "Oh! No, miss. You're the disrespectful one from earlier."

This is some shit! Constance thought to herself. Destiny stopped in her tracks and saw that he was not going to let Constance in. She went back to the steps and to the bouncer, pouted, and asked him to let her friend up. "Pretty please?"

The bouncer still refused as Constance stood at the bottom of the steps at a complete stop and her hands folded in front of her chest. Destiny leaned over to the bouncer, whispered something in his ear, and he lit up like a Christmas tree. He let Constance in VIP. "Thank me later," Destiny said.

"What the hell did you say to that man?" Constance asked.

"Do you really want to know?" Destiny asked.

"On second thought, um, I don't want to know," Constance responded, smiling from ear to ear.

"Look at your boy over there, acting the fuck out. Who is that trick he is talking to? She looks a hot damn mess!"

"Destiny, I told you that he is a regular dude with groupies. I still don't get it. Let me go over there and break that shit up!"

Destiny responded, "Do your thing, boo, I'm not mad at you," as Constance walked through the crowd and straight to Damon.

"Hey, baby! Did you miss me?"

"Oh, shit! Constance, hey, baby. I didn't see you make your way up here."

"I can clearly see that you were too occupied with this trick."

The girl with Damon just looked Constance up and down. "Damon, you betta get your little girlfriend before I bust her ass."

Constance responded, "There is no need for any of that, boo, she was just leaving."

As the girl got up and walked away, Damon and Constance began arguing.

"Why is it that every time I leave you alone, some bitch randomly appears in your face?"

"Baby! I don't have the answer to that question. What I can tell you is that I love you and there is no other woman for me, so stop acting like that." As Damon kissed Constance on the forehead and pulled her close to him, she began to blush.

Radiance, Unique, and Destiny just looked over and start laughing.

"That nigga got more game than Michael Jordan," Radiance commented. "I wish Constance could see that. I don't want her to get hurt."

"Radiance, sometimes it's best to keep your comments to yourself," Unique responded, "especially when it comes to matters of the heart. It's okay to want the best for your friends, but sometimes in life people have to go through things in order to learn from their mistakes. Trust me, I know."

"Well, I guess you're right, Unique, but it would be good to get out of something before it causes hurt and pain."

"You girls are getting too deep over here, we should be partying," Destiny said. "So can we get a drink and let Constance handle her own business over there?" She grabbed their hands, began pulling them downstairs, and started walking to the bar. Destiny ordered two Rum and Cokes and a cranberry juice with vodka.

As the bartender handed the girls the drinks, they went over to the dance floor and began dancing and watching everyone party. "Man, it's so hot in here. I know my hair is no more," Radiance commented. "I'm glad I came, but I'm going to go and stand over here, you two. I'm tired and my feet hurt."

"Girl, you complain like an old woman," Destiny responded, laughing.

"Yeah, yeah, yeah," Radiance responded, as she headed towards the wall. As Radiance leaned against the wall and began trying to find creative ways to rest her feet, the sound of women's voices began to rise in the background. When she lifted up her head, she noticed three ladies standing in front of her. It appeared to be a circle. As Radiance began to move, the ladies blocked her. "Excuse me, ladies, I'm trying to move."

"Oh! Honey, I can see that, but I'm afraid that I will not allow you to pass through," one of the ladies responded.

"Excuse me, miss, but I need for you to understand that I'm not requesting that you move, but I am telling you that I am moving," Radiance responded. "Now for the last time, excuse me." Radiance then attempted to walk away and immediately the three ladies blocked her in. Out of the crowd, from what appeared to be nowhere, another woman dressed in all black came around. As she got close, Radiance noticed that it was Jewel.

"Oh! It's my old friend, Radiance. *Fancy* meeting you here, bitch! I told you that the shit between us was far from over."

" Look, Jewel, once again I am not for your shit! So on that note, I'm leaving or would you prefer that I fuck you up once again in front of your little girlfriends?"

"Oh, see boo, I think you've got the game fucked up because I'm fixing to whip your ass up in this place and my little girlfriends are going to assist me in doing so," Jewel replied and followed up by pushing Radiance up against the wall. As Radiance swung and hit Jewel in her face, one of her friends came from behind Radiance and grabbed her arms, while the other lady came from the side and swung and hit Radiance in her rib cage. Jewel then came towards Radiance and began swinging for her face. Radiance just picked up her leg and kicked Jewel in her stomach, while still being hit on her other side over and over again by Jewel's other girlfriend. Destiny looked over to the wall to check on Radiance. From the dance floor she noticed that there was a fight going on and realized that it was Radiance who was getting banked.

"Oh shit, Unique, that's Radiance!" She then started running through the crowd, pushing every one out of the way. As she got to the wall where Radiance was getting attacked, she pulled the lady off of her who was holding her from behind, and started swinging punches at her. Unique then went to jump in between Jewel and Radiance, trying to break up the fight; when Jewel's other girlfriend came from the side and stole Unique in her jaw. As the music stopped and the security started running, Constance stopped talking to Damon and began adjusting her clothes. "What is going on around here?"

"Baby, I have to go and find where my girls are. It is way too much going on here."

As Constance stood up, she reached over, gave Damon a kiss on the cheek, and exited the VIP area; only to see her girlfriends being carried out by bouncers and the other girls being escorted out the back door. Another woman was stretched out on the nasty club floor. It appeared that liquor had been thrown on her from the looks of her clothing and face. *I always miss all of the fun*, Constance giggled to herself as she walked to the parking lot. She saw her girlfriends standing next to the car.

"Can someone please explain what just occurred here?" Constance asked." Radiance, girl, your dress is torn up and you have scratches all on your face. Are you okay?"

"Girl, I'm fine. That bitch is worse off, though," she responded back to Constance.

"Who did this to you, girl?

"Jewel and her little friends were here and tried to bank me, girl, that's all. Don't sweat it though, Constance."

"We busted their asses," Destiny and Unique both interrupted.

"This has been one hell of a night," Radiance replied.

"Oh, no, Radiance we can go and find those bitches and put one last smash down on them one last time."

"Constance, it's really okay. I will see that bitch again and when I do it will be on and cracking."

"Are you sure, Radiance? You know a bitch like me loves a good fight," Constance replied.

"Girl, we know that already, but we straight for the moment."

"Man, what a night," Destiny said. "I must admit that in spite of everything, I still had the time of my life. It's been a long time since I had the pleasure of whipping a bitch's ass. I must admit, I still got it."

"Spoken like a real crazy person," Unique responded.

"I'm just saying," Destiny responded back.

"So, Radiance, what's the beef with you and Jewel anyway?" Unique asked.

"Girl, she thinks that me and her boyfriend have something going on. The thing that is so crazy is that I don't even know who the fool is," Radiance laughed

"And you all call me crazy," Destiny commented. "Jewel seems like she is the one with some real issues."

"You girls are all crazy. I can never take you out without you all acting out," said Constance.

"Whatever, Constance," Radiance responded, "you are the one who always acts out, C, everyone knows that."

"I beg to differ, Radiance," Constance immediately responded. "I'm not the one sitting here with the torn clothing and scratches on my face. You're such a troublemaker," Constance smiled at Radiance.

"Whatever, C. You always have something to say about everything."

"Will you two quit it," Destiny responded. "Constance, you need to focus on the road." As the girls argued back and forth, Constance continued to drive faster. "I'm just ready to go home and go to bed, so let me get everyone there as quickly as possible. I'm way too tipsy to deal with this shit right now!"

"Constance, why don't you pull over at the next exit and I will make sure that I get everyone home safely. I will just stay over at your house tonight," Destiny responded.

"You know what, Destiny, that is exactly what I'm going to do. Let me pull over right now before we get on the beltway."

As Constance pulled over and switched seats with Destiny, she got in the passenger seat and went to sleep instantly. Not long after that, Destiny looked in her rearview mirror and noticed that Radiance and Unique were asleep as well. As she continued to drive, she got on the beltway and switched stations. She drove and listened to the music, as she cruised the beltway. She noticed that she was getting sleepy and began opening the windows and turning up the music. Soon she realized that her eyes were getting heavy and before she knew it, she dozed off to sleep for a second. She woke up instantly, as soon as she noticed that she was swerving into the opposite lane.

As she rolled down the windows trying to get herself together, she heard sirens and noticed the flashing lights in back of her. *Shit! It's the police.* She started calling out the girls' names as loud as she could and no one responded. Everyone was in a deep sleep. *This is just fucking great!* As she pulled over, she noticed the officer get out of the car. He walked over and she noticed that he was not your average cop. He had the body of a god. His skin complexion was the color of roasted almonds and his arms were defined like a sculpture's. As he walked over to the car, he requested to see Destiny's driver license and registration. He then smiled at her as she handed him her license. She noticed that his teeth were as white as snow. The officer then began talking to Destiny. "Miss, the reason why I'm pulling you over is because your brake light is out."

"Oh, really officer? I didn't realize that it was out. I will get it fixed first thing in the morning."

"You also have a tire in the back that is going flat and you will not get very far with it like that. You have to put a spare on it right away."

"That would explain why the wheel has been shaking so badly," Destiny responded. " Well, if you give me a minute to go in the back of the trunk, I can grab a spare. Could you please assist me in putting it on, Mr. Officer?"

"Sure I can," the officer responded. "I'm always willing to help a lovely lady."

As Destiny opened the door and walked to the back of the trunk to get the spare tire, the officer couldn't keep his eyes off her perfectly round ass and her long slender legs. He found himself lusting over Destiny as he watched her bend over trying to reach in the trunk to grab the spare tire. As she bent over, her dress began to rise higher and higher. He then realized that Destiny had no underwear on. He noticed that she was just as free as it got. As he looked at her, he tried to turn his head, but soon noticed that his eyes kept moving back towards her. As he stared, his penis began to grow inside of his uniform pants.

"I think I got it," Destiny yelled out. "Officer, can you please help me?" The officer was puzzled for just a moment. "Yes, certainly," he responded, as he tried to adjust his dick inside of his pants, hoping that Destiny would not turn around and notice. As he walked over towards the car and picked up the spare tire, Destiny noticed his bulging muscles in his arms. He lifted up the spare tire and began walking over to the back tire well.

"Are you okay, young lady?" the officer asked Destiny.

"Well, yes I am, Officer. I was just noticing what nice arms you have. Looks like you can carry weight pretty easy in that case."

The officer then chuckled and responded, "Well, yes I can. No disrespect, young lady, but it seems like you're curious to find out."

"Well, what if I told you that I was and I wanted to test your guns out, Officer? Would that be a problem?" Destiny responded. The officer then dropped the last lug nut and then picked it up quickly. He began to place it on the wheel quickly.

"So, Mr. Officer, I take it that you are the strong, silent type."

"Well, I'm not silent at all, actually," the officer responded back.

"So if that's the case, please answer this one thing for me..." She then walked closer to the officer, closed the trunk, and hiked up her skirt revealing her pussy to the officer. "...if I unbuttoned your uniform pants and pulled them down, placing my pussy on your stiff dick, would you lock me up for assault with a deadly weapon?"

Destiny then noticed that the officer's dick expanded in his pants and he was completely speechless. She then leaned over towards him, putting her breasts right in front of his face. As she grabbed his hand and he stood up, they began walking towards the patrol car.

"It's always been a fantasy of mine to fuck in the back of a police car. I want you help me live out my fantasy."

The officer then responded, "It would be my pleasure."

"So you do speak," Destiny replied, as she smirked at him and he opened up the back of the police car. As Destiny crawled in the back seat, the officer followed, but not before smacking her ass. He continued by lifting up her dress and then kissing her ass.

"Ouch, Daddy! You better watch it, I like that freaky shit!"

"You have no idea how much I do, but you will soon find out."

As they entered the car, she reached over and unbuttoned the officer's pants followed by unzipping them. She pulled out his dick which was as hard as steel. She then inserted it into her mouth, sucking it as if her life depended on it. The officer grabbed her head, forcing her to put his dick further and further in her mouth. He began to moan very loudly and he started biting his lower lip. Destiny was sucking his dick and the officer noticed that her hair was getting in the way. He then began to grab it as she continued. She stopped and came up to catch some air, but not before she climbed on top of him and grabbed his dick, inserting it inside of her wet pussy. The moans then turned into screams. "Oh shit! Your pussy is the fucking best! I love the way that it feels on my dick!"

He then removed her breasts from her dress and began squeezing them both together. While allowing his tongue to travel over and explore each one of them, he then grabbed her right breast and began sucking it as if it was sweet honey. Destiny then began to moan and her body began to shake as he sucked her breasts and continued to grab her waist, forcing her to take every inch of his dick inside her walls. "Take this dick, girl.

You asked for it, so I am giving you all of it. No need to scream, take this shit!" He then lifted her up, turned her around on the back of the seat, and reinserted his dick back inside of her. He then began humping on her as hard as he could, while she continued to moan and scream, "Give me that dick, baby! I love it," cheering him on as he kissed her on her shoulder. His moans became louder as he yelled out loud, "I'm ready to cum!" Destiny then yelled, "Cum for me, baby!" She then felt a sudden burst in the inside of her. As he climaxed, it felt like a volcano that just erupted.

As they both climbed to opposite seats to catch their breath, they started to fix their clothing. They started laughing at the same time, "Now *that* was a good damn time."

"Thanks for a great time, Officer. I got to live out my fantasy and I owe that all to you. But I must get going. I have three very sleepy friends in the back seat and it is already 4 a.m. So, would this be a good time to ask for my license, registration, and repair order, sir?" The officer then reached in his pocket to hand her the license and registration.

"Don't worry about the repair order, pretty lady, or should I say, Destiny. Just get the brake light fixed as soon as possible." As he glanced at the license before handing it to her he asked, "Is this a valid address for you?"

"No, it isn't, officer. I have moved since then."

"So, Miss Destiny, how can I reach you? Do you have a number for me?"

"I do have a number, but I will not give it to you at this present time." She then grabbed her license and registration from him, as she exited the door that was left wide open during their sex session.

"So it's like that, Miss Destiny? I have no address or phone number to contact you," the officer laughed. "So how will I find you again?"

She then replied, "If I'm a part of your destiny, we will see each other again." She licked her lips, ran to the car, and pulled off. As Destiny drove off in the car, grinning to herself about what just took place with Mr. Officer, she suddenly heard the sound of Constance's voice coming from the passenger seat. "Damn! Girl, we are not home yet? I could have sworn that when I dozed off to sleep a while ago, I was in this exact same location. Was I, or is this liquor getting to me?"

" Girl! Just blame it on the liquor," Destiny responded, laughing the whole time. "No, but seriously, we were here and we caught a flat and the officer had to assist me in putting the spare on."

"Damn! Where was I when all of this was going on?"

"C, you were right there where you are sitting, in a damn coma. Radiance and Unique's asses were in the back seat knocked the hell out. You three shouldn't drink if you can't handle your damn liquor. Really, it's a crying shame."

"Whatever, Destiny. I'm not in the mood for your shit at 4:30 in the damn morning," Constance replied, rolling her eyes and smiling.

Destiny just replied, "Let me get us home. I am dumb tired and I need a good night's sleep. It has been a long night."

"Girl, you telling me," Constance answered back. "But before you get home, could you please fix your dress? Your tit is halfway out your top. What kind of mess is that?"

"Oh shit, C, let me take care of that immediately!" Destiny just burst out laughing.

"From the looks of it, Destiny, it seems like you are the one who had a wild evening."

"C, you have no idea."

"I'm confused. Do you need to tell me something? Destiny, you have that devious look in your eyes."

"No, girl, there's nothing to tell. Nothing at all.

"Why is it that I don't believe you at all, honey?" Constance just shook her head and they drove for ten minutes. They finally pulled up to Constance's house.

"Girl, let's get these drunk ones from the car and get into your crib. I'm crashing here for a few hours. I'm beyond exhausted."

"That sounds like a pretty good damn plan," Constance replied. "Now how are we going to get these drunk bitches up? Look at Radiance's drunk-ass mouth all open. We should stick some paper in it or something," Constance giggled as she was talking to Destiny.

"Girl, you are so silly; maybe next time. I'm more interested in getting them inside quickly and lying across your couch. Radiance, Unique, get your drunk asses up. We're home," Destiny yelled from the top of her lungs. Neither one of them responded. "C, hand me that cup in front, in the cup holder. It still has ice in it." As Constance handed Destiny the cup, she then asked Destiny, "Are you getting ready to do what I think you're about to do?"

"Oh yeah, you know it. Without a doubt." She reached inside of the cup and grabbed some ice and put it in the back of Radiance's dress.

"Oh shit! What the fuck?" Radiance jumped up, screaming while kicking Unique in the back and waking her up, too.

"Mission accomplished," Destiny laughed, while standing outside of the car, looking at Radiance with her arms folded. "It's time to go inside and catch some sleep. It's late and I'm tired," Destiny and Constance both responded at the same time.

"I'm with you on that note," Unique replied. "Radiance, girl, you kicked me in my back and now it hurts pretty bad. You lucky I love you, little girl, that's some shit to fight about," Unique started laughing to herself.

Radiance responded, "Girl you would win, too. My head is pounding and I can't take this shit!"

"Next time you will think before you have that big-girl drink," Destiny said to Radiance.

"Girl, I only had some cranberry juice."

"Oh, yeah. I have been meaning to tell you about that. It was some Grey Goose in that, boo. Sorry for that, girly!"

"Oh, no you didn't! You know that you're wrong for that one, Destiny. I would expect that from Constance but not you," Radiance smiled at the girls.

"Now that's some bull," Constance interrupted, while opening up the door to her house. "Why do I have to be the one that is always the bad one? I'm a perfect angel."

"We all better move out of the way before Constance is hit by lightning," Unique commented.

"You all are on some stuff," Constance laughed, while running inside of the house.

"The first one to the bedroom gets the bed. The rest will get the couch and floor."

"Oh, hell no!" everyone responded, while running up the hallway.

Chapter Three: The Morning After

◇◇◇

AS THE MORNING CAME AND THE SMELL OF smoke filled the air, the fire detector beeped on and on. "What the hell is going on here?" Destiny said, as she got off the couch and started stretching. As she walked in the kitchen, she found Radiance, Unique, and Constance in the kitchen trying to prepare pancakes and sausage for breakfast. "You know, for future reference, you all should leave a memo when you all get together and decide to prepare a meal. None of you can cook. Where are the cereal and milk? And for Christ's sake, please open a window. As a matter of fact, open all of the windows," Destiny laughed.

"Well, Miss Destiny, let me be the first to let you know that I am an excellent cook. The best chef that ever lived," Radiance said.

"Negro, please!" Constance responded to Radiance. "Your ass can't even make toast."

"Girl, please, you're just a hater!" Radiance responded back, laughing. Unique just shook her head and asked Destiny to pass the cereal and milk over. They all sat down and decided to go with the cereal and milk option.

"Girls, I want to let you know that I truly appreciate your friendship and I'm so blessed to have such great girlfriends."

"Where did that random thought come from?" Radiance interrupted Unique's comment. "You are so deep early in the morning. Too deep for me," Radiance said smiling. "On that note, I have to get ready to leave and go home to check on Walter." She stood up, picked up her bowl, and walked it to the sink.

Constance began speaking to Radiance, "You better get that ass home before your mother comes home."

Destiny then asked, "Is your mother still on that crazy shit? It's been going on for way too long. I don't understand it for the life of me."

"Well, Destiny, it is what it is. Somebody has to look after Walter, he's just a kid," Radiance responded, while picking up her shoes and walking towards the door.

"That may be the case, baby girl, but you're still a teenager and you have your own life to live. Just food for thought. At what point do you start living for yourself instead of others? Think about it," Destiny yelled at Radiance as she exited.

Constance then began questioning Destiny. "Honey, why do you even bother trying to talk to Radiance about the things that she has going on in her life? She has been dealing with them for years now."

"I know, C, I just hate to see her let her life pass her by without living a little. She will have time to be an adult soon enough. I just want her to enjoy what's left of her youth."

Unique then looked at Destiny and Constance while they were talking and said, "I know that you guys mean well when discussing Radiance, but sometimes things are better left unsaid. I'm sure she already knows what she needs to do to better herself. But before she is able to do that, she has to desire it. When she desires it, everything else will fall into place. To desire is the first step to success." As they all looked at each other with puzzled looks on their faces, they all collaborated and said at the same time, "Yeah, to desire is the first step."

As Radiance entered her house and put her keys on the shelf, she stretched open up the refrigerator and pulled out the eggs and bacon. She then went to the dishwasher and pulled out the frying pans. She began singing in her Michel'le voice, "You took my love and I'm willing, there's no limit to the love I'm giving... the love I'm giving." She began thinking to herself, *Today is Saturday and the day that I can officially say that I'm a woman. Jermaine has no idea what kind of shit I have under my sleeve.* She then giggled and said, "I'm going to give him all of this sweet pussy." As she continued to laugh, the bacon sizzled on the frying pan and she started to scramble the eggs in the other frying pan. The phone rang and when she picked it up, she heard her mother's voice on the other end.

"It's about fucking time your ass decided to pick up the phone. I called you around eleven last night. Why in the fuck did you decide that it was okay not to answer the goddamn phone! Where the fuck were you and the answer better be in the goddamn bed sleep, because if it's not, I'm going to whip your ass!"

"Good morning to you, too, Mom. I *was* in the bed at eleven."

"I told your ass about popping slick out your mouth when I'm talking to you, little girl. Don't get fucked up. I will deal with your smart ass when I get home. Make sure you do your chores around the house, and make sure your brother eats and makes it to basketball practice."

As she hung up the phone and put breakfast on the plate, she went to the end of the hall to yell up the steps, "Walter, breakfast is done. Walter, I know you hear me. Bring your ass down here and get off that damn game. I know you're still up playing with it. Don't make me walk up there because if I do, it won't be pretty." She stood at the end of the hallway, quiet, with her hands on her hips waiting for Walter to respond and finally he did.

"DANG! Radiance, you always tripping. You're starting to sound like Mom, always yelling like a crazy person." As he peeked around the corner of the hallway stairs, flashing his smile and wearing his basketball uniform, Radiance just started shaking her head.

"Boy, just get your butt down here and eat this breakfast."

Walter then responded, "Why do you look like something from a video and why is your face scratched up?"

"Boy, mind your business and eat all this food, man!"

"Radiance, why did you give me this nasty bacon? I can't eat this. Brother Hakeem from that Muslim restaurant on the corner of Liberty Heights told me that pork was straight from hell and a part of the white man's plans to kill off black men."

Radiance then burst out laughing. "Boy, that is the most ridiculous and racist shit I've heard all day! Boy, you better eat that breakfast. I promise you that you will not die from eating a piece of bacon."

Walter just laughed and said "I'm just saying, you never know with this society."

Radiance then asked Walter, "Society? Boy, where are you learning these big words from?"

Walter replied, "That's no big word. I just know proper English, you feel me!"

"Yes, little brother, I feel you. Please remind me to go through your video games and DVD's to see what kind of foolishness they have on them later on today. I'm about to get ready for work right quick. Make sure you eat and that you're ready when I get back down here, crazy."

As Radiance ran upstairs to get ready, Walter continued to eat breakfast. While upstairs, she picked up the phone and called Jermaine to confirm their plans for later that evening. As she started dialing, the feeling of butterflies moving around came into her stomach. The phone rang a few times and finally Jermaine picked up. His voice was so soothing.

"Hey, Jermaine, it's me."

"Well, hello, angel of mine. I was just thinking about you."

Radiance giggled on the other end, girlish like.

"What's so funny?" Jermaine smiled on the other end.

"Nothing at all," Radiance responded right back. "Well, what do you have planned for us tonight?"

"There you go again, Radiance. Why do you keep asking me the same old thing over and over again? I told you not to worry about it and that I got you. Just let me surprise you, woman."

"Okay, Jermaine, it's just that I'm not that into surprises. I tend to like to know what's going on."

"I see," Jermaine responded, "well you have never been that into surprises until you met me, Miss Lady. I'm fixin' to change all of that around because dealing with a brother like myself is one big surprise."

Radiance then asked, "Is that right, now?"

"It sure is, angel," Jermaine answered. "All that you need to know is to be ready around 8:00 p.m. Where do you need me to pick you up?"

"Jermaine, about that. I much rather meet you. Is that okay?"

Jermaine then said, "I guess. That is not the way that I do things. I have always been a gentleman and believe in picking up my date, but if this is something that you want to do, I guess we can do that. Just meet me at the movie theater at Owings Mill at 7:30 p.m. Can you do that for me?"

"I sure can, Jermaine," Radiance answered. "I'm so excited."

"As you should be. Radiance, baby, I'm going to make this evening one to remember."

"Is that right, Jermaine? I'm so looking forward to this evening," Radiance responded back. "A night on the town is exactly what I need right about now."

"Well, baby, I'm going to make sure that you get just that," Jermaine responded. "But, angel, can you do me one small favor and wear something comfortable yet sexy for me? Possibly some really nice-fitting jeans or those stretch pants that show off your perfectly round ass and hug your hips, oh so nicely."

"We'll see, Jermaine," Radiance laughed on the other end.

"Well, baby 'we'll see' is better than you saying no, I guess," Jermaine replied. "I guess that I will see you at 7:30 p.m."

"You certainly will, Jermaine. I will see you then."

"Okay, Radiance. Try to have a good day today and if for some reason it's not, just know that I will make it all better later on. Talk to you soon."

As Radiance hung up the phone she grabbed her uniform, went in the bathroom to take a shower, and get dressed for work. Thirty minutes had passed and Radiance exited the bathroom. She grabbed her purse and ran down the stairs. Walter was sitting on the living room couch with Radiance's journal, trying to read all that was inside of it and stumbling over words he was unable to pronounce.

"Boy, give me that book."

"No way," Walter replied. I think someone's got a boyfriend."

"Child, please." She then reached over and snatched her book back from him and put it in her purse. "Boy, let's get you to basketball practice. Remember that Miguel is picking you up today and taking you with him to stay the night in his new apartment."

Walter just replied, "Okay, I better go pack my bag."

"Don't worry, I did it already. Here it is. Make sure you put it in the locker when you get to practice so that you won't forget it."

As they left outside, they found Constance leaving the house to take Unique and Destiny home. "Girl, you still trying to drive?" Radiance yelled. "You know you don't have any skills." Constance then turned her head and started laughing. "Girl, where are you heading?"

"I told you I had to go to work this morning, but I have to drop Walter off at basketball practice first."

"Girl, come on. I will give you a lift."

Walter's eyes got big and he then asked his sister, "Are you sure about this? Can Constance even drive?"

"Come on, Walter, we will be okay."

"I certainly hope so."

As they got in the car, Unique, Destiny, and Constance greeted Walter.

"What's up, Walter? Look at you, getting all big and handsome," Destiny commented. "You will be old enough to be my boyfriend in a little bit."

"There's no time like the present," Walter commented. "I'm a grown man." Everyone just started laughing.

"What's so funny? I really am a man," Walter responded.

"You sure are, little brother," Radiance commented. As they pulled up in front of the youth center, Walter grabbed his things and said, "Well, it was good talking to you ladies, but I have to go now. I will talk to you ladies later."

"See you later, Walter," the ladies all said in harmony. They then pulled off.

"That brother of yours is something, Radiance. He's too cute," Unique commented.

"Girl, don't let cuteness fool you. He is bad as hell."

"Girl, there's no way he is bad," Destiny responded.

"Shit, you all need to see his little ass in rare form," Constance responded. "Here's your stop. Unique and Destiny, it was cool kicking it with you, now get the hell out of my mother's car. I have one stop left and I have to get over to Damon's. We're spending the day together today and I can't be late messing around with you ladies."

"Girl, please, that nigga will be around, I'm quite sure," Destiny responded.

Unique agreed, "You know he will, but hey, I understand how it is when you have a nice, black, silky dick waiting for you, so let's keep it moving, Destiny." She then grabbed her by the arm and pulled her away from the car, closing the door.

"So, Radiance, you're my next stop and then I'm off to my man's house. We have a lot of talking to do..."

"Talking my ass, Constance," Radiance commented as she smiled, "fucking is more like it." "Is that all you guys do? Do you two ever discuss your future, being in love, having a family, being married, and fulfilling your dreams together?"

"Girl, please. That is spoken like a true virgin who has never had any dick in her life."

Constance started laughing at Radiance. "We do discuss other things, but I'm seventeen and that other shit can wait right now. I'm more interested in getting fucked and living my life like its golden. I will save the fairytales for you, ladybug. What time are you getting off today?"

"I'm off at 6:00 p.m. today?

"Do you need me to pick you up?"

"I don't know. Will you be done fucking by then, Constance?"

"Oh, no you didn't, Radiance! For your information I will be done fucking by then. Damon has to work at the studio tonight. Don't hate because I'm getting fucked on the regular and you're not ,Radiance! But, I guess if you never had dick, then you couldn't possibly miss it."

"I hear you, C, but today will be the last day that you will ever be able to tease me about not getting dick."

"Come again? You about to give somebody the pussy?!" Constance asked, nearly hitting the car in front of her. "My little girl is all grown up. Tell me more about this. I'm so excited for you! It's Jermaine, isn't it? What time and where? Do tell."

"Constance, this is my stop," Radiance replied. "I have to go, lady. Pull over right quick."

"I know that's right. I'm pulling over right now to get all of the juicy details," Constance responded. As she pulled over, her eyes got large and Radiance had all of her attention.

"So what you waiting for, tell me everything. I'm listening," Constance commented.

"Girl, please, I have to go to work," Radiance smirked, while getting out of the car. "I will take you up on your offer for a ride, and maybe just maybe I will tell you a little bit of information when I get off. "

Constance said, "Oh, it's like that, Radiance? You know you on some bullcrap for that one. You just going to leave a sister hanging with no information."

"Bye, Constance. See you later," Radiance said, as she closed the car door while waving goodbye. She entered the dollar store where she worked and standing at the doorway, tapping her foot was her friend, Charisma. "Well, look at what the wind blew in."

"Hey, Charisma, what's going on?" Radiance giggled, while going over to greet her friend with a hug.

"Don't be coming over here hugging nobody," Charisma replied, while fussing at Radiance. "I called you last week to see what you were up to, and I got no response. You show no love girl, just no love at all."

"I know, Charisma, I missed you, too," Radiance responded back.

"Yeah, I bet you did," Charisma replied while grinning. Charisma was the assistant manager at the store. She was twenty-one and often appeared to many as much older.

"You are such a mother," Radiance responded to Charisma.

"Someone needs to look out for you," Charisma responded back.

"Yeah, I know, Charisma," Radiance replied. "So, what's been going on in this lovely place since I have been gone? Is it all work or have you been playing with David in the back room again?" Radiance asked Charisma.

"Radiance, please, how juvenile would that be? I can assure you that I have better things to do other than chase after some man. You're so young and have not lived. You have so much to learn. Maybe you should start by taking some time to get to know yourself and think about your dreams and creating a bright future for yourself. Before you can fall in love and be a blessing to someone else, you have to have something to bring to the table. If I were to present the perfect guy to you right now, what would you have to offer him?"

Radiance then responded to Charisma, "Nothing but my sparkling personality. I still don't get how we got on me when I simply asked have you been playing with David in the back again." "Whatever, Radiance, count your drawer and do some work," Charisma responded, while walking to the back office.

"Make sure you tell David hello for me, Charisma."

"Yeah, whatever Radiance," Charisma yelled back at her.

Radiance then started to count her drawer. When she finished, she stared at the clock and began wishing that it was time to clock out. She thought about what Charisma had said about having something to bring to the table when she met the perfect man. She then began thinking to herself, *What would the perfect man have to offer me? All that I ever want to do is make the love of my life happy and in return receive the same from my mate.* She then closed her eyes and tried to picture what true happiness would feel like. She thought about it often and wondered if she would ever have the chance to truly be happy.

Could it be that finally in my life, I have reached a point of happiness? Accepting the things that we have no control over, realizing that eventually patience pays off. Finding that drive that keeps you moving on, accepting that even the weak can become strong. Happiness is a gift and life is only what you make it. Maintaining faith in yourself and striving toward those goals that you may feel are impossible to reach. Loving yourself and knowing yourself as well. Understanding that determination keeps you strong. Happiness comes from your soul and it's up to you to let it glow. Happiness, so many seek it and never come in contact with it. Maybe it's because they're not satisfied within themselves. Part of being happy is creating a purpose for your life. Not wasting time and energy. Instead, focus on thinking positively.

Six hours had passed and Radiance hadn't noticed as she put the rest of the stock up. She then looked at the clock and realized that there were only twenty minutes left before quitting time. She picked up the phone and called Constance. The phone rang a couple of times and she then heard Constance on the other end. "I will be there in about fifteen minutes, Radiance," Constance said. "You know that I wasn't going to be late. You still have to tell me all the details about you and Jermaine."

"Damn! Constance, you didn't even give me a chance to speak," Radiance laughed on the other end. "Girl, just be silent until I get there."

"Don't worry, you going to have plenty to speak about in fifteen minutes. I will see you soon. "Later, lady.

As Radiance hung up, she picked up the phone again, took a deep breath, and called Jermaine. As the phone rang, she began fixing her hair and putting her lip gloss on as if Jermaine could see her on the other end. She realized that she was nervous and was being silly for no reason at all. A female picked up on the other end and Radiance asked if she could speak to Jermaine. The lady on the other end told her to hold on. She then began yelling out, "Jermaine, telephone!" Radiance felt a chill go up her spine when she heard the woman call his name. "Who is it?" Jermaine asked. Radiance could hear his soothing voice on the other end.

"I don't know, boy," the lady said in the background, "it's some young lady. You have so many calling my house, you need to tell them to stop calling so damn much! Here boy, take this phone."

"Hello," Jermaine responded on the other end.

"Hey, playboy, it's Radiance. I was just calling to see if we are still kicking it today."

Jermaine then responded, "Playboy! Baby, I can assure you that I'm no playboy. That's just my mother talking to hear herself." Again, Jermaine chuckled.

"Sure you're not," Radiance replied on the other end of the phone, "only time will tell..."

Jermaine interrupted Radiance before she finished her statement, "Of course we're still on, darling, I wouldn't miss it for the world. You're the only thing I've been thinking about all week. I will meet you at the movies at Owings Mills at 7:00 p.m. Please don't be late."

Radiance's smile was as bright as a shining star on the end of the phone. "I won't be," she then responded. "I will see you then. Goodbye, Jermaine"

"Please don't say goodbye, beautiful, simply say 'until then,'" Jermaine said on the other end.

"Okay," Radiance replied, "until then."

As she hung up the phone, she noticed Charisma staring at her with her hands on her hips, tapping her feet once again.

"Oh man! Charisma where did you come from?"

"Honey, I have been standing here for a good five minutes."

"I hadn't noticed," Radiance responded to Charisma.

"So I see," Charisma responded back, "and from the look in your eyes, I take it that you have met the young man who will steal your heart and take God's precious gift from you. I know your ride is outside, honey, but before you go, I want to ask you something. Are you ready to give such a precious gift away?"

Radiance just looked at Charisma with a blank stare.

Charisma then said, "Never mind. When your mind is made up, it's made up. I have something to give you, Radiance," Charisma added, while digging in her purse. She then pulled out a golden package and handed it to Radiance. "Make sure that he uses it when you're in the heat of the moment. Tell him to put it on."

Radiance's eyes got big.

"Don't comment, just take it," Charisma said in a very calming voice. "Now stop looking puzzled and grab your things and clock out. Your ride is waiting for you. Enjoy yourself this evening." Charisma waved goodbye to Radiance and went right back into her office.

As Radiance swiped her time card to punch out, she grabbed her bags, put on her coat, and headed out the door. As she opened the car door, Constance responded, "Goodness, girl, I thought you were never going to leave work. Are you okay?" she asked Radiance.

"Yeah, C, I'm cool. Just thinking to myself," Radiance responded.

"Oh, okay," Constance commented. "So you know what's coming next. What's up with you, Jermaine, and this love thing you two got going on? You have my attention."

"Listen to you, all up in my business and stuff," Radiance responded to Constance. "There's really nothing to tell. We are going out tonight and I will have more to tell afterwards. I have to go and get ready. Is it cool with you if I get dressed at your place tonight?"

"Yeah, that's fine, Radiance," Constance answered, "but what are you going to do about Walter?"

"Miguel is picking him up from basketball practice and taking him over to his spot tonight."

"Is that okay with your Mom?"

"Lord only knows. I left a message on her voicemail letting her know that Miguel is picking him up. She will probably be too busy entertaining one of her boyfriends to realize that Walter is even gone."

As they pulled up to the house and Radiance got out of the car, she grabbed her bags. She was anxious to get inside and get dressed. There was no way that she was going to miss her date with Jermaine. That's why she didn't bother going home. There was a strong possibility that her mother would come in and start bossing her around, giving her a list of demands to follow. Radiance knew that one of the demands would include her forbidding her to leave the house. She often felt like she was living in a Cinderella horror show with no happy endings. That included no prince holding a glass slipper, ready to take her to a fantasy land.

Constance opened the door and glanced over at Radiance and said, "If you are going on a date with Jermaine, you have to look great! So let's do something with this hair and throw a little makeup on. Give me thirty minutes and I will have you looking like something from Essence Magazine." After Radiance went inside, washed up, and got dressed, Constance said, "Sit at this vanity set please. Turn away from the mirror." She plugged up the flat irons and began combing Radiance's hair, not leaving one strand of hair out of place. She then reached in her makeup bag and began putting eye shadow on Radiance's lids. After she did that, she put lip gloss on Radiance as a finishing touch. "Now you look like a million bucks."

"Wow, Constance!" Radiance responded. "I look like a model of some sort. Thanks so much! I hardly recognize myself."

Constance replied, "Please don't sleep on my skills. Beauty is my craft. So when is Jermaine coming to get you?" Constance asked.

"He's not. I told him that I would meet him there," Radiance said. "I didn't want any drama so I asked if it was cool that I meet him at Owings Mills. We're catching a movie and then he's taking me out to eat. So, I have to run."

"You need me to run you up there?"

Radiance responded, "No, Constance, I'm cool. A bus is coming in ten minutes, and besides you have done enough. If you run into my mom, cover for me."

"I got you," Constance responded while Radiance grabbed her purse and headed to the door. "Damn! C, I have been so caught up with my own stuff I forgot to ask you about your date with Damon."

"There was no date. He postponed on me, that damn clown. He gave me some bullshit about he forgot that he told his boy that they were going to shoot some ball. I'm going to see him later on tonight!"

"Well have fun, lady! I've got to go."

"Okay, Radiance, you do the same and don't do anything I wouldn't do," Constance smirked, while winking at her.

Radiance left the house and she walked about a block up the street to the bus stop. As she waited, she glanced at her watch to make sure that she had not missed her bus. She began to think to herself, *Maybe I should have taken Constance up on that ride.* As she stood there, she noticed that Eric was across the street and instantly began to feel her stomach flutter. Eric was kind of like a forbidden fruit that was tempting. The fruit appeared to be so ripe and full of sweetness. Radiance began to think, *If only I could taste the juice that this fruit contains inside of it,* as she stood there trying not to stare at Eric across the street. She noticed that he was walking across the street and heading towards her. As he came closer, her hands began to tremble, so she placed them in her jean pockets so that Eric wouldn't notice them.

He was wearing a Polo sweat suit with a pair of tennis shoes. Radiance could smell the scent of his cologne before he got close to her. As he got closer, he said, "Hello. Wait a minute, don't tell me. It's Radiance right?"

Radiance then replied, "As a matter of fact it is, Eric. How are you doing?"

"I'm good," Eric then responded back. "I'm amazed that you remember my name."

"Yes, I remember your name. I very seldom forget names and faces," Radiance smiled while batting her eyes at Eric. She then thought to herself, *How could I ever forget you, Eric? I have the biggest crush in the world on you.*

Eric then commented, "I always see you and Constance around and I made a promise to myself that the next time I saw you, I would come over and make it my business to speak. It's really rude for me not to speak. We live in the same neighborhood and I would very much like it if we could be friends, if possible."

Radiance then replied, "Sure it's possible. I wouldn't have it any other way."

"Great," Eric said, "it's good to know that we are on the same page. You look stunning, Miss Radiance, where are you headed?"

Radiance began to blush and replied, "I'm actually on my way to Owings Mills to catch a movie with a friend."

Eric smiled at Radiance, looking her up and down and said, "Must be a very special friend."

"I guess you can say that," Radiance commented, as she looked Eric in his eyes and wondered if he could look into her soul.

Eric then replied, "I'm going to get going now. Your bus is coming up the street... not unless you want me to take you to your destination."

Radiance then replied in a very light whisper, "Please take me to my destination."

Eric then said, "I'm sorry, Radiance, did you say something?"

Radiance then caught herself thinking out loud and responded, "Oh! No thank you, Eric. I will be just fine. Maybe I will take you up on a rain check for that offer. It was so nice talking to you." As the bus pulled up, Radiance got on and turned around.

Eric replied, "It was nice talking to you, be safe, and I will see you around."

As the door to the bus closed, Radiance noticed Eric walking in the opposite direction. She then reached in her purse, paid her fare, and grabbed the first seat. She watched Eric walk off. He turned around once and caught eye contact with Radiance. He then turned back around and continued to walk away. Radiance continued to watch Eric until he was out of her vision. The bus moved away very slowly. Her heart began to sing its own song, beating to its own rhythm. As Radiance sat down, she went into her purse and grabbed her mirror and began fixing her hair and checking her makeup to make sure there were no flaws on her face. Radiance wanted to look perfect for Jermaine. As she closed her mirror compact and put it away, she looked out of the window of the bus once more. She still had the image of Eric in her head. He seemed like such a perfect gentleman. As she turned back around, Radiance noticed that her stop was coming up, so she pressed the bell on the bus and gathered her things to exit the back door.

In the meantime, Jermaine was at home getting ready. As he exited the shower, water began dripping down his chest, passing his eight-pack abs and stopping right at his twelve inch manhood. Jermaine grabbed his towel and began drying himself off. Jermaine then reached for his boxers and put them on. He left the bathroom after he grabbed the lotion. Jermaine had a thought of Radiance and wondered if she would be wearing those form-fitting jeans that he loved so much and that showed every curve of her body from her hips to her perfectly round ass. That very thought made his penis rock hard. He picked up the lotion bottle and started pouring it in his hand and lubricating his body. The image of Radiance's smile came to his mind. He really loved her smile. Jermaine suddenly remembered how soft her lips felt when he kissed her at the locker the other day. "Damn, I wanted her!" he said out loud. Jermaine thought of relieving himself from sexual frustration before he saw Radiance, but decided against it. Jermaine already had it in his mind that there was no way he wasn't getting sex this evening. A smirk then came to his face. Jermaine grabbed for his jeans and shirt and started getting dressed. He was running a little late and didn't want Radiance to be standing outside of the movies alone too long. As Jermaine finished dressing, he sprayed his cologne on, brushed his hair, grabbed his coat and car keys, and left out the door. As he drove off, he looked at his watch on his wrist. He wanted to make sure that he was not running too late.

Jermaine thought to himself, *I wish she would have just let me pick her up.* As he pulled in front of the movie theatre, he noticed Radiance getting off of the bus and he thought to himself, *Damn! She did it to me again. Those jeans are fitting her like a fucking glove* "and she has no idea what kind of strange things I would do to her," he then said out loud. "God give me the strength, I'm trying to be a gentleman." As he looked over again, he saw Radiance walking inside of the theatre. He had the perfect view of her perfectly round ass. His dick started to get hard instantly. "Down, boy!" he said out loud as he shook his head, got out of his car, and started to walk over to the theatre.

Jermaine opened the door to the movie theatre and noticed Radiance looking at the show times for the movies. Radiance hadn't even noticed him come in. He tip-toed behind her and grabbed her waist from behind, as he kissed her neck. Radiance jumped and turned around instantly, ready to fight! "What the fuck!?" As she turned around she noticed that it was none other than Jermaine, and her mood changed instantly.

"Boy! You almost got knocked the hell out! Quit coming from behind me like that!" She started laughing and continued, "You know I don't play that."

Jermaine responded back, "You think you tough, don't you?"

Radiance said, "Just a little bit."

"Whatever, girl. Hush with all of that and give me my kiss. You know I've been waiting for that all day." Radiance extended her arms, giving him a hug and followed up with giving Jermaine a peck on the cheek.

Jermaine responded, "Radiance you play too much for that punk ass kiss. That's not exactly what I had in mind. Close your eyes and let me show you a sneak preview of my vision." As he grabbed her tightly, he kissed her cheek and then stuck his tongue down her throat. He felt himself getting excited and he let her go slowly and pulled away. He didn't want Radiance to feel his manhood just yet.

"Well, Jermaine your vision is much better than mine," Radiance replied while fanning herself. Is it hot in here or is it just me?"

Jermaine responded, "It's pretty hot." He laughed while looking at Radiance. "So, beautiful, what movie did you have in mind?" Jermaine asked in a seductive voice.

"I was thinking about that movie called, 'A Love Story.'" Radiance answered.

"Never heard of it," Jermaine responded, "is it one of those girl flicks?"

Radiance replied, "It doesn't have to be. Maybe you will like it, Jermaine."

"I don't know about that, beautiful," Jermaine interrupted, "but it doesn't matter. I have the best companion and as long as I'm with you, nothing else even matters."

Jermaine then reached in his pocket and pulled out money, and went to the front of the line to purchase their tickets. Radiance watched him as he walked to the front and began admiring everything about Jermaine. He made her feel like a priceless gem and he appeared to be sincere in any and every thing that he said. Radiance truly felt like a woman whenever she was in Jermaine's presence, and in her heart, Radiance believed that such acts of kindness should be rewarded. Radiance thought to herself, *I can't wait to give Jermaine all of this love that I have inside of me.* As Jermaine walked back over, Radiance couldn't help but smile. Jermaine then responded, "I love your smile." He then grabbed Radiance by the hand and walked inside of the theatre. Radiance just followed her heart. It began to race and she began to feel overwhelmed with emotions she never felt before. Radiance began thinking to herself, *I have never felt this way before.* Radiance then asked herself, "Could this be what being in love feels like?"

As Jermaine and Radiance entered the movie theatre and found seating, they gazed into each other's eyes until the lights went out. Radiance tried to get comfortable and Jermaine slowly lifted his arm to reach behind Radiance and pull her closer. He kissed her on the forehead and whispered to her, "You are as pretty as a picture." Radiance started blushing and gently placed her head on Jermaine's shoulder as the movie played. Radiance's eyes became heavy and she fell asleep on Jermaine's shoulder. Radiance was awakened by kisses on her cheek. Jermaine managed to have his fingers travel to Radiance's forbidden area. He was sticking his fingers in her wet pussy and started moving them around inside both gently and roughly. Radiance moaned softly, trying not to draw attention to herself. She found her lips kissing Jermaine's shoulders, softly and gently. Radiance's legs began to shake back and forth and her pussy became more moist by the second. Radiance then began to nibble on Jermaine's ear lobe softly and whispered in his ear, "I'm so horny right now." Jermaine just bit his lower lip and his dick began to expand inch by inch, causing his jeans to bulge up. Radiance then whispered, "I want to feel your dick in my hands." Jermaine took Radiance's hands and placed them on his dick. Radiance began to rub his dick slowly yet firmly. Radiance thought to herself, *Wow! Jermaine's dick is huge!* Radiance's hands glided up and down the shaft of his dick and her legs began to tremble, shaking back and forth. Radiance then moved closer to Jermaine and started nibbling on his ear lobe and whispering so lightly and softly, "I think I'm ready to leave this movie theatre and go get something to eat. Dessert will follow. I have worked up a serious appetite and only you can fulfill it." Jermaine had a puzzled look on his face and agreed to Radiance's suggestion. Jermaine responded," If that's what you want to do, beautiful, then I'm all for it. I just want to enjoy you and be embraced with your beauty."

Radiance responded, "Come on, big boy and I do mean, big boy." Jermaine glanced over at Radiance and began smiling. Radiance reached over and grabbed her purse and headed to the exit door. Jermaine followed behind while looking at her ass. He suddenly became hypnotized by the movement of her ass as it swayed left to right. When they left the movies and went to the car, Jermaine opened the car door for Radiance and kissed her on her cheek as he closed her door. Jermaine entered on the other side and put the keys into the ignition. The sounds of Jodeci filled the airwaves. Jermaine started singing, 'Forever My Lady'.

Radiance interrupted, "Jermaine, I'm going to want to let you leave the singing to the professionals."

Jermaine responded back, "I have a great voice. You're just jealous." He smiled at Radiance, showing her his pearly white teeth.

Radiance responded back, "You're right. That's it. I'm jealous of your soothing voice." Her eyes began to roll up in her head and she busted out in laughter.

Jermaine responded, "Dang! Radiance it's that funny? That's just cold, girl."

Radiance laughed, "The truth hurts sometimes."

As they drove off and listened to the sweet melodies playing on the radio, Jermaine told Radiance that he had to make one more pit stop for their special date. He then pulled up to a pizza shop in the neighborhood and asked Radiance to stay put while he went inside. For a moment, Jermaine left and went inside. Radiance's eyes followed him in every direction he traveled. Radiance then began thinking to herself, *I wonder what Jermaine has planned for the rest of our date*. Radiance then saw Jermaine leaving the pizza shop with what appeared to be a very large bag and a fake rose in his mouth. Radiance giggled and started shaking her head. *This guy is a foolish one.*

Jermaine jumped back in the vehicle and handed Radiance the fake rose from his mouth. Radiance said, "Thanks, Jermaine. Where ever did you get this rose from, silly?"

Jermaine responded, "There was a man inside selling them and I wanted to get it as a token of my affection. Real corny, right?"

Radiance responded very quickly, "Oh, no, Jermaine! I think that it's the sweetest thing anyone has ever done for me and for that I thank you."

Jermaine just smirked and start scratching his head. Jermaine then said, "I'm glad that I was the one who made you feel that way because in my eyes you're special and unique."

Radiance and Jermaine pulled up to the school's football field. Jermaine parked the car and reached in the back. He grabbed his bag, went inside of it, pulled out a blindfold, and asked Radiance to put it on. Radiance said, "I don't know what kind of crazy shit you've got going on, Jermaine, but I'm not into all this extra stuff."

Jermaine responded back, "You know that I would never do anything to harm you." He then asked Radiance, "Do you trust me?"

Radiance had a blank stare on her face and replied, "For the most part I do."

Jermaine responded, "Well if that's the case, put the blindfold on and let me surprise you, beautiful."

Radiance pondered the idea and decided to trust Jermaine. She didn't feel that he would do anything to ever harm her. Radiance felt herself falling in love for the very first time. Jermaine then glanced over at Radiance and looked into her beautiful eyes while reaching for her purse and placing it on her shoulder. Jermaine said, "This will certainly be a night to remember. I give you my word on that, Radiance. Now, baby, close your eyes and allow me to guide you from this moment on. Just listen to the sound of my voice and trust me the way that I trust you. Please know that I would never do anything to harm you. All I want to do is protect you." Jermaine then reached over and tied the blindfold over Radiance's eyes. "Now keep those eyes closed or you will ruin my surprise."

Radiance then responded, "Whatever!"

Radiance heard the sound of rattling bags followed by Jermaine's car door closing. Jermaine walked over to the passenger side of his car with bags in his hands, almost falling down. Jermaine then put a bag in his mouth and opened the door for Radiance. As he closed the door, he took Radiance by the hand and took the bag out of his mouth. He asked Radiance to please carry the lightest bag and placed it in her hand while laughing.

Jermaine then said," I have far too much to carry."

Radiance caught an attitude and responded, "Now Negro, how do you expect me to carry anything while blindfolded?"

Jermaine responded back, "Easy, just follow my lead." He then took Radiance by her hand and led her down a hill. As they walked down the hill slowly, they finally came to their destination. Jermaine took Radiance to the lower bleachers of the football field and responded, "Sit here, Radiance and don't touch anything! I have to set up a few things."

As Radiance sat down, she sucked her teeth and began wondering what in the world did Jermaine have planned that would cause her to have to remain blindfolded and sitting patiently. Meanwhile, Jermaine was over in the middle of the field pulling out all of his special surprises. He placed a blanket in the middle of the football field and he had pizza sitting next to the blanket with a few candles along the side of the blanket. Jermaine then start thinking out loud and whispered, "You're a bad man...the mood is perfect. If I was a female and a dude did all this for me, he could get it!" Jermaine then started laughing and walked over to the bleachers where Radiance was sitting. Jermaine extended his hand, grabbed her by the hand, and asked Radiance, "Are you ready, precious?"

Radiance responded, "I've been ready!"

Jermaine then escorted Radiance over to the blanket, went behind her, and removed the blindfold. As Radiance slowly opened her eyes, her mouth dropped open wide. Radiance was completely shocked about the atmosphere Jermaine created in such a short time and water filled her eyes. She responded to Jermaine, "No one has done anything so sweet for me, ever. What's the occasion?" Radiance asked in a very soft-spoken voice. Jermaine smiled and responded, "What do you mean? This is our first date of many more to follow. Now don't you think that's worth celebrating, Radiance?"

"Well, since you put it that way Jermaine, I guess you're right," Radiance replied back while licking her lips. Jermaine looked over at Radiance and responded, "You better stop licking your lips like that or you might find yourself in a lot of trouble." Radiance commented, "Is that right? Well I like a little trouble once in a while." Jermaine then walked over to the blanket, waved his hand at Radiance, and replied, "Come on, the pizza is getting cold." Radiance walked over towards the blanket while grinning. As she got to the blanket and sat down, Radiance took her purse off her shoulder and threw it on the ground. As Radiance's purse hit the ground, her pink journal fell out. Jermaine looked down on the ground and his eyebrows rose.

Jermaine then asked, "Radiance, what's in the little pink book?" Radiance responded while biting her lip, "Oh it's nothing. Just my book of poetry. I write a lot when I have things on my mind. But enough of that. Let's talk about something else."

Jermaine interrupted Radiance and replied, "Not so fast. I didn't know that you wrote poetry. Radiance, can you read me something?"

Radiance replied back to Jermaine, "I don't know about that. I normally don't share my work. It's very personal to me."

Jermaine responded, "Radiance, you told me that you trust me, right?"

Radiance responded back, "Yes, I do."

Jermaine responded, "If that's the case, read me something."

Radiance responded, "Okay, Jermaine, I will read you something this one time. Please don't joke me afterwards." Radiance simply smiled at Jermaine, opened her book and said, "This is entitled, 'Everlasting Love!'"

"Does everlasting love have an end and if it doesn't where does it begin? Somewhere in the middle or in between. Some special place in your heart that only allows you to love unconditionally, feeling a certain way all of the time, finding yourself smiling inside and out, understanding this feeling that lies underneath; finding yourself daydreaming about a series of events. Showering each other with love all of the time; that special way you look at each other and get lost in one's eyes. Never ending kisses and romance, planning your future and enjoying every waking minute of it. Everlasting love, from the beginning to the end; then you face many different challenges. Together you will stay or suddenly it will go. Everlasting love forever together equals the formula to everlasting love and success is the key element to happiness." "That was beautiful, Radiance," Jermaine responded as he gazed into her eyes. "You should write more. I believe that there is such a thing as everlasting love. Many seek it and never find it."

He then handed Radiance a slice of pizza and told her to eat up. Radiance took the pizza and remained silent. The wind started blowing and her hair began blowing in the wind. Jermaine became mesmerized and replied, "Radiance, you are far too beautiful for any words to ever describe and I could find myself spending a lot more time with you in the event that you would let me." Jermaine moved in closer to Radiance and said, "You have something dangling from your chin. It's the cheese from the pizza. Let me get that for you, beautiful." Jermaine then stuck out his tongue and licked the cheese off Radiance's chin.

Radiance then replied with an attitude and started laughing, "Don't be licking anything off me, I'm no dog."

Jermaine started laughing out loud, "You going to stop talking to me like that. I got something for that ass the next time you get out of line."

Radiance then commented, "If you're feeling like a frog, Jermaine, I suggest you leap."

Jermaine then commented, "That line is lame." He then started tickling Radiance, causing her to roll around and beg for mercy, laughing as hard as she could with tears rolling down her eyes. Jermaine continued to tickle her.

"Quit it!" Radiance started yelling from the top of her lungs.

Jermaine responded, "Say, 'pretty please!'"

Radiance replied back, "Hell no!"

"Say, 'pretty please!'" Jermaine demanded once again.

Radiance continued laughing and eventually said, "Okay, pretty please!"

As they rolled on the blanket back and forth, Jermaine stopped and kissed Radiance on the forehead and hugged her tightly. Jermaine then whispered in Radiance's ear, "Look up at the stars. Each one sparkles brightly. I kind of look at the stars as representations of lost souls looking down at their loved ones."

Radiance looked over in Jermaine's direction and said, "I'm seeing a side of you that I never witnessed before and I love it." She then grabbed Jermaine by the face and kissed his lips gently. Jermaine just held Radiance tight in his arms and continued to kiss her firmly. He stuck his tongue in her mouth and locked his tongue with hers. As Jermaine kissed Radiance passionately and rubbed her back softly, the wind started blowing intensely and raindrops started drizzling slowly.

As the raindrops' pace started to pick up faster in speed, Radiance stop kissing Jermaine and suggested that they get back to the car before they got soaking wet. Jermaine responded, "Why do you want to leave? Making love in the rain has always been a fantasy of mine," Radiance became nervous and started shivering. The coldness of the raindrops began to make her nipples perk up from her wet tee shirt. Jermaine noticed Radiance's nipples perk up and commented while laughing, "Your nipples look like perfect doorknobs ready to be turned." He then took off his hoodie and placed it on Radiance in an attempt to keep her from shivering. Although his hoodie was wet as well, he figured anything would be better than a thin, wet shirt. As he removed his hoodie with no shirt underneath, you could see his eight-pack abs. His chest was defined to perfection. He reminded her of a perfect sculpture; not one thing out of place. Radiance's eyes enlarged and her mind thought of creative ways to fuck Jermaine. She'd read a few books and even studied a few movies so that when the time came for her to make love for the first time, she would be well prepared.

Jermaine noticed Radiance staring and asked, "Do you like what you see?"

Radiance replied, "As a matter of fact, I do." Jermaine then moved in closer to her and started slowly inching his fingers underneath Radiance's shirt and started fondling her breast. He used his other free hand to unbutton her pants. Jermaine then replied, "You still haven't allowed me to taste my dessert. Is it okay if I take a lick of it? I bet you it's as sweet as cherries."

Radiance commented, "I guess there's only one way to find out." Jermaine then moved her jeans further down and pulled her underwear down. He dove his head into her moist pussy as if he was scuba diving. He gapped her legs far apart and started using his serpent tongue, licking every part of her clit, causing her to moan. Radiance tried to keep herself together, but she started grabbing his head and shoving it further into her pussy. Her moans increased and she started gripping the blanket. Then she started squeezing her breast and shaking her head in circular motions. Jermaine continued to tongue kiss her pussy while blowing in it. The feeling drove Radiance insane. She never felt such pleasure. Her body began to shake rapidly and Radiance's juices squirted in Jermaine's mouth and he gladly guzzled all of Radiance's secretions. He finally came up for air and told Radiance that he wanted to enter her pussy. Radiance responded, "I don't know if I'm ready for all of that, Jermaine. This seems like a bit much." Jermaine wiped his mouth and told Radiance, "I think you are so ready. I'm going to take my time. As stingy as you are, love, I think you're ready." Jermaine pulled down his pants as the water continued to pour all over him. Radiance started licking her lips as she looked at Jermaine's dick and replied, "All this time you had King Kong in your pants. Good God!" Jermaine then replied, "It's time for you to meet my friend. His name is little Jermaine. He will soon be your best friend, baby girl! Lay back for me and let me take you to ecstasy. We will be arriving there in a matter of minutes."

"Well, take me there," Radiance replied. She then heard Charisma's voice in her head, "If it happens, it happens, but hand him this when the moment is right."

"Wait, Jermaine, one second." Radiance reached in the bag and handed Jermaine the gold wrapping. "Do you mind putting this on?"

Jermaine smiled and replied, "Not at all. He then opened the packet with his teeth and placed the condom on his twelve inch dick. He proceeded with spreading Radiance's legs apart and whispered very sexily, "Ready or not, here I come."

Radiance then responded, "Please be mindful that this is my first time, Jermaine."

Jermaine smiled and replied, "I will take my time and learn each part of your body. You are going to feel pressure inside of you for a minute." He then added, "If the feeling gets too intense, just grab me tightly, bite me, or do whatever comes to mind naturally." Jermaine slowly inserted his dick inside of her inch by inch. The moans turned into screams. Radiance's nails dug into Jermaine's back and his soft gentle strokes turned into rough strides. He gyrated his hips and pumped in and out. Radiance screamed from the top of her lungs. She then replied, "It hurts too much."

He responded, "I will take it slow."

Suddenly the pain turned into pleasure and they continued to kiss passionately. Radiance could feel her heartbeat race. Jermaine's heartbeat followed the rhythm and the two became one. As Jermaine gently kissed her neck down to her breast, the sensation traveled to his dick. Radiance then told Jermaine never to stop. He finally said in a loud voice, "Baby, I'm about to cum!" His eyes traveled to the back of his head and an avalanche collapsed inside of Radiance's walls. She felt a tingling sensation inside of her and she grabbed him tightly as he relieved himself. Jermaine kissed Radiance's cheek and lay on her soft breast. He started caressing her face and reminded her that she was beautiful and special. Radiance felt loved for the very first time and from that point on she knew that her life was about to change for the better. Even though Radiance had a wonderful evening she couldn't help but wonder what she would have to face when she went back home and encountered her mother. Radiance was convinced that whatever she was faced with, she would be able to face it.

Bring the pain, I have been through it all and I'm still standing. Prepared to deal with life's challenges, dealing with all of the curveballs life's throwing at me. I was always told that misery enjoys company. I'm still standing waiting for life to bring me the pain. Still dealing with others' negative energy. Still trying to remain happy, realizing life has so many lessons. Bring the pain. I've been through it all, no problems are too large or too small. Sleepless nights, heartache & pain; lies, scandals, and others' misery. Bring the pain. I'm still standing, walking through eternal darkness, stepping on broken glass along the way. Trying to find my way; so many paths to take.

Which path leads me to my destiny? Bring the pain. I won't be discouraged. I carry the world on my shoulders and I'm still standing as I stand tired and weak. I pray to God to be delivered in my destiny, and give me strength. Bring the pain. I'm still here. I'm able to face all of my fears. Even though I'm not sure what's next, the faith that I have can take on any obstacle. Bring the pain. I can handle everything as long as I'm able to speak Gods' name. Sometimes life is unpredictable. It reminds you of a jigsaw puzzle not yet put together. But if you remain patient and study each piece, eventually it will end up as a masterpiece. When you bring the pain and you're still able to stand tall, you suddenly realize that you can conquer all. Bring the pain.

Chapter Four: The Showdown

◇◇

*A*s Radiance got dressed, Jermaine simply watched as he buttoned up his pants. He couldn't believe what had just taken place. He now looked at the football field differently. Radiance walked over to Jermaine, grabbed his hand, and they slowly walked off. As they arrived at the car, Jermaine opened the door for Radiance and closed the door after she entered. Jermaine then ran over to the driver's side, opened the door, and took the bag filled with all of the items from his special evening with Radiance and threw it in the back seat. He took the keys and put them in the ignition and immediately turned the heat on. He looked over at Radiance and saw that she was shivering. Her clothes were soaked and so were Jermaine's. He then asked, "Are you okay, beautiful?"

Radiance responded, "I'm better than okay, I'm great. Just a little wet."

Jermaine smiled and said, "We know how wet you can get," as he smirked.

Radiance responded while laughing, "Do we, really?"

"Of course we do," Jermaine responded, as he pulled off in the car and reached over and started rubbing Radiance's leg. Jermaine then commented, "I hope that you enjoyed tonight! I really wanted it to be special. I think that you are an amazing person and that you should be reminded of that every day."

Radiance responded, "It was very special for me. It's all I ever imagined it would be and more." Jermaine just looked at Radiance and stared for a moment. It made Radiance very nervous. Jermaine then responded to her, "I'm glad that it was." He continued to gaze into her eyes. Radiance said, "Quit staring at me like that, it makes me feel weird. Why are you looking at me like that?"

Jermaine just laughed at Radiance and responded, "I would never want to make you nervous, but the eyes tend to tell a story and if you look a person straight in the eyes long enough, it's like entering her soul. You should try it sometime."

Radiance interrupted Jermaine and said, "Yeah, right! If that's the case, what did my soul just tell you?"

Jermaine responded, "I'll tell you what I see when I look into your eyes. I see a very beautiful woman who has hope, ambition, determination, and unfulfilled dreams. I see someone trying to find her way in a very difficult world, and someone who is in need of love. But not just any kind of love. Your heart desires true love."

Radiance's mouth dropped as Jermaine was speaking and she wondered if he was a psychic because there was no way he would say such things or know exactly what it was that she was feeling deep down inside. Radiance quickly closed her mouth and started shaking her head. She then replied, "Maybe you're right about a few things, but not everything." Radiance then started instructing Jermaine on the best directions to get her home. Jermaine laughed and replied, "I think I'm right about more versus less, though. But it's cool, Radiance, you never have to admit to it." Jermaine chuckled as he pulled in front of Constance's house. Radiance just looked at Jermaine and rolled her eyes. "Whatever, Jermaine!" She then leaned over, kissed him on the cheek, and exited the car quickly.

"Damn, Radiance!" Jermaine exclaimed as he rolled down the window. "Is that all I receive after such a great night?"

Radiance turned around and commented, "It sure is. You already received too much; some things which I can never get back, even if I wanted to."

Radiance turned back around and continued walking. Jermaine smiled at Radiance's ass for the last time and pulled off. As Radiance walked towards Constance's door, she noticed that Jermaine pulled off, and she then headed towards her own house. She knew Constance was with Damon, but she couldn't have Jermaine drop her off in front of her door. Her mother was home and would have zapped out if she saw Radiance in Jermaine's car. As Radiance approached the door, she noticed her mother in the kitchen fixing Thomas a plate. She looked like hell and had bruises on her back that Radiance could see through the sheer robe she was wearing.

Radiance closed the door and her mother stopped what she was doing and turned around and saw Radiance. Her mother then responded, "Where the fuck have you been and where the fuck is Walter?" Radiance responded, "Walter is with Miguel..." Her mother interrupted Radiance in the middle of speaking and yelled from the top of her lungs, "WHAT THE HELL do you mean he is with Miguel?! No one told you or Miguel to make decisions on Walter's whereabouts! I should smack the shit out of you for not using your goddamn brain."

Radiance responded, "I don't see what the big deal is. You know that he is safe with Miguel." Radiance's mom then commented, "I don't know who the hell your fast ass is talking to, but I suggest you get your tone under control before I knock your goddamn teeth out your mouth and you will then be picking them up off the ground! You must have been smelling yourself lately. Hell, look at you biting your lip like you want to say something. If you are feeling like a frog, then I suggest you leap, bitch! I'm waiting."

Radiance responded, "I'm so sick and tired of you treating me like this. I've done nothing to deserve this mistreatment. All that I have been doing is being a mother to your child, working like an adult and putting my life on pause to accommodate your lifestyle. On this day, all of that ends! All you do is lay down with these sorry-ass men. First Victor, then John, Mike, Terry, Robert, and now Thomas. I don't know why you're the way that you are towards me and why you let these men mishandle you, and it appears that your latest boyfriend is putting his goddamn hands on you, leaving bruises all over you. If I ever see him doing that shit, I'm going to kill him!"

Radiance's mom walked over to her and smacked her face as hard as she could. Radiance closed her hand creating a fist, and hit the wall. She then walked away from her mother and out of the door. Radiance's mom then responded, "Get your ass back in here right now! Don't make me come after you!"

Radiance continued walking and her mother followed. They were interrupted by Thomas's voice at the end of the step. Radiance's mom looked over and saw Thomas. He said, "Woman, where is my plate of food? I sent you down here over an hour ago and my patience is running out. You're too busy worrying about your daughter's fast ass! Let her go. She knows how to get back home. And make it *fast*!" Radiance's mom went inside the house, closed the door, grabbed the plate in the kitchen, and went upstairs behind Thomas, not uttering one word. Thomas commented, "The next time that I send you to do something, you better do it quickly! I work hard and I don't have time to supervise your ass. When I give you specific instructions, I'm trying to be nice to your simple ass. But it seems as though the only time you listen is when I'm fucking you up or the dick is up in you. Don't make me send your simple ass to intensive care, woman. Do you fucking understand?"

Radiance's mom responded, "I'm about sick of your sorry ass! Who the fuck do you think you're talking to like that? Grab your shit and leave, nigga! Get the fuck out of my house! This is the last straw!"

She then traveled to her closet and started pulling down all of Thomas's clothes and throwing them at him. She then responded, "That's all your shit! Now roll out!"

Thomas replied, "You are a disrespectful bitch! I'm going to teach you some damn manners!" Thomas walked to the ironing board, grabbed a belt, walked over to Radiance's mom and began hitting her with it. She attempted to fight back but her efforts were in vain. Thomas was much stronger. He continued to hit her over and over again, causing her screams to intensify.

As Radiance's mom whimpered while trying to block the belt from hitting her, Miguel and Walter pulled up in front of the house. They both jumped out of the car. Miguel said, "Damn, Walter! I can't believe you made me drive all the way over here to get your Playstation." Miguel then laughed and told Walter to come on, as they headed towards the door. Walter reached for his keys around his neck and opened the door. They heard crying and loud screams as soon as they entered the house. Walter's eyes enlarged and Miguel raced upstairs. He noticed that the screams were coming from his mother's room. He kicked in the bedroom door and noticed Thomas hitting his mother. You could see the rage and anger in Miguel's eyes. "Nigga, get the fuck off my mother!" he yelled. "I'm going to kill your bitch ass!" Miguel added, as he ran over to Thomas and started swinging at him. The two began wrestling and started rolling on the floor. Miguel elbowed Thomas in the jaw and got up and started kicking Thomas in the head over and over again, leaving his Timberland boot print on the side of Thomas's face. Miguel's mother was screaming in the background. She exclaimed, "Miguel, please stop! You're going to kill him!" She slowly picked herself up off the ground and started to move towards Miguel. She began grabbing him from behind, using what strength she had left to hold him back. "Stop this animalistic shit right now!"

Miguel replied, "Fuck that! He hit you! I'm going to put his bitch ass six feet under!" Miguel pushed his mother out of the way. His mother then reached for the phone and dialed the police. Walter came in from behind with tears streaming down his face and a bike in both his hands. He walked in the room, pushed Miguel with his bike, and threw it on

Thomas. Miguel turned around and went over to Walter, "Okay, lil' man, I think he learned his lesson." Miguel added, "There is no need to do anything further."

Miguel then started thinking to himself, *Damn! I forgot about Walter. I don't want this shit to affect him.* Miguel then instructed Walter to go in his room, grab his Playstation, and wait for him outside near the car. Walter just looked at Miguel and didn't move an inch. Miguel then asked louder, "What did I just tell you? Don't make me say it again!" Walter hesitantly left and went in his room. Miguel found his mother helping Thomas up off the ground and escorting him to the bed. Miguel then asked, "Why are you helping this sorry son of a bitch? Mom, he just whipped your ass damn near senseless!"

Miguel's mother responded, "On the real, I want you to get the fuck out of my house! I'm so sick of my ungrateful-ass children trying to run my life. I'm more than capable of living my own life! Get the fuck out of here now and take Walter with you!"

Miguel responded, "Fine, I will. Maybe I should have allowed that nigga to continue hitting you since you seem to like it. That shit is just crazy!"

Miguel's mother then replied, "Watch your mouth and get the fuck out of my house right now!"

"Fine, Mom, I will," Miguel responded, as he exited her room. He went over to Walter's room, grabbed a bag filled with Walter's clothes, and headed towards the staircase and out the door.

I feel so alone, out in a world that's not my own. Wondering about life and all that it has to offer. So many questions come to mind. I often feel like I'm running out of time. Trying to remain positive and striving towards my dreams. Thinking about my future and all of the joy that it will bring. Walking ahead, just to get pushed back. I often feel like I'm under attack. Alone is how I feel. No one could possibly relate to the changes going on deep down within. Trying to figure out my true identity. Still remaining a mystery to many. Alone, waiting to get touched by an angel. Waiting for that other person who is identical to me. Then I realize that I'm so unique. Alone is what I am and life is what you make it. Walking on a path all alone, you tend to learn patience. While traveling you experience some inclement weather, but within my journey I discover strength, ambition, and determination. Then suddenly, I take a deep breath and realize that life is just a big test. I feel all alone for a reason. My destiny is within my reach and my walk is my own. Not everyone can sit on my throne. Therefore it is intended for me to be alone.

Chapter Five: It's So Hard to Say Goodbye

◇◇

RADIANCE WALKED ALONE DOWN THE DARK street of her neighborhood feeling completely lost and all alone. She started thinking to herself, *How could an evening that started off being so lovely end up this way?* "This is not exactly what I had planned," she mumbled out loud, while shaking her head and trying to hold back her tears. Her tears were a mixture of joy and pain, all at the same time. She started smiling when she thought about Jermaine and the way he made her feel. He handled her with plenty of tender love and care. Radiance knew in her heart that what they shared was special and rare. Radiance began thinking about her life and how being close to her mother would feel; being able to experience true love for the first time; and enjoying her youth hanging out with her friends and living her life to the fullest. It was then that she realized that things like that only happened in fairytales and she whispered softly, "Life's no fairytale."

As Radiance continued to walk up the long, dark road, she soon came to Joe's sub shop. She noticed that Lisa was standing at her usual spot, waiting for her next client. Radiance remembered that she didn't pay her the rest of the money for taking her to school. So she felt the need to pay her for all of her help and what she thought at the time was useless information about life. Radiance went into her jean pockets, pulled out some cash, and started walking over to Lisa. Radiance noticed that her back was turned. As Radiance got closer, she reached out to Lisa and tapped her on the shoulder. Lisa jumped instantly and replied, "Damn! Baby girl, you shouldn't go around scaring people like that. You almost gave me a heart attack!"

Lisa noticed that Radiance's eyes were a little more glassy than normal. "Are you okay, baby?" Lisa asked.

Radiance responded, "Yes, I'm just fine. I just came over to give you this and to tell you thank you for helping me in my time of desperate need." She then handed Lisa the money. Lisa took the money and said, "Thanks, honey, but I don't want your money. I'm okay at the moment. Please take it back and buy yourself something nice."

Radiance responded, "No way! I try to keep my word. Someone once told me that if you don't have your word, you don't have anything." Radiance attempted to crack a smile but didn't manage to do so. Instead, she scratched her head and commented out loud, "The thing is, I can't remember who that was exactly." Lisa just looked at Radiance and said, "Well, whoever it was, it sounds like they're wise and know a few things about life."

Lisa smiled at Radiance and remembered that it was indeed her who told Radiance that without your word you have nothing, when she was walking her to school. *Maybe she was listening after all!* Lisa knew that Radiance's head was as hard as a rock. Radiance attempted to walk away, but Lisa stopped her dead in her tracks. "Not so fast, hot stuff!" Lisa said. "Come back! I want to talk to you for just a minute. There's something different about you today. You normally shine so bright, but for some reason you appear to be very dim today. Why is that the case?" Radiance stopped and replied, "Just life stuff, Lisa. You know how it is. I'm going through some changes at home with my mother. She always tripping on me and putting these men before her kids, and even more importantly, herself. It's crazy and downright wrong."

Lisa responded to Radiance, "Try not to judge your mother too harshly. Everyone has a story to tell. The problem is that not all of us want to tell it. Some people choose to march to the beat of their own drum. One beat, one person, one walk, and the only sound that we hear is the one we create, baby girl! This might not make sense now, but it will in due time."

Radiance just looked at Lisa and rolled her eyes. "Damn, Lisa, you are always giving some advice. The problem is that I don't understand any of the shit you be kicking!" Radiance then asked, "Can you speak regular language for me next time?"

Lisa commented, "Girl, all I do is speak English. It's nothing complicated about it. You just have to open up your mind and hear what's being told to you, instead of what you want to hear." Radiance laughed and replied, "Whatever!" Radiance attempted to walk away one more time. "Hold up, Radiance," Lisa yelled out. "Come back! You're walking differently and baby, I know that walk. You got fucked! So tell me, darling, was it good?"

Radiance's eyes enlarged and suddenly she felt embarrassed. Lisa said, "No need to be speechless, doll! Fucking is a way of life. Just enjoy it and protect yourself. *And* remember, just because it sparkles brightly doesn't mean that it's a carat, honey! It could be a piece of costume jewelry with no value to it at all. You feel me, diva?"

Radiance turned around, smiled at Lisa, and replied, "I feel you."

"Now that's what I'm talking about," Lisa responded back, as she went in her purse, grabbed her lip balm, put it on, and started to walk over to a black Ford Explorer. Radiance called out Lisa's name and Lisa turned around. "What's up, honey? I got to get back to work and get this money." Radiance then asked, "Why don't you just chill out tonight and we can finish having some girl talk?"

Lisa responded back, "Honey, I would love to, but bills have to get paid. So that means I have to go make the doughnuts. Come and talk to me tomorrow, same time."

Radiance yelled back at Lisa, "It's a date!" Immediately after she replied, she felt uneasy as Lisa walked over to the Explorer, opened the door, and climbed inside.

Radiance went inside of Joe's sub shop and got something to drink. She noticed the pay phone on the wall and went over to it to call Destiny. She knew that Destiny would give some good advice about everything that was going on in her life presently. As she dug deep down in her purse for change, she noticed a red Navigator and wondered if it could be Eric. Radiance smiled at the thought of it possibly being Eric. There was something about him she was curious about. She smiled as she dialed Destiny. It didn't take her long to pick up on the other end. "Talk to me," Destiny replied on the other end.

"Hey, Destiny, it's Radiance. Girl, I need to talk to you. I'm in a mess and I need to talk to someone. I'm feeling a little lost right now."

Destiny responded, "What's going on? Is somebody fucking with you?! Let me put my sweats on. I'm on my way!"

Radiance burst out laughing on the other end. "No, girl, you don't have to whip anyone's ass. I just got into it with my mom dukes and I'm tired of her shit. There is no way I'm going back in there right now. I can't take it."

Destiny replied, "Understood. I'm on my way to you. Are you at Constance's?"

"No, girl, she is with Damon."

Radiance commented, "Okay, then. I have my homeboy's car. I'm going to come scoop you.

Where are you?"

Radiance responded, "I'm at Joe's sub shop."

"Oh, okay," Destiny said, "I'm on my way. Don't move."

"Okay," Radiance responded, "I'm going to chill until you get here."

Meanwhile, Lisa was in the black Explorer with an older male. She asked the man, "Hey, Daddy, what's your pleasure tonight?" The man then responded, "I always wanted to make love to a beautiful woman at the park, on a night just like tonight."

Lisa responded, "Oh, that's a nice fantasy, honey! But unfortunately, I don't travel further than the alley about two blocks from here or to a hotel that's pretty close to the area that I'm working." The man just looked over at Lisa, as he reached in his pocket and pulled out a stack of hundred dollar bills and asked, "What if I pay you triple your price? Come on, sexy. Look at me, I would never hurt you. And with the money you make tonight, you can afford to take a day off and go and treat yourself to something nice."

Lisa responded, "I don't know about this, sugar, but I could use the extra cash. So, I will make an exception to the rule this one time only. Let's go live out your fantasy." Lisa winked and the man pulled off and headed towards the park.

As they pulled up to the park and put the car in park, Lisa got close to the guy and said, "So what do you want me to do to fulfill your fantasy?"

The man responded, "Suck my dick in this car. Start off very slow and then go into overdrive. That drives me wild!

"No problem, Daddy! Your wish is my command," Lisa said, as she unzipped his pants and pulled his dick out. She placed her mouth on his dick and started licking it nice and slow. She gradually picked up the pace, making her tongue bend around the head of his dick. The man moaned and climaxed quickly inside of Lisa's mouth. She swallowed his secretions, came up for air, wiped her mouth, and asked, "Were there any other requests?"

The man responded, "No, there are no other requests, you dirty, filthy whore! You have no fucking respect for yourself. My dick is the last one you will ever suck because I'm about to kill your nasty ass tonight!" The man reached over and smacked Lisa in the face. Lisa attempted to go in her bag for pepper spray, but the man snatched her purse and threw it out of the truck's window. Lisa reached for the door in an attempt to get out, but the man placed the locks on all the doors.

The man exclaimed, "You fucking cock sucker! You're not going any-fucking-where today! Your ass will never see light again!"

Lisa replied, "Oh, no, bastard! I will see light. You got me fucked up in this game. All my fucking life I had to fight, and your dumb ass is no fucking exception to the rule! Bring it on, you sick bitch!" Lisa reached over and poked the man in the eyes and then took her stiletto shoe off and began hitting the man in the face with her heel. The man reached over and punched Lisa in the stomach causing wind to leave her body, but Lisa kept fighting. She started punching and scratching and kicking. She reached down for his dick and began squeezing his scrotum sack. The man yelled out, "You disgusting bitch!"

As he grabbed his dick, Lisa managed to get the door unlocked and attempted to reach for the handle of the door and open it. She eventu-ally was successful, but the man grabbed her by her hair. Lisa continued to fight and scratch and yell, but the man took his other free hand, went into his pocket, and grabbed his pocket knife. He pushed the button causing the sharp metal to appear. Lisa bit his arm and attempted to get out, but the man grabbed her by her neck, took the knife, and slit her throat. Lisa's screams were no more and blood was pouring everywhere. The man said, "That fucking whore had no idea what was coming to her." The man looked around to make sure that the coast was clear, and no-ticed that there was not another person in sight. He kicked Lisa's lifeless body out of his truck, closed the door, and pulled off as he licked the blood off his knife. He laughed out loud and responded, "At least the bitch tasted good."

Chapter Six: The Freaks Come Out at Night

◇◇

RADIANCE CONTINUED TO STAND IN JOE'S SUB shop waiting on Destiny to come. She started looking down at her watch and she grew impatient by the minute. *What the hell is Destiny doing?* Radiance thought to herself, as she walked back over to the pay phone and called Destiny once again. "Who is calling me?" Destiny asked, as she wobbled over to the phone with one shoe on and the other one off. She looked over at the Caller ID and didn't recognize the number. "Damn! It's probably just Radiance," she commented out loud. "I'm not going to answer that. I told her that I was on my way. That girl has no patience." Destiny put on her other shoe, grabbed the keys off the kitchen counter, left out the back door, and started walking over to the alley where she parked.

Destiny started hearing sounds and looked around in an attempt to see what was going on. She looked over to her left and then looked over to the right, and noticed nothing. "Damn! My mind must be playing tricks on me," she whispered. Much to her surprise, she started hearing footsteps that sounded as if they were far away and suddenly they became closer. Destiny started putting a little extra pep in her step as she went over to the car. The alley was pitch black. Destiny attempted to push her light keychain on her keys and noticed instantly that it was not working.

"Shit!" she screamed out loud. "This is just a fine time for this keychain not to work!" Destiny looked again, first to her left and then to her right, and saw nothing. Then she heard a voice from behind her that whispered, "It appears as though you are looking for something. Well, now you found it." Destiny turned around and saw a man dressed in all black with a bat in his hand. "Put your fucking hands above your head!"

Destiny looked at him and said, "Hell, no! I'm not doing that," and attempted to get inside the car. The man kicked the car door and said, "Now, we can do this the easy way or the hard way. Which one do you prefer?" It was at that moment that Destiny knew that this man was not playing.

The man said, "Now, put your hands on top of your head." Destiny followed the instruction that she was given and replied, "I don't have any money or valuable items, if that's what you want." The mystery man dressed in all black replied, "Shut up and don't speak unless spoken to, miss. It's not your money or jewelry that I want, it's your pussy." Destiny's heart started racing fast and she became terrified. She replied, "Please don't do this to me! I don't have much money, but I will give you what I have."

The man answered, "I told you that it was not your money that I desire, but instead it is your pussy!" He swung the bat in front of her and said, "Don't worry. If you just listen to what I say, step-by-step, and follow instructions that are given to you, this will be all over before you know it. Now, lift up your dress and pull off your underwear right now, before I rip them off you! Tears began streaming down Destiny's face as she lifted her dress and pulled off her underwear. Destiny started thinking to herself, *What can I do to protect myself and get away from this sick bastard?* Nothing came to her mind. The man appeared to be cut up and much larger than she was. The masked man went over to Destiny and said, "Now, turn around so you don't have to look at me."

Destiny turned around and her life started flashing before her eyes. The next thing Destiny felt was a dick inside of her, pounding against her walls. She screamed as loud as she could and kept trying to get away. She saw that a stick was on the hood of her car which was well within reach. Destiny extended her arms in an attempt to get the stick. The man noticed it and grabbed her by the hair. He said, "Now don't make any funny moves!" He started pumping her from the back and Destiny's screams turned into sexy moans. Destiny started enjoying the sex more and more and began thinking, *I must be a sick lady, but this dick feels all too familiar.*

Suddenly, her body went into a relaxed mode and she found herself enjoying the sex. "Good girl," the man said, "not everything has to be hard. You're starting to learn the easy way. Now keep still. I want to take a minute to just enjoy you." The man lifted his hands slowly, removed his mask, and threw it on the ground. Destiny noticed the mask on the ground and attempted to turn around. The man replied, "Don't even try it!" He then took his lips and began kissing on her shoulder gently. He took his tongue and traveled to her ear, sticking his tongue inside and licking the inside of her ear as if his tongue was a Q-tip and he was trying to clean her ear canal. Destiny couldn't take it anymore. Her body began to shake and the man started moaning. He then responded, "Your pussy is as wet as an ocean. Don't move. I'm about to bust!" His moans then turned into screams and their bodies trembled as one together.

There was a moment of pause in between and after a minute the man removed his dick, and instructed Destiny to turn around. Destiny turned around and noticed who it was. She exclaimed, "Mr. Officer!" She pulled down her dress, walked over to him, and smacked his face. "You sick fuck! Why did you scare me half to death and how did you find out where I lived?"

"I guess it was a part of my destiny," Mr. Officer replied. "Don't act like you didn't enjoy it." Destiny smiled and replied, "Ironically, I did." She shook her head in complete embarrassment as she watched Mr. Officer adjust his clothes. Mr. Officer then said, "You have no idea what I went through to find you again!"

"What did you have to go through and how did you find me?" Destiny asked.

Mr. Officer responded, "Don't worry about that. Just know that I did. And what do you mean how did I find you? I'm the law, baby. I can find out anything," he smiled, showing off his dimples.

Destiny responded, "I guess you're right."

"Sure I am," Mr. Officer then responded. I went through a lot to find you again. Is there anywhere that we can go to talk?

Destiny said, "Sure. We can go inside my apartment for a minute."

One hour had passed and Radiance was still at Joe's sub shop waiting on Destiny. She was beyond upset. "This is it! I'm out of here." Radiance left out of the sub shop and started walking back home. When she left outside of the door, she noticed the same black Explorer truck that Lisa got in about an hour ago. But there was no Lisa. Radiance started thinking to herself, *Maybe I'm bugging out and that wasn't the same truck.* Radiance continued to walk and noticed that the truck turned the corner slowly and gradually pulled up next to her. *It was the same truck and man for sure*, Radiance thought. The man replied, "Hey, sugar. You need a lift?" Radiance felt scared and replied, "No, thank you. I'm good."

The man commented, "Now this is no place for a little lady like you, so let me get you home safely."

Radiance responded again, "Listen, I said no, and no means no. So bounce!"

"The man replied, "I can see that you're not used to a gentleman. I'm just trying to be nice to you. Please don't make me have to teach you some manners."

Radiance answered, "On the real, Mister, please roll out! I said that I don't want your damn ride." Radiance started to walk faster. The next thing she heard was, "Okay, I get the hint." The man put his car in park with hazards on, jumped out of the car, slammed the door, and walked over to Radiance. He said, "Get your ass in this car right now!" He reached for her arm, but Radiance pushed him and started running.

The red Navigator from earlier turned the corner with music jumping. It was Eric. He noticed Radiance running and a strange man following. He thought to himself, *What the fuck is going on?* He sped up and called Radiance's name. "Radiance, get in this fucking truck right now!" He placed his car in park, went in his glove compartment, and grabbed his gun. He cocked it back as Radiance went to the truck and hopped inside. The man stopped and Eric went over to him. He asked, "What the fuck is the problem, homeboy?"

The man just looked at him and responded, "There is no problem. I just offered that bitch a ride and she tried to play me."

Eric responded, "That *bitch* is a friend of mine, and if she didn't want the ride you should have taken the fucking hint!"

The man looked at Eric with hateful eyes and said, "I don't want no beef, so I'm going to leave." Eric responded, "Good! I think that's a great idea. I would hate to have to blow your fucking head off!"

"Please, young man, I don't want any trouble," the man said, while thinking to himself, *I'm going to kill this nigga the next time I see him.* The man went to his car and pulled off. Eric got back in the truck and asked Radiance, "Are you okay, sweetheart?"

"Yes, Eric, I'm okay," Radiance replied, while looking at his gun. She then commented, "Thanks for helping me. I thought that man was going to attack me."

"No problem," Eric responded. "I'm glad I came up this way. I forgot my wallet and had to go home. I was on my way to the strip club with a few of my homeboys. Thank God I forgot it. Anything could have happened to you roaming these streets at this hour. Why are you out here so late?"

"I was just meeting my homegirl, but her ass never showed up. It's been a long day, or night rather, and I needed to clear my mind. You know how it is!"

"No, actually I don't," Eric replied, while laughing, "but I'm a great listener if you need a friend."

"I actually do need a friend right now," Radiance responded. "So how much time do you have for me?"

Eric answered, "As much time as you need."

"Well, that could take up most of your night," Radiance giggled.

Eric responded, "Well, I'm willing to take up some of my night for you, so go for it. You seem like cool people. But, before we get into that, who in the hell was that nigga whose head I almost blew off?"

Radiance said, "I don't know, but Lisa got in the car with him about an hour ago. He came back but she didn't. I'm worried about her. If he tried to attack me, Lord only knows what he did to her. I'm going to call the police. Can I please hold your phone?"

Eric replied, "Now hold up, now. Me and the law don't get along. Are you going to do a report?"

"No, I want to report an incident as an anonymous caller," Radiance responded, "that man could be dangerous and go after some other woman out in the street."

Eric responded, "True that," and handed Radiance his cell phone to make the call.

So many desire me just wanting to get close to me. To feel my touch will make them complete. My name is Destiny. As you walk up this pathway called life and you travel to far and mysterious places, you look around and still feel as if you're in a maze. Searching all over, wondering what your purpose in life is. You're confused and uncertain about everything and everybody. You first call on God and then he appoints you to me. I'm so pleased to meet you. My name is Destiny. As you lie down in your bed, wonder about your talents, and envision all of your dreams, you write down a plan or a road map that leads you to me. I'm so glad to meet you again. Let me re-introduce myself to you. My name is Destiny. I am known as the one who predetermines events and many say that I'm personified as a goddess who links you to your fate. My name is Destiny.

Chapter Seven: The Fairytale

◇◇

"HEY, BABY! WE SPENT ALL DAY TOGETHER," DAmon commented as he looked over at Constance as she continued to eat her crab cake dinner. "I really enjoyed spending the day with you. I don't get to spend any time with my baby because I'm always grinding trying to get this paper. I meant to tell you how sexy you look tonight. Those pants are grabbing your ass so perfectly, and your hips are speaking their own language and causing my dick to rise." Constance finished chewing her food and then replied, "Well, you know, baby, I try to make it do what it do with what little I have!"

Damon responded, "With what little you have?! Baby, I can promise you that nothing on your body is little and I love it. You truly are my queen. You are fit for royalty and baby, I'm going to give you all of that and more. I only have a little way to go to get this money out, and I'm going to get you out of your mother's house and wife you. All you will have to do is look beautiful and keep me satisfied mentally, physically, and emotionally. Can you handle that, baby?"

Constance replied, "Of course I can do that, but baby, is there a reason you're talking this wife stuff to me?"

Damon said, "Well, actually there is. Constance, I feel like my soul is connected to yours in a way that I'm not able to describe in words. Baby, you are my heart and I know that if you ever left me that my heart would never beat the same way again. Listen, C, we are young, but you are the one thing that keeps me going. You're the first thing that I think about in the morning and you're the last person I think of at night. You're my first true love. Sometimes I find myself desiring you in the middle of the day." Damon then went over to the seat in which Constance was sitting in the restaurant and got down on one knee. He took Constance by the hand and kissed it gently. He went into his sweat suit pocket and grabbed a black velvet box. He cracked it open and then said, "Baby, you're my diamond. Will you marry me and help me sparkle for the rest of my, well I mean, our lives?" Constance started shaking her leg nervously and attempted to speak, but no words came out. Damon then asked her again, "Baby, I love you! Will you do me the honor of being my wife?" Constance finally got the words to clear her mouth and replied, "Yes, baby, I will be your wife!"

Damon smiled brightly and went to Constance and embraced her, hugging her with all of the strength that he had. Constance grabbed his face and kissed his lips so tenderly. Damon pushed Constance away for a second and said, "I just turned nineteen, C, and I don't have it all figured out yet. But I promise you that I will do my best to make you happy. I do have something that I want to show you. Grab your bag and let's go!"

Constance grabbed her bag. She appeared to be so excited about whatever surprise Damon had in store. Although she had no clue what it was, she had a feeling that it was going to be a pleasant one. Damon grabbed Constance's hand and started walking swiftly. Damon then said, "It won't be long now. The surprise is about a block up the street. We don't even have to drive there. Besides, I want to take the time to enjoy my fiancée." Constance just smiled and replied, "I like the way that sounds."

Damon and Constance soon arrived at a duplex house on the corner of the block. Damon reached in his pocket, grabbed some keys, walked over to the house door and opened it. He waved at Constance, instructing her to come inside. With a very puzzled look on her face, Constance went inside and asked Damon, "What is this?"

Damon replied, "This is home, baby! Listen, don't judge the spot too harshly right now. All we need is a little patience and love, and we can paint the unfinished picture."

Constance said, "Baby! No need to explain anything! I love it and we can make it work in spite of anything."

Damon responded, "Now that's why I love you so much!"

Constance just laughed, "You better!"

Damon replied, "Oh, baby! You have no idea what you mean to me, but you will soon find out. Come over here." Constance walked over to the door that led into the bedroom. "Now you're talking my language," Constance whispered softly. "Can you please take me to paradise tonight?"

Damon said," Baby, I will take you wherever you want to go, if you just follow my lead."

As they entered the room, Damon said, "I know that this isn't what you had in mind for a house, but we can turn this house into a home. I'm not a romantic type dude, but I tried to make tonight a little romantic.

Constance just laughed and replied, "Yeah, I see the mismatched rose petals everywhere! Damon, do your thing, boo. I respect the effort you put into this, but tonight I'm going to make this Paradise Island. Close your eyes and imagine us lying on the beach in Jamaica. Relax and take a deep breath."

Damon answered, "No, baby, I told you to follow my lead. So, let's flip the script and *you* close your eyes and *you* imagine that we are on the beach of Jamaica, and let me take it from there." Constance just said, "Anything you say, Daddy! I like it when you start acting all hard and stuff."

Damon responded, "Enough talking. Just lie down on the floor and gap your legs open for Daddy."

Constance just went along with the idea and lay down and gapped her legs open. Damon kneeled down and instructed Constance to lift up her right leg. Damon took Constance's high heel shoe off and placed her toes in his mouth. He began licking them in circular motions and up and down, as if he were eating an ice cream cone. Damon started rubbing on her breasts while still sucking Constance's toes. The more he rubbed her breasts, the more her body began to shake to a point of no control. Constance then screamed out, "Daddy, stop it! I can't take anymore!" Damon then took her toes out of his mouth and traveled to her legs. Then he moved to her inner thighs, with his tongue licking her up and down. His tongue moved as rapidly as a serpent's tongue, stopping for no one in between licks. Damon stole a few kisses, inserting his tongue in her pussy hole and French kissing it. Constance started shouting and started pulling at her hair weave, loosening up her tracks. Damon stopped and said, "Relax, baby, and keep your eyes closed. Remember, we are in Jamaica and were lying on the beach. The sand is in your hair and the water is beating your skin. As you gaze at the moonlight, you're reaching for my dick and begging me to insert it in your pussy, which is as wet as the ocean."

"Oh, Daddy, you've got me so hot right now!" Constance replied, as she reached for Damon's dick which was as hard as steel. She inserted it in her pussy while breathing heavily. Damon's mouth opened wide and he closed his eyes as he felt the moistness of her pussy. As he gyrated his hips, Constance could feel the girth of his dick as it touched every angle of her walls. His dick stroked in and out of Constance's slippery pussy and the breathing between both of them increased. Damon said, "Hold up, Constance, let me lie down on my back and you ride this dick like you're participating in a rodeo, boo! Ride that shit backwards! Get your cowgirl on, baby!" Constance replied, "Whatever you say, Daddy!"

Damon eased his dick out of her pussy, laid on his back, and Constance climbed on top and rode his big black dick as if it were the last ride of his life. Damon moaned, grabbed the sheets, and cried out, "Damn, girl! Your pussy is the fucking best in the world! Tell me you want this monster, boo!"

Constance replied, "Oh, shit! Baby, yes I want the monster!"

"How bad you want it?"

"Damon, oh I want it bad! Baby, I crave the shit!"

Damon replied, "Turn around and take this dick from the back!"

"Oh, baby! I can't move. The monster feels too good to me."

Damon said, "Turn that ass around! It's about to feel even better!"

Constance pulled away from the dick, turned around, and arched her back as her body was positioned on all fours. Damon's dick became hard instantly and he said, "Relax while I put this dick in your ass."

Constance replied, "Baby, I never done that before."

Damon interrupted her and said, "Remember, we are on the beach in Jamaica and you are on all fours. You can feel the sand in between your fingers and on your knees. The water is moving towards your feet. As I'm inserting the monster, you say my name."

"Oh, Daddy," Constance moaned, as Damon inserted his dick centimeter by centimeter, and then inch by inch. Constance started pulling away from his dick but Damon gripped her by the hair and asked, "Where the fuck are you going? I'm not done giving you this thug passion!" Constance started yelling as Damon continued fucking her in the ass. Her pussy began dripping as she climaxed all over the sheets. "Oh, Daddy! I can't control it!"

Damon replied, "Let it go! Are you ready for me to cum inside of you?"

"Oh, yes Daddy!

"Here I come!"

"Oh, Daddy! Cum for me!"

Damon climaxed as sweat trickled down his chest and landed right on Constance's perfectly plump ass. Damon and Constance just collapsed on the floor ass-naked, and caught their breath. Constance then thought to herself, *Maybe I was wrong about this nigga. He just put the shit down on me.* She then looked over at Damon, smiled, and said, "Baby, I think you have the capability to truly make me happy."

Damon responded, "Of course I do, and I have the rest of my life to prove that to you."

I waited for you for so long and then you came to me one day, a little different than what I expected, because you didn't display a halo or wings. My angel, I often envisioned you in my mind and wanted to know everything about you. I felt your presence when I felt so alone My angel, when I thought that times were too tough, you appeared on my shoulder, never revealing your face but instead whispering to me that everything was going to be all right. My angel, whenever I felt like I was in trouble, I thought of you and suddenly, I felt courage. My angel, you kept me warm when I encountered so much coldness deep down inside. Your warmth melted all of the ice that I had within. You helped me by showing me how to trust again. My angel, you showed me how to love again. You became my lover and my friend. I was once a woman who didn't believe in fairytales and then you appeared with a horse and carriage. My angel, you chased away all of the demons and put your magical cloak on me to protect me from living in fear. My angel, you taught me how to live again. With you, I have learned the true definition of love and friendship. My angel, you taught me how to live out my dreams and also how to make fantasies, reality. My angel, now I know that fairytales can come true, my angel. And I owe that all to you, my angel.

Chapter Eight: Going Through Some Changes

◇◇◇

ESTINY AND MR. OFFICER TALKED ON THE couch for what seemed like hours. Mr. Officer said, "You are a very interesting individual, Destiny, and I would love to see more of you." Destiny interrupted Mr. Officer in the middle of his comment and asked, "What time is it?"

Mr. Officer said, "It is just a little past 11 p.m." Destiny responded loudly, "Oh, shit! I forgot all about my girlfriend, Radiance! She is going to kill me. I'm so sorry, I have to go. But before I go, Mr. Officer, what is your real name?"

Mr. Officer replied, "In due time you will know everything, Miss Destiny." He then winked at her and headed towards the door.

"Wait one damn minute, sir! Don't be walking away from me while I'm talking to you. What is your name? I asked you a question."

Mr. Officer continued to walk off. She then called out, "You are lucky I have to pick up my girlfriend! And just for the record, you should know that I'm not into playing games with grown ass men." Destiny then mumbled under her breath, "That guy got me messed up. I don't have time for foolishness."

Destiny then walked over to the couch and grabbed her keys and headed toward the door. She started thinking to herself, *What in the world am I going to tell Radiance when I see her? She is going to kill me.*

Well at least I have a good excuse for my lateness. Destiny sat in the car and started having flashbacks of what just took place. She began smiling as she pulled off.

In the meantime, Radiance was in the truck with Eric, looking out the window. Eric asked, "What's wrong, Radiance? I know that you had a wild evening and you were just almost attacked. It's okay to display emotion. That's way too much going on for one day. Then on top of it all, you have to deal with all of the issues with your mom. I told you that I am a great listener in the event that you want to talk."

Radiance responded, "I truly appreciate all that you are doing and I'm so thankful that you pulled around the corner when you did. I was truly afraid and I had no idea what was going to happen out there. When I saw you, I knew that everything was going to be okay. I feel like I'm living in a world all of my own most of the time, and no one understands me. I feel like an outcast, maybe even a rebel, most of the time. I'm faced with so many changes and Eric, I'm just a teenager in a fucked up world with real-life responsibilities. So how do you bounce back to just living?"

Eric said to Radiance, "Life is fucked up anyway and you're often dealt a bad set of cards. You're forced to play them the best way you can. Sometimes you win and other times you don't. But it's all in how you play them. If you sit back and watch what everybody else is playing, from their hand you can get a general idea of what's coming up next. Just sit back and look for that big joker, shorty. You feel me!" Radiance just looked at Eric with a blank stare and eventually said, "Yes, boo, I feel you." Eric looked over at Radiance and smiled, and Radiance noticed a twinkle in his eye. Eric responded, "Come here, shorty!" Radiance moved in closer to Eric and he extended his arms to give Radiance the biggest hug. She lay on Eric's chest and began crying. "It's okay, Radiance. Just let it go. There's nothing wrong with crying. It's just another way of cleansing yourself. Just let it go." Eric looked up at the roof of the car and began thinking to himself, *This woman is truly special and I barely know her, yet she feels so close to me. It's as if she's been here forever.* He looked down and started stroking her hair back. "It's okay. Just let it go," he said.

Radiance picked up her head and started wiping her face. "I'm so sorry, Eric she said, "we barely know each other and already I caused you to act out on a crazy person. And now, I have soaked your shirt!" She then laughed, "Where are my manners?" Eric responded while looking at Radiance, revealing a smile and his eyes twinkling in the moonlight, "Please don't apologize. The shirt will dry and friends look out for one another, right?"

"Well, I guess they do. I'm glad to have a new friend."

Eric responded, "The feeling is mutual." Eric then asked, "Where is our next stop?"

Radiance asked, "Can you please take me home? It's time for me to face the music. I'm quite sure my mother is waiting for that."

Eric then asked, "Are you sure?"

Radiance responded, "I'm positive."

Eric then commented, "Well, let's go and face the music."

Radiance just looked over and said, "Let's ride." Radiance gazed out the window and started trying to mentally prepare herself to go home and deal with her mother. Eric and Radiance soon pulled up to her house and found a police car pulling off.

"Thanks, Eric. I appreciate everything you did for me tonight, but I've got to go."

"Are you good, Radiance?" Eric asked. "Do you need me to come with you?"

Radiance replied, "No, I'm good, thanks." She raced off and Eric continued to gaze as she left. He began thinking, *Her night keeps getting better by the minute.* Eric shook his head and pulled off.

Radiance walked in her house and found her mother sitting on the couch, sipping on a glass of wine. She asked her mother, "Why was the police here?" Her mother put her glass of wine down and asked her in a serious tone, "Where the hell have you been?" Radiance responded,

"I had to get some fresh air." Her mother then said, "You are starting to smell yourself. You should have stayed wherever the hell you were! The police was here to lock Miguel's ass up!" Radiance then asked her mother, "Lock Miguel up? What are you talking about?" Her mother said, "He brought Walter to get that dumb ass video game system and Thomas and I was having a disagreement that led to some fighting. It was nothing I couldn't handle, and Miguel came in minding grown folks' business. He started fighting on Thomas for no reason."

Radiance said, "That just doesn't sound right to me. Where the fuck is that nigga? Is he the one putting these marks on you?" Radiance's mom responded, "Calm your fucking ass down! I can handle my own fucking affairs. I'm so tired of my children minding my fucking business. I didn't sign up for this shit! You, Miguel, and Walter, can get the fuck out of my house."

"Listen to yourself, Radiance responded, "do you understand what you're saying?"

"I understand exactly what I'm saying." Radiance's mother shouted, "Get the fuck out of my house."

Radiance just looked at her. "Are you serious right now?"

Her mother then responded, "Yes, I am."

Radiance said, "You're going to jeopardize your children for that no good nigga upstairs who has no respect for you whatsoever? Fine then! Fuck it! I will go and you don't ever have to worry about me returning." Radiance's mom sat back on the couch and continued sipping her wine. She yelled at Radiance as she went upstairs, "Please do me that favor and don't return! Make sure you take all of your shit with you! I have my own life to live. I don't want to worry about yours."

" Trust me, you don't have to worry!" Radiance responded, as she ran up the stairway to her room and immediately started packing her belongings. As she filled her backpack up, she looked at her room and knew that it would be the last time that she would ever see it. She left her room and found Thomas standing in her mother's bedroom doorway, staring at her with lustful eyes. "What the fuck are you looking at, you sick bastard?"

Radiance went over to him and pushed him as hard as she could. She yelled out, "This shit is far from over, and if you hit my mother again, I swear I will put you six feet under!" Radiance walked down the stairs, looked at her mother with an evil glare in her eyes, and walked out the door.

My walk is long and the road is unfamiliar. The sky is midnight and within me is complete darkness. Faced with the evil that lurks within, suddenly my aura turns into deep sadness. Walking on a dark road and not knowing where the road starts or when it ends. Questioning the ones that I love and so called friendships. Wondering why people experience hurt, heartache, and pain. Trying to figure how to get over internal suffering. Trying to find unusual strength, instead you display weakness. Trying to make yourself whole again, knowing that there is a piece missing. Looking for someone to fill your void, not knowing while doing this, you're giving away your joy. Suddenly you begin building up walls, trying to protect that precious gem known as your heart. Trying to display a hard exterior because of the fear of rejection. Not knowing all along you're the one in need of protection. It's midnight and my vision is unclear. My heart is dark and I'm living in fear.

Chapter Nine: Lessons Learned

◇◇

RADIANCE WALKED OUT OF THE HOUSE WITH all of her belongings, upset with everyone and anybody. I can't believe I have all of this nonsense going on. *Life is not fair,* she thought to herself, as she walked, nervously looking around at her surroundings and still nervous about the strange man that attempted to attack her earlier that day. Radiance continued to walk and hear the strange sounds. "Shit! Where am I going? Constance isn't home and Lord only knows where Destiny is." Radiance soon noticed a phone booth across the street. She crossed over and headed towards the phone booth. She reached in her pocket and she attempted to call Unique, just to find no response at all. "Damn!" Radiance yelled out. Frustrated tears began to pour down her face once more and her heart felt like it was in the pit of her stomach. "Why the fuck is this shit happening to me? This shit should not be going on right now!"

Radiance picked up the phone once more to call Destiny, and there was no answer. Then she hung up and called Constance's cell phone, to still get no answer. She fell down on the ground and buried her head in her lap. She started talking to herself: "Get it together. You're so much stronger than this." Radiance continued to try to instill encouragement in herself as she sat with her head in her lap. Destiny pulled up to Joe's sub shop and was surprised to see Radiance was gone. "Shit!" Destiny said. "Maybe her ass went home." She hopped back to her car and proceeded to head up the road towards Radiance's house.

In the meantime, Radiance managed to get herself off the ground and thought to call Charisma. She reached for the phone and Charisma picked up on the first ring. "Hello?" Charisma replied on the other end.

"Hey! Charisma, girl, I'm sorry to bother you so late, but you were the only one that I could think of," Radiance replied, while wiping her eyes and sniffling.

Charisma asked, "Girl, what's wrong with you? Why do you sound the way that you do?"

Radiance answered, "My mother just asked me to leave her house and I don't have anywhere to go." Charisma interrupted Radiance and said, "Don't say anything else. Just come on over. You're more than welcome to come over. Besides, I could use the company. How are you traveling?"

"I'm going to walk over there."

"The hell you are!" Charisma responded. "Where are you?"

"I'm about a block away from my house, at the Laundromat."

Radiance suddenly heard a horn honking loudly and her name being called. Charisma started asking questions on the other end. "Who is that Radiance?"

Radiance replied, "It's my girlfriend, Destiny."

Charisma then asked, "Are you going with her or are you getting dropped off over my house?" Radiance replied, "I'm going to ask her to drop me off over there to you. I really need to talk to you."

Charisma responded, "Okay, ladybug. I'm going to wait up for you, but don't take too long. I have to still catch up on my beauty rest."

Radiance replied, "I'm on my way."

"Okay, now, do you still know how to get over here?"

"Yes, I do! I won't be long. I promise I'm on my way right now."

Charisma giggled on the other end and responded, "All right then. Try to smile for me, Radiance. It will get better, I promise you. I can't imagine what you just went through, but I can assure you that it is a little storm that carries a lot of thunder. In due time it will calm down. I will see you when you get here."

"Okay, see you soon."

Radiance hung up the phone and stomped over to Destiny's car. She asked, "Where the hell have you been? My whole life has been flashing before my eyes! I lost my home, virginity, and damn near lost my life in just one day!"

Destiny just replied, "Come again? Radiance cut it with all of the extra shit! What's with all of the bags? Did your mother really tell you to bounce? And who in the hell you been fucking? That's some mess, Radiance. You should have told me about that. And what do you mean you almost lost your life? Your mother tried to kill your ass again?" Destiny laughed, but then she looked over at Radiance and noticed the tears in her eyes. Destiny replied, "You're not playing right now." Suddenly her laughter left and a look of concern came over her face. "I'm so sorry, Radiance! I didn't know. I should have been here. I just got caught up in my own stuff. But I'm here now and we can figure it out together, little girl. So wipe your face and let's talk about it. We can come up with an awesome plan."

Radiance replied, "Right now, all I want to do is get to my girlfriend Charisma's house. Can you please take me there?" Destiny just looked over and replied, "Sure I can, but do you want to talk about anything else that went on today, like getting ready to lose your life?" Radiance said, "No, I really don't want to talk about that. I'm still shook up about that. Thank God Eric showed up when he did and scared that man off." Destiny responded, "What man?" Radiance looked at her and stated, "The one that tried to sexually assault me. Can we please change the subject? I don't want to get into this shit!"

Destiny replied, "I understand. I will not ask you anything else, but know that I'm concerned and ready to talk to you when you are. But, before I let this go, I have to ask you about your experience with Jermaine. You finally gave someone the pussy! We need to toast on that one!"

Radiance attempted to crack a smile but couldn't. She said, "Damn! I didn't call Jermaine back. I have too much on my plate. I hope he will understand."

Destiny responded, "He will be just fine and if he isn't, fuck him. That's just the way I see things." Radiance responded, "I guess you're right, but I don't want to be rude. The evening was romantic and filled with passion. And his acts of kindness meant a lot to me. He went all out with candles, food, and the perfect ambiance. He made me feel like a real woman. I felt special and completely safe when I was with him. The way that he looked at me even put me in a trance." Destiny replied, "I hear that. He was supposed to make you feel special. You're a great lady and a wonderful person." Radiance responded, "Thanks, Destiny."

As they pulled up to Charisma's house, Radiance asked, "Are you coming inside, Destiny?"

"No, I have to get going. And besides, it's late and I don't want to be rude. Call me in the morning so that I know that you are okay!"

Radiance replied, "Will do, Destiny. I will hit you up later."

Destiny responded, "Okay, lady, be easy."

Radiance left the car and headed towards the apartment community. Radiance went down the steps to Charisma's apartment and began knocking on the door. Charisma answered the door, yawning. "Hey, girl! Come on inside and make yourself comfortable. Let's talk for a little while so I can find out what's going on with you."

Radiance replied, "The same stuff is going on, Charisma. My mother asked me to leave, her boyfriend is hitting on her, and my brother almost went to jail for trying to protect her. She blames us for her unhappiness in her love life. This has been taking a serious toll on me and lately I don't know whether I'm coming or going. Just to put the icing on the cake, I was almost sexually assaulted by a strange man today. Thank God for my friend Eric showing up when he did, and scaring him away. I have nowhere to go and you were the only one that I could turn to. Charisma, I don't know what to do."

Charisma responded, "Little child, you have to place your faith into God and know that He is in control of all situations. This battle is not your own. Sometimes, before you are abundantly blessed with a harvest, you have to walk naked in the wilderness. This way, you will always know how you got clothed once you receive your threads. You must maintain your faith always, and remember that we go through storms often. You may often walk in a tunnel of darkness and you may feel that you need night vision in order to get to where you need to go. There are blind spots all of the time, but once you finally reach the end of the tunnel and go outside, you may still see fog. But, if you look above, through the mist of the falling rain and the gloomy clouds, the sun peeks out for just a minute. That's God's way of letting you know that He has been with you the whole time."

Radiance just looked at Charisma and responded, "I never thought of it that way before. That helps me out a lot. I have faith that has no limit to it and I try to remain strong, but lately I have come to realize that even the strongest individual can become weak."

Charisma replied, "It is okay to get weak, but you just have to find your strength to keep striving towards your dreams and ask God to reveal your purpose."

Radiance said, "If it was only that simple."

Charisma then responded, "It is just that simple. But in the meantime, honey, you are welcome to stay here as long as you like. Let me give you the grand tour. The bathroom is here, guest room is here, and linen closet is here. Now, there you have it. Make yourself at home. I have to get some rest. I have to be at work tomorrow and I believe you do, too. Charisma headed towards her bedroom and called out, "Good night!"

Radiance responded, "Good night, Charisma!" Radiance sat down and started thinking about her life and in what direction it was heading.

I woke up today feeling so pleasant and free. The birds were chirping and the flowers appeared to have bloomed so beautifully. I stood and thanked God for his blessings in advance. The breeze put me in a trance.

I closed my eyes and envisioned me dancing all alone to a very unique song. The butterflies appeared to be so colorful and full of life. The feeling of love filled the air. I opened my eyes and no one was there. So I continued dancing while singing a melody; as I started walking and admiring my surroundings. The children played so anxiously. The feeling of joy overwhelmed me. I felt so free. Suddenly clouds appeared and the feeling of raindrops touched my head. The children jumped up and ran inside their homes. The butterflies disappeared and so did my joy that I felt inside. No longer did I want to sing my song. Everything appeared to have gone wrong, but for a moment I felt peace. It was like being in a sweet dream or fantasy. Everyone was happy including me. Then, naturally, reality came back, making me leave my fantasy. But every now and again, it's okay to dream.

Chapter Ten: On My Own

◇◇◇

ONSTANCE CONTINUED STARING AT DAMON until he drifted off to sleep. She gazed at her ring and start envisioning what it would be like to be a devoted wife to Damon. *How lucky am I to have such an amazing man?* It was an honor for her to wear Damon's ring proudly. She thought back to how hard it was for her to get close or trust any man after being raped by her stepfather. Constance always had that awful experience in the back of her head, but tried to take a different approach towards it. She felt that it was okay to forgive, but she could never forget. She managed to keep her rage under control, but she was afraid that eventually it might come out and show its ugly face.

"I've got this thing called life all figured out," Constance whispered to herself. "There is no way that I could fall down now. I'm on top of the world and I'm ready to take on any obstacle by force." Constance kept whispering the same thing over and over again. She figured that if she stated it enough, eventually she would trick herself into believing in it. Constance knew that she didn't have it all figured out, but she thought that at least if she had a general idea then she was still one step closer to her dream. Constance continued looking at Damon and leaned over and kissed him on his forehead ever so gently. He appeared to be at peace when he was sleeping and she didn't want to wake him. Constance got up and tip-toed into the bathroom to wash up a little. She realized that she had no bathroom supplies and she had no wet napkins in her purse. She reached for her clothing on the floor and started putting it on. She reached for her shoes, grabbed her purse, and left out the door closing it gently behind her. She was trying to prevent Damon from hearing her leave out. Constance started heading towards the store and instantly started smiling as she glanced at her hand. She thought about Damon and she was really excited.

She wanted to inform her girlfriends right away, but decided against it. She thought to herself, *I'm going to gather them all together at dinner so that I can break the exciting news to them*! She commented out loud as she giggled, "They will never believe this!" Constance crossed the street and went inside of the convenient store. She grabbed a cart as she went to purchase some stuff for the house. Constance walked through each aisle, gathering everything she needed from toothpaste to soap. Constance became frustrated when she couldn't find the toilet paper. Constance said, "Shit! Where are the fucking toilet paper and napkins?" Constance heard a voice with an accent from behind her, "If you keep talking to yourself, you might find you're answering your own questions like a crazy person." Constance turned around and looked at the woman standing right in front of her. It was Virtue.

"How are you doing?" Virtue asked Constance.

"I'm good. And yourself?"

Constance noticed that Virtue wasn't alone. She started thinking to herself, *I'm not for any bullshit today*. Virtue said, "I'm so rude. This is my friend, Ambiance. We got a junk food rush and wanted to come and get some snacks to munch on."

Constance replied, "I can understand that! I'm going to grab the rest of my stuff and bounce as soon as I find what I was looking for." Virtue started laughing as Constance resumed looking for the toilet paper. She said, "Girl, I think this is what you were looking for." Virtue handed Constance the toilet paper. Constance took the toilet paper hesitantly and replied, "Where the hell was this?"

Virtue smiled and said it was in the bottom bin. Ambiance looked at Constance's hand. "Tell me what you did to get that ice on your finger, so

I can take some notes and go and get me a man to wife me!" Constance replied, "I hate to tell you but I didn't use a potion, boo. My man just recognized a quality woman when he saw one." Constance glanced at her hand once more and then commented, "But my ring is pretty breathtaking, isn't it?"

Virtue just looked over at Constance and shook her head with a smirk on her face. Ambiance responded with a little sarcasm in her voice, "I guess he did."

Constance replied, "Oh, but he did! Well, ladies, it's been nice talking to you, but I got to go before my baby wakes up in our new apartment and realizes that I'm gone." Constance winked at Ambiance and Virtue and added, "See you later, kitty cats."

Virtue responded, "See you, later."

Ambiance just looked at Constance with a slight smile on her face. Constance rolled her eyes in a friendly way and walked off. Ambiance just looked at her and then turned to Virtue and asked, "What's up with your girl? All of her extra attitude was not needed. That's exactly why you can't give a bitch a compliment, damn! All that extra shit is uncalled for!"

Virtue replied, "Ambiance, I think that you are looking a little bit too much into the situation."

"Shit you say," Ambiance commented, "that shit was just ludicrous!"

"Girl, please!" Virtue replied. "You're either tripping or hating on that ring on her finger. One or the other." Ambiance replied, "Bitch, please! I don't have any hate up in my blood. Have you looked at me lately? I'm simply fabulous. That big bitch could only wish she looked this good on her best day, and I'm dressed *down!*" Ambiance then reached in her purse, grabbed her compact mirror, opened it, and started staring at herself. She reached in her purse again for her lipstick and started applying it on her full lips. "Being this fucking beautiful has got to be a curse!"

Virtue just looked at Ambiance and said, "You know, Ambiance, you are a very beautiful girl, this is true, but sometimes your attitude makes you ugly. To be so vain isn't a great quality."

Ambiance replied, "Girl, please! I'm not vain, but I am confident. There isn't anything wrong with that." Ambiance put her compact mirror and lipstick away, smiled at Virtue, and replied, "Let's get our snacks and go."

Constance walked back into the house to find Damon awake. "Hey, baby! Did you enjoy your nap?" Constance asked Damon.

He replied, "Yes, baby! Where did you go? I was worried. Please don't leave me like that ever again."

Constance replied, "I won't, baby! You're such a dear worrying about me and stuff. I just had to go across the street to get some stuff for our new place and I didn't want to wake you up. I promise that I will never do that again."

Damon said, "You better not. Now bring that ass over here so I can punish you with my monster, baby!"

Constance responded, "Baby! You already tortured me with that monster enough today."

Damon answered, "You were a bad girl, so Daddy is going to have to spank that ass for leaving and not letting me know. Now bring that ass to me."

Constance smiled and went over to Damon. He grabbed her closely, turned off the light, and said, "Round two. Don't try to put up a fight."

Meanwhile, Radiance just finished taking a shower and she went into the guest room. She lay on the bed and stared at the ceiling. She began having a conversation with God. Radiance began, "Lord, I have no idea what you have in store for me, nor do I understand why you selected me to go through it. But, I know that you love me. Can you please shine your light upon me and guide me in the right direction that leads me to the way of my destiny? I'm so alone and confused at the same time. Fatigue takes over my body and strength is something that I no longer possess. I'm forced to take on the responsibility of an adult and I'm just a young woman. I'm in a cruel world that has no slack for anything or anybody. Whatever your will is, let it be done, but could you cushion things up just a little bit, especially in the love department? I think I may have met the love of my life. His name is Jermaine. He is so amazingly wonderful and I love him. Please make him feel the same way about me, so we can spend the rest of our days together. Maybe when we're older, we will get married. Bless him and his family. Please watch over my family and friends, too. In Jesus' name. Amen.

My journey is long and my will is weak. I can barely pick up my feet, walking through muddy water and hard stones. Taking on this journey all alone; so many twists, turns and delays every day. I pray the way of the world never ceases to amaze me. It's a war going on outside. Nothing seems to pass my eyes. So many unfulfilled promises and broken dreams. Many people confused about their true identity. Walking on this journey, you have to ask yourself, who in this world can I trust? So many people relying on me. Trying to keep my sanity. I often feel like I'm walking on a tightrope. Trying to keep my balance becomes a challenge. My journey is long and my days are short. My faith is powerful and my heart is pure. My love is unconditional and my vision is clear. My focus is to complete my journey and finally select a resting place.

Chapter Eleven: Day Dreaming

◇◇

*D*ESTINY PULLED UP IN FRONT OF HER HOUSE and went inside her apartment. She took off her shoes, threw her purse on the couch, and her keys on the kitchen counter. "Man, it has been a long day," Destiny said to herself, as she went in the bathroom to turn on the shower. Destiny tied up her hair, looked in the mirror, and started imagining Mr. Officer coming from behind, moving her hair away from her shoulder, while kissing on her neck. She envisioned him inserting his fingers in her pussy and ass. Mr. Officer eventually removed his fingers and began licking each finger separately. He managed to leave one finger un-licked, as he placed it on the tip of her full lips. Destiny imagined Mr. Officer's nice, soothing voice instructing her to taste her pussy juices. "What does it taste like?" He asked, "Is it as sweet as a honey nectar tree? Does your pussy smell as fresh as roses?" Destiny sat down on the toilet, lifted her legs up, and started finger-popping her pussy while massaging her breasts. She could smell the scent of his cologne. Destiny remembered how inviting Mr. Officer's arms were as he held her so tightly! Destiny's silence eventually turned into intense moans. Her fingers became very moist and she felt a sense of relief as she stood up and entered the shower. *That damn officer got me fucked up and I can't take this shit!* Destiny thought to herself, as she started washing her naked body and closed her eyes. Flashbacks of everything that took place outside in the alley came back to her mind.

Destiny could remember everything about Mr. Officer, from his touch to his scent. She had a photographic memory. As she entered fantasy land, the phone from the living room rang. "Damn! Destiny yelled. "That damn phone can mess up a fantasy. "Fuck it. I'm not going to answer." She closed her eyes again and tried to remember. The phone stopped for a minute. "Good, they hung up," she said, as she started rinsing her body off. Then, the phone started ringing again. "Man, whoever that is on the phone is going to catch it." Destiny turned off the shower, grabbed her towel, wrapped it around her body, and stomped over to the phone. "Hello!" Destiny answered.

"What the hell are you doing?" Unique asked on the other end.

Destiny caught an attitude instantly. "Well, I'm glad you asked. I was trying to enjoy a nice shower until your rude ass kept calling my phone."

Unique responded, "Girl, please! You will be all right!"

Destiny asked, while shaking her head on the other end, "What do you want?"

"Girl, I want to see if you want to meet for dinner tomorrow."

"Unique, I know your ass didn't call me at damn near 1 a.m. to ask about some dinner."

Unique said "It is not 1 a.m., it's 12:50 a.m."

Destiny responded, "Yeah! Like I said, damn near 1 a.m.!"

Unique started laughing. "So are you down or not?"

"Sure, Unique, I will meet you for dinner."

"Cool! I'm going to call Radiance and Constance to see if they want to roll."

Destiny said, "You may want to call Constance in the a.m. She is with Damon and Radiance and her mom got into it, so she packed up her shit and rolled out."

"Get out of here, Destiny!" Unique replied. "What happened?"

Destiny responded, "I'm not a lady to carry stories, so I'm going to let her tell you, because it's not my place to do so."

Unique responded, "I know that's your motto to live by, so I will leave well enough alone." Destiny said, "Good. Listen, girlie, I'm tired so I'm about to carry my ass to bed. I will talk to you tomorrow."

" Okay," Unique responded, "I will see you at dinner!"

Destiny hung up the phone and went in her room, opened the window, walked over to the bed, and lay down--falling to sleep almost instantly.

Meanwhile over Charisma's apartment, Radiance finally managed to go to sleep with hopes of entering a fantasy land where there were no worries, only happiness and unconditional love. In that world, all dreams came true and every woman had her own Prince Charming. There were many fairies that were assigned to make all wishes come true. No drama took place in this magical world and unicorns were considered your best friends. Cupid shot everybody with his arrow of love and animals gathered around and danced, as everyone sang a sweet tune.

Charisma was in the other room sleeping and suddenly she woke up with a stream of tears flowing from her eyes. "I have to stop doing this," she said. "There is no reason for me to wake up every night, looking over next to me for a man who doesn't exist. My heart should not feel this heavy and the feeling of loneliness should not try to take over my soul. I rebuke you Satan, in the name of Jesus!" Charisma then dropped on her knees and start praying to God for her soul mate. "Lord, you know that I'm a good woman, so why not send me a good man? I have been a good woman and I have been obedient. Granted, I backslid once or twice, but Lord you know my heart better than anyone. I just want someone who's designed just for me. Someone to grow old with and be with till the end of my days. Maybe you can bless me with some beautiful children with hearts as pure as gold, and dreams that are bigger than the universe. Please grant me that one request, Lord, I think I deserve it." Charisma got up and left her room. She walked over to the guest room to see if Radiance managed to get herself together. She cracked the door and peeked in to see Radiance fast asleep. Charisma closed the door back and looked up towards the ceiling. She said, "One last thing, Lord. Please look out for Radiance. She is walking in a maze over and over again, with no idea how to get out of it." Charisma went back into her room, lay down, and went back to sleep.

My soul is crying for true love. Every good woman deserves to be loved. Hoping and praying for someone designed for me. Together, we can walk towards our destiny. Praying to stay forever young. Taking a sip of water together at the fountain of youth. Finally feeling comfortable with giving my heart to someone that I can trust. Knowing that you will guard my treasure with your life because you realize how valuable and priceless it truly is.

To give my heart to another will be forbidden. The way that you love me is so special. You find me to be beautiful, even when I'm feeling ugly. Without you, I'm missing a piece, but when we're together I feel complete. You make me feel sexy and free, and you're attentive when I tell you my dreams. You're all that I ever wanted and everything that I need, baby! You're the one for me. Together forever, we will always be. You were sent from heaven straight to me. Designed to love me unconditionally!

Chapter Twelve: Missing in Action

◇◇◇

*C*ONSTANCE WOKE UP FROM HER SLUMBER AND noticed that Damon was not there. She went in the bathroom to wash up. She plugged up her hot curlers, washed her face, and started putting on her makeup. She started thinking to herself, *Damn! I didn't check my cell phone one time yesterday.* Constance walked over to the living room, grabbed her purse off the floor, and went inside it to see who had been trying to call her. She noticed that Radiance had been trying to call her, back-to-back-to-back. Constance started to get worried. *Why in the hell was she calling me like this?* She instantly called Radiance back. Radiance's mother picked up the phone and replied, "Hello?" Constance responded, "Good morning, Miss Renee! Is Radiance home? I know that it is early, but I looked at my phone this morning and noticed that she was trying to call me since last night." Radiance's mother replied, "I'm sure her fast ass did. I kicked her ass out of my house last night, as well as her brothers. So dear, I'm afraid to tell you that I have no idea where she is and to be honest, I really don't care. So, with that being said, you might want to remove this number from your cell phone because you have no reason to call here ever again. But before I let you go, if you happen to talk to her ass, tell her to make sure that she took all her stuff with her and to put her rent money in my mailbox for the time that she resided here. I received a notice of eviction in the mail and I need her funds to help cover it.

Constance replied, "Excuse me!"

Radiance's mother responded, "Girl, you heard me. You're not deaf, so stop acting like you are. Thanks for relaying that message to her and you have a good day, Constance. I have to get ready for work." Radiance's mother hung up the phone.

Constance just took the phone away from her ear and looked at it with irritation. "I can't believe Miss Renee is trying to go hard like this," she said to herself. "Then again, what the fuck am I talking about? I shouldn't expect anything less than that coming from her. It's really a shame that she is that way." Constance started dialing Destiny's number and the phone rang over and over again. She got no response so she hung up and called Unique. The phone rang a few times and then Unique picked up the phone. "What's up, diva?"

Constance responded, "Good morning, Unique. I'm trying to get in contact with Radiance. Is she with you or Destiny?"

Unique said, "No, she isn't with me or Destiny."

"This shit is crazy! Can somebody please tell me what the hell is going on?"

"Girl, I don't really know what is going on," Unique said. "All that I can tell you is that Destiny dropped her off over her homegirl Charisma's house last night after she got into it with her mother."

Constance asked, "What the hell happened?"

"Girl, I don't know. I got this information from Destiny and you know she lives by her motto on not carrying any stories. She would prefer that Radiance tell us versus her, because she feels uncomfortable talking about anyone's business with another person."

Constance responded, "Thanks, Unique! I'm about to try to call Destiny back so I can get Charisma's address, phone number, or something."

"Cool. But before you go, I was going to try to get all of us together later. We can grab a bite to eat and talk a little."

Constance responded, "That would be great because I was going to suggest that to you ladies today, anyway, because I have some great news to share with you all. But I can't talk about it until we are all together, so Unique, don't even ask!"

Unique laughed on the other end, "Damn! You stopped me before I had a chance to ask."

"I know how your ass can get, so I figured that I would stop you before you got to it," Constance smiled on the other end of the phone. "I got to go now. I'm worried about Radiance."

Unique responded, "Okay, diva, I'm going to let you go. I will see you later."

Constance hung up the phone and attempted to call Destiny back. This time, Destiny picked the phone up right away. "Hello," Destiny replied on the other end of the phone. Constance said, "Hey, Destiny. I just got off the phone with Unique and she told me that Radiance was over Charisma's house because she and her mother had some words. I know that you are not into carrying stories, so I won't ask you to tell me what you know already. But can you please give me Charisma's number or tell me where she lives or something? Radiance once mentioned her staying near Gwynn Oak Avenue, but I have no idea exactly where that is."

Destiny replied, "I dropped her off last night. Radiance gave me instructions on how to get there and I have a slight clue on how to get there, but I'm not one hundred percent on how to get there, if you know what I mean. But if it helps any, she said that she was going to work today for a little while."

Constance sighed and stated, "That's right. It is the weekend. She would be at work. What was I thinking? She should be there for about four hours today. I'm going to go past there as soon as I get dressed. Are you meeting up with us later, Destiny, to go and grab a bite to eat?"

Destiny replied, "I sure am."

Constance said, "Sounds like a plan, then. I will talk to you soon. Let me get ready."

Destiny responded, "Okay, C! I will see you later."

Constance plugged her cell phone into the charger in the bathroom and continued applying her makeup. She heard the apartment door slam. "Baby! Where you at?" Damon asked, as he walked in the door. Constance yelled back, "I'm in the bathroom getting dressed!" Damon walked back towards the bathroom and replied, "You getting all dolled up, gorgeous," and reached over and kissed Constance on the cheek.

Constance smiled. "Where did you go so early in the morning?"

Damon responded, "I just went to grab a bite to eat. I started to bring you some, but I forgot to place an order for you."

Constance replied, "Now you know you're wrong for that one, Damon. Your ass wasn't thinking about me. You see how you do? I love you anyway," she smiled, as she put her hot curlers away.

Damon laughed, "So where you about to go, Miss Lady?"

Constance responded, "I'm about to go past Radiance's job right quick. She got into it with her mother and when I called over her crib, her mother told me not to call there anymore because she is not living there anymore."

Damon just looked at Constance and shook his head. "Now that sounds like some bullshit! For real, I feel bad for your girl, but you probably won't get to talk to her much at work."

"I know, baby! Constance replied. "That's why I'm meeting up with my friends later for dinner. I hope you don't mind. I want to tell them my news about getting engaged. Girl stuff, sugar! You know how it is."

Damon replied, "Yeah, I know how it is. But don't stay gone too long and don't forget to go past your crib and grab some clothes, because I need you with me every night. I don't know how your mother and stepfather will take the news, but all I can tell you is that I'm excited to have you here with me forever." Damon then said, "But enough of that stuff. I don't want to sound like some sweet-ass dude."

Constance replied, "But, Damon, you are very sweet."

Damon responded, "Cut that shit out! Constance, there is nothing sweet about me. Anyway, Constance, I'm getting ready to go and meet up with the fellas at the basketball court. I have to show those cats how to play basketball."

Constance just laughed and said, "Enjoy yourself, baby! I will talk to you later."

Damon replied, "Okay, baby, let me just grab my basketball and change this shirt right quick." Damon removed his shirt, revealing his tattoos and his abs, making Constance wet by the second. She looked at Damon's lion tattoo on his abs. In the tattoo, the lion was trying to claw something with his paw. It was reaching for Damon's dip, just before you got to his pelvic area. "Damn, baby," Constance said, "hurry up and get out of here before I throw your ass on this couch and make my pussy accidently land right on your dick."

Damon bit his lower lip and replied, "You lucky my homeboy is waiting outside for me or I would punish your ass with the monster, boo. Your pretty ass is in for it later."

Constance just replied, "I like the way that sounds, Daddy!"

Damon licked his lips and walked out of the door. Constance just smiled to herself and yelled out at Damon as he left, "Make sure that you save some energy for me later on tonight. You might want go to the store and get your ass some Wheaties. You know that I'm like the Energizer bunny that keeps going and going!"

Damon was already gone and Constance continued getting herself together. She just smiled when she thought about Damon. She felt that he truly made her happy.

Your friendship is all that I need. You were always there for me in my time of need. With you, I shared my pleasure and pain. You were always there for me, every step of the way. Together we prayed, smiled, and cried. We often took on the role of each other's guide. Even when we were both walking blindly, you always stood right beside me. Giving me words of encouragement in my times of bad decisions and disasters. You have always been truthful with me, never displaying any acts of deceit. Ready to stick by me through good times or bad. You're the best friend that anyone could ever have. Thank you for being exactly what God designed you to be. Thank you for never passing any judgment on me. Even when I was dead wrong, you found the right words to keep me strong. You're so awesome and always sincere. Many would refer to you as a dear. Always positive and appearing to shine as bright as a ray of sun. Even when you're going through your own issues, you have time to address mine. My friend is what you are, and together forever we will stand tall. Never letting any storms damage us. Together like a bud of flowers. We will bloom. Nurturing each other with bare essentials. Helping one another find power. Together we will stand as high as a tower. Indestructible.

Chapter Thirteen: True Friendship

◇◇◇

RADIANCE GOT UP, GATHERED HER CLOTHES, and started getting dressed. Charisma was in the living room waiting for her to get ready so they could head to work. Radiance yelled out to Charisma, "Here I come! I just have to brush my teeth and wash my face."

Charisma responded, "Okay! But make it quick. I will be waiting in the truck."

Radiance said, "Okay! I will be down in a second." Charisma left the apartment and went to the truck to wait for Radiance. She turned on the truck to warm it up and turned on the radio. She started to bop her head to the sound of R&B playing on the radio. She started singing, "If you think you're lonely now, wait until tonight, baby!" She went in her purse to reach for her lipstick. When she got it, she adjusted her rearview mirror and began putting it on. As she was putting on her lipstick, she noticed a good-looking man walking over to the dumpster. He was wearing a pair of sweat pants, a white tank top, and a pair of slippers. His arms appeared to be toned and strong. His chest filled up his tank top well, and his skin was a smooth chocolate complexion.

"Damn!" Charisma exclaimed, as she dropped her lipstick on her lap, causing it to get all over her pants. "Shit!" she said, as she reached in her glove compartment to get a wet napkin pack to get the lipstick off her clothes. As she was reaching for the napkin, her eyes managed to still concentrate on the rearview mirror, watching what she thought was a chocolate wonder. Charisma began thinking to herself, *I would eat his ass up like some good barbeque!* Her eyes watched every step he made from walking towards the dumpster to walking back to the apartment building. *He must be new to the area because I have never seen that sexy man around here before.* Charisma lost sight of the man as he opened his apartment building door and went inside of the building. She continued to stare at the rearview mirror although there was no reflection to see other than her own. The door to the truck opened and Charisma jumped.

Radiance then asked, "What are you jumping for and why do you keep looking in the rearview mirror?" Charisma just looked over at Radiance and replied, "Nothing, girl. Just fixing my makeup." Radiance laughed and commented, "Looks like you're wearing your lipstick on your pants instead of your lips. When I got in the truck you looked like you were daydreaming. Did I miss something?" Charisma smiled at Radiance and said, "No, you didn't miss anything. Enough with the million questions. We have to get to work".

Radiance giggled and replied, "Whatever you say, lady. Ten minutes later, Charisma and Radiance pulled up in front of work. Radiance hopped out of the truck and Charisma continued to park. Radiance opened the door, clocked in, and the first person she thought about was Jermaine. She immediately picked up the phone and dialed Jermaine's phone. Radiance was disappointed when she received no answer. Charisma walked in and told Radiance to count her drawer and if she needed her she would be in the back trying to get everything together and making herself a cup of coffee.

Radiance started counting her drawer and heard the door alarm. She noticed Constance. "Girl, I'm so sorry! I seen that you called me and I wasn't there for you when you needed me! Radiance, girl, I'm so sorry! Come here!" Constance cried, as she walked over to Radiance with her arms open in an attempt to hug her.

Radiance responded, "Girl, I'm okay! You tripping. There is no need for all of this extra stuff."

Constance replied, "Destiny told me without telling me that you and your mother had a falling out. Can you please tell me what in the world happened?"

Radiance said, "There isn't a lot to tell. She put a nigga before her children again. The only thing different this time is the fact that she told us to get the fuck out! Walter is with Miguel and I'm staying with my girlfriend, Charisma. She told me that I can stay with her as long as I need."

Constance asked, "What are you going to do about school?"

Radiance answered, "I'm going to keep going, but I have to work more now to save up, so that when I turn eighteen I can have some cash saved. Maybe if I'm still dealing with Jermaine, we can get a place of our own."

Constance replied, "Girl, let's take it one day at a time for now. Radiance, I told you that you can't always rely on these guys out here. But anyway, I know you are working, but the girls are getting together later and we are going to grab something to eat. I have some really important news to tell you guys, but everyone has to be all together when I break the news. So, if you need me to pick you up, let me know. I will still have my mom's car for a few more days. When she gets back in town, I know that she will take it from me. But, my baby told me that he would buy me a car to get me from point a to point b next week. I swear I love that man of mine. He is all that I ever wanted and all that I need!"

Radiance said, "Okay! Enough with that crap!" Radiance rolled her eyes while smiling at Constance. "I will be there. I can't wait to hear the news."

Constance twisted her lips and commented, "I know you can't wait to hear the news!" Constance turned around and went to the door to exit. "I know you're working, so do me a favor and hit me later. You can bring Charisma with you if you like. She seems like a nice lady and I would like to get to know her a little better."

Radiance's mouth dropped open and she asked, "Girl, you feel okay?! Wanting to meet anyone outside of your circle! Let me find out you're growing up a little bit."

Constance replied, "Whatever!" She waved her hand and switched out the door. Radiance continued to stare at the clock in the hopes of time speeding up so that she could get off soon and find out what big news Constance had to reveal.

I'm searching for a new beginning. Looking forward to leaving my past behind. No longer worried about the sake of time. Suddenly, for once in a very long time, everything appears to be crystal clear. Learning to leave painful memories in the past. Envisioning my life the way that it should be. No longer responsible for anyone other than me. Planning my future and living out all of my dreams. Things are not always as hard as they seem. Ready to expose myself to the world. No longer am I a little girl. Wanting to spread my ray of light. Learning more about my sexual appetite. Traveling alone, but living life at the same time. Realizing that the world is mine. Going after all that I want and ever desired. Making mistakes, but learning in the process. Discovering how much inner beauty I possess. Realizing life is merely a test. Learning myself and growing up. Now I know the way of the life. My decisions are my own and my faith is what I make it. And throughout it all, I discover patience.

Chapter Fourteen: The Gathering

◇◇

*D*AMON PULLED UP IN FRONT OF THE BAS-
ketball court and discovered Jermaine and Charles outside
hooping already. He parked his car and got out. He grabbed his basketball and went over to the middle of the court. He took his basketball
and twirled it on his finger. Damon asked, "Are you two niggas ready to
get rid of that bullshit basketball and play with a real one? *And* take this
tough ass whipping?"

Jermaine replied, "Negro, please." Jermaine took off his shirt revealing his eight-pack abs. Charles just looked at him and asked, "Dude, what
was the point of you taking off your shirt? Like that's going to help your
sorry ass win or something."

Jermaine said, "Yeah, whatever, nigga! Let's see if you will be still
singing that tune when I dunk on your ass!" Charles attempted to block
Jermaine's shot and was unable to.

"Buckets!" Jermaine shouted, as he shot a three from the sideline of
the court.

Charles replied, "Man, you were just lucky that time. Trust me, it will
not happen again." Charles went and grabbed the basketball and threw it
to the side. He asked Damon to hand him the other basketball. Charles
said, "I'm going to dust you off, pretty boy. Come get some of this!" Damon just laughed and said, "Let's play ball!"

The gentlemen started playing hard core ball, racing up and down
the court. Jermaine appeared to be unstoppable on the court. He crossed

over on Damon and Charles like Allen Iverson. As he proceeded to elevate and dunk, he was blocked by Damon. "Okay!" Jermaine said, as
the ball was stolen from him and Damon dodged him and Charles. As
he leaped up in the air like Jordan in his prime days with his tongue out,
and as Damon landed back on his feet, Jermaine yelled out loudly, "Who
is the man, niggas?! I just made you two my sons!"

Damon walked over to the side to grab his water bottle and noticed
a woman walking down the street. "Damn!" he exclaimed, causing Jermaine and Charles to turn around. All of their eyes got big as they noticed this woman walking down the street.

"Damn! That broad's body is sick."

Jermaine replied, "Yeah, you right! She looks like she has two midg-
ets in the back of her shorts!"

Damon stated, "I would put the smash down on her."

"Slow your roll, playboy," Charles replied. "You are damn near married. And Jermaine, what happened to that girl you was seeing? What's
her name? Radiance, I think it was, right?"

Jermaine replied, "Yeah. Shorty is okay, but I think she wants more
from me than what I can offer right now. She wants a relationship and
I like friendship and sex. I'm too young to be involved in a relationship.
I'm still living my life, you feel me homeboy?"

Charles replied, "Yeah, but you have to tell her. That shit isn't right."

"Listen to you," Jermaine laughed. "You always trying to be like Den-
zel Washington to some female."

Charles just said, "No, I just think they should be given options."

"I hear you," Jermaine replied.

Charles then asked Damon, "What's your story?"

Damon answered, "Hold that thought while I go and book this female. There is no way I can let her ass get away from me."

Charles responded, "Man, you know that isn't right!" Damon replied, "Dude, stop minding my business. I can handle this situation."

I sure hope so, Charles thought to himself.

Damon headed towards the female and said, "Excuse me, beautiful. I'm not trying to be rude, but I just couldn't let you leave my eyesight without asking your name."

The female just looked over at Damon and responded, "My name is Ambiance. Is that all you needed to know?"

Damon replied, "Well, is it okay if I ask you something else?"

Ambiance smiled while chewing her gum and said, "Well, I'm not sure. Am I mentally prepared for your next question?"

Damon responded, "Well, lovely, it is a real easy question. I think you can handle it."

Ambiance smirked and commented, "Sure, go for it."

Damon then asked, "Do you have a man?"

Ambiance replied, "No, sir I don't, if that makes you happy."

"Well, is it possible that I could get your number and talk to you later?"

"I guess it would be okay. You are fine, a little bit." Ambiance gave him her number. She then reached over and grabbed Damon's arm, blew a kiss, and switched away. Damon felt his dick getting aroused as he watched her ass sway back and forth as she walked away. Jermaine had his head on the fence and said, "That bitch was fine!"

Damon replied, "She sure was."

Charles then added, "You niggas are always looking at a fat ass."

Damon said, "Yeah! I know. I just want you to know that it is some gay-ass shit that you don't."

Charles replied, "Brother, trust me, I do look at all of that. But I like to see what her mind has to offer, too. It's good to go with the total package. You niggas need to get with it. I need a lady to elevate and motivate me. That requires more than a fat ass and perky breasts."

Damon then responded, "I will keep that in mind while the dick is up in her and I'm smacking her ass from behind."

Jermaine warned, "Your girl is going to kick your ass if she ever finds out."

Damon replied, "Don't worry. Real gangstas don't get caught up."

Charles interrupted, "For your sake, I hope you're right."

Charles stood there while dribbling the ball and heard his name being called. He turned around and saw Lamont walking over to him. Lamont was the biggest drug dealer on the west side. He had power that every man wanted and more swag than any average person.

"What's good with you?" Charles asked as Lamont walked over. Lamont extended handshakes to Damon and Jermaine. Lamont then responded, "I don't have a whole lot going on and I just wanted to come over and show some love. I seen you all hooping. My main man over here got some serious game."

Jermaine just responded, "I know. I try."

"That shit was pretty impressive! If you keep playing like that, you may get to go off to college and get drafted.

Let me know if you ever want to make that happen. I know some people that scout."

Jermaine answered excitedly, "I'm definitely interested. Let me know if you can make that happen."

Lamont responded, "For sure, big homey! Consider it done. Let me bounce. You know money never sleeps."

"I hear that shit!" Charles replied. "I will get up with your ass later."

Lamont walked away and Jermaine grabbed his shirt off the ground. Damon reached down for his water and Charles proceeded to walk off the court. "Let's roll out!" he said to Damon and Jermaine.

In the meantime, Radiance was clocking out at work. After watching the clock for four hours, it was finally time to go. Radiance yelled out to Charisma in the back, "It's time to go!"

Charisma replied back, "Okay, let me finish writing up this report for the next shift. Hold up one minute." Radiance responded, "Okay." She started rolling her eyes. "I hate waiting around for people," she mumbled to herself. She then yelled out, "I will be waiting outside!" Charisma responded, "Okay, fine."

Radiance started grabbing her things and noticed an older man walking in the door. She could smell the fragrance of his cologne before he even walked over close to her. She started biting her lower lip and thought to herself, *He smells delightful!* As he walked closer, everything seemed to stand still. It was like an old romantic movie when a man walks in and the wind blows on his designer suit, causing it to move in the wind. His eyes twinkled as he walked over to Radiance and smiled pleasantly. He asked her for directions: "Can you please tell me how to get back on 695? I'm not from around here and I'm lost." Radiance stuttered with her words for a minute and eventually got herself together. She stated, "You are not that far away. 695 is only about a block up. If you keep straight there is no way that you can miss it." The gentleman then responded, "I'm so rude. My name is Stephen. And your name would be, madam?"

Radiance giggled like a school girl and answered, "My name is Radiance."

Stephen responded, "And radiant you truly are. Not trying to be out of line, but you are simply gorgeous."

Radiance continued to smile as bright as the sun. She then replied, "Thank you. I'm flattered that you think so." Stephen then asked, "Can I ask you a question? Is someone as lovely as yourself single?"

Radiance paused for a minute thinking about Jermaine, and remembered that he had not returned any of her phone calls. She responded, "As a matter of fact, I am." Stephen then reached in his suit pocket, grabbed a business card, and handed it to Radiance. As he handed her his business card, Stephen then asked, "Do you believe in fate?"

Radiance responded, "Why yes, I do."

Stephen then asked, "What about love at first sight?"

"I never had that happen to me, but I believe that anything is possible."

Stephen smiled as he walked towards the door. "Well, I do, and I can teach you how to believe in love at first sight. Call me. I'm on my way to a meeting, but I will be awaiting your call." As Stephen left the store, the scent of his cologne still filled the air. Radiance continued looking at the store totally and completely in amazement, even after he was gone. Charisma came out right after and smelled the aroma. "Damn, something smells good!" As she proceeded to walk towards Radiance, she asked, "What did you just spray?"

Radiance replied, "Nothing actually."

Charisma responded, "Well it certainly smells like something. Let's get on out of here, lil' child."

Radiance replied, "Come on, let's go. But before we head back to the apartment, me and a couple of my girlfriends are going out to eat I told everyone about you and they're simply dying to meet you. I know you usually don't go out, but can you make an exception to the rule this one time? Pretty please?"

Charisma responded, "Well I don't know..."

Radiance interrupted "Don't say no, Charisma. Let's go. It would mean a lot to me." Radiance looked at Charisma, batting her eyelashes. "So what do you say?" Charisma shook her head and replied, "Okay, Radiance, but just this one time. I can't believe you talked me into this," as they got inside of the car.

True love is so hard to find. That special one that you have in your mind. Your image is installed in my memory. The way that you walk, the sound of your voice, the movement in your body, and the lasting impression you left in my heart. Your smile is so reassuring to me. Remembering the touch of your skin as you touched my hand in the middle of a handshake. Remembering the echo of your voice as you introduced yourself to me for the very first time. It was love at first sight and I knew instantly that you would belong to me. You were truly a vision of pure beauty and you represented all that love was intended to be. When our eyes connected, I gave you permission to enter my soul and when you did, you made it glow. From that moment on, I knew nothing would ever be the same. With you, I felt much joy and knew that you could never cause pain. Encountering new love that will last forever until the end of time. I'm yours and you are mine. True Love.

Chapter Fifteen: Girls Just Want to Have Fun

◇◇

*U*NIQUE STOOD ON THE PORCH SMOKING her black and mild. She didn't want her grandmother to see her. She kept looking from the corner of her eyes, trying to make herself aware of her surroundings. The last thing she ever wanted was for her grandmother to come out yelling and quoting Scripture. Unique dropped her black and mild on the ground, stepped on it, kicked it to the side, and went inside to get ready for dinner with her girlfriends. When she entered the house, she heard her grandmother calling, "Gal, what were you outside doing?"

Unique replied, "Nothing, Nana. I was just getting some fresh air outside."

Unique's grandmother said, "Well, you smell like tobacco smoke and I hope you were not out there smoking that stuff that's going to kill you child."

"No, Nana, I wasn't!"

"Well, okay!" Then her grandmother added, "But you better be telling the truth. It's something in the water that's not quite right. Just know that, all right?!"

"Nana!" Unique responded. Her grandmother commented back, "I thought you were going out with your girlfriends for dinner."

Unique responded, "I still am, Nana." Her grandmother looked Unique up and down and replied, "Well, I hope you plan on putting some clothes on! Maybe a dress or something. You hardly wear dresses. I have some good pantyhose up in the drawer if you feel the need to get dainty a little bit, like most young ladies at this age. Maybe you should put some pearls on or something."

Unique just laughed and said, "Okay, Nana! I will keep that in mind if I need some pantyhose."

Unique's grandmother replied, "Well, I tried. Go get yourself all cleaned up now. Put some lipstick on or something." Unique's grandmother then asked, "Is that little gal that I like with the nice hair going with you?" Unique asked, "Which one, Nana?"

"You know, the pretty one with the short hair and cluster curls." Unique smiled and responded, "Destiny is her name, Nana, and yes she is going."

Unique grandmother responded, "Well, I think that's nice. She is a nice little gal. Maybe she will teach you to put makeup on. She does her own so nicely."

Unique shook her head, went to her bedroom, and started looking through her closet to find something to wear. Suddenly there was a knock at her bedroom door and it was Constance. Unique turned around and replied, "Damn! How did you get in here? I just left my living room less than a minute ago." Constance just laughed and replied, "Yeah, your grandmother let me in a few seconds ago and told me to go back, straight ahead, and that I would find you. She also told me to mention pearls to you. I have no idea why she told me that, though!"

Unique just giggled to herself and told Constance that it was an inside joke between her and her Nana. Unique then asked Constance, "So what are you here for so early? I thought we were going to meet up in about an hour or so." Constance replied, "Yeah, I know. But I figured I would stop past and hang out with you until you get ready, and that we could leave together." Unique replied, "That's cool. If you go wait for me in the living room with Nana, I will take a shower, and then we can call Radiance and Destiny and roll out. Give me about twenty minutes." Constance replied, "That's fine. I will go and talk to your Nana for a while. She is quite an amazing woman."

Constance left out the bedroom and headed right back up to the living room and called out, "Nana are you still out here?" Unique's grandmother's head peeped from around the kitchen and replied, "What do you need child?"

Constance said, "Nothing, Nana. I just wanted to come and hang out with you until Unique gets dressed." Unique's grandmother responded, "Well, all right! I can use some girl talk, but talk to me while helping me peel these potatoes. Here is a knife. Now you do know how to use one of them, don't you?" Constance replied, "I think I do, Nana. I have peeled potatoes before." Unique's grandmother just smiled pleasantly and instructed Constance to wash her hands before she started peeling anything. Constance walked over to the sink and washed her hands and smiled. She said to Nana, "I think that this is nice. I enjoy cooking. When I get married and have a family, I'm going to cook, clean, and be a good wife, just like ladies did in your day." Unique's grandmother replied, "That's nice, but you know that I'm only twenty-one, right?"

Constance giggled and said, "Yes, Nana! I'm aware of that."

Unique's grandmother replied in a joking tone, "Well, as long as you know that I'm twenty-one, we are straight. But honestly, love bug, I think that you will be a great mother and wife one day. Take your time, however. You still have to live a little. Go to school and enjoy your old man, and *then* get married. Travel and learn each other inside and out. Friendship is so important in a marriage, and trust is the key to a successful relationship. Because, if you can't trust who you are with, then your partnership is out the door. Remember that, love bug, and hurry on up with my potatoes, child. My bacon grease is just about ready on the stove and I have a taste for some fried potatoes, and I need peeled potatoes for that!" Unique's grandmother continued to smile as Constance replied, "Nana, I'm sorry."

As she handed the potatoes that she already peeled over to her, Constance then asked Nana, "Do you think that eighteen is too early to marry?" Nana replied, "Well, I don't think so, if your guy is the right one. In my day, they arranged marriages as early as sixteen, but in these days folk don't operate like that. Marriage is the way of life, but like I told you earlier, you have to live a little. Days and times has changed. You have to make sure that your guy wants you and only you, before you walk down the aisle." Constance started thinking about Damon and sharing the rest of her life with him. She knew that he was the only one for her and she trusted him with everything in her heart. Damon would never do her wrong. Unique's grandmother kept cooking and the potatoes and the aroma filled the air.

"Smells good, Nana!"

Unique's grandmother responded, "Well, gal, I try to cook good meals. Come over on a Saturday and I could teach you how to get around the kitchen, so that when you are ready after living a little, you will be a great wife. Because they way to a man's heart is through his appetite."

Unique walked in the kitchen with her jeans, sweater, and her grandmother's pearls around her neck. "See, Nana, I have on pearls," Unique commented. Her grandmother shook her head and replied, "Now that's not exactly the look I had in mind, but it's a start. Come give Nana sugar." Unique went over and kissed her Nana on the cheek, grabbed her purse, and told Constance to come on. "Not so fast!" Nana yelled out at Constance. "Bring your butt over here and give me my sugar." Constance replied, "I'm sorry, Nana," and walked over to her and kissed her cheek. "Now that's more like it," Unique's grandmother said. "Unique, make sure you're back at a reasonable hour and don't dare come back in here smelling like tobacco smoke, gal!"

"I won't!" Unique yelled out, as she walked out of the door.

Constance waved her hand at Nana and followed Unique out the door. Unique asked Constance, "Where did you park?" Constance replied, "Right across the street." Unique said, "Girl! I know your Mom is back from down South, so why do you still have her car?"

Constance replied, "Yeah, girl, she is back. But she is in the house with my stepfather. I texted her earlier asking if I could hold the car. She said yes even though I only have a permit. She just told me to drive safely in the text message. She must have plans with that sorry-ass stepfather of mine. I fucking hate his ass and wish that he would just die. He is not worthy of living, but my mother thinks that he is the best thing on God's green earth."

Unique responded, "Damn! That's pretty hard, wouldn't you say?" Constance replied, "Hell no! I mean that from the bottom of my heart!" Constance felt rage coming back stronger than ever before and tried to tame it by changing the subject. Unique just glanced at Constance and was wondering what her next reaction was going to be. She was surprised when Constance jumped into another topic, asking Unique to call Destiny and Charisma so they could hurry up and meet them at the crab shack. Unique replied, "Cool. Let me hit them up." She picked up the phone to call and noticed when she picked up, Destiny was already calling her. Unique exclaimed, "Damn, bitch! You must be psychic! I was just picking up the phone to call you to see if you can meet us a little earlier." Destiny said, "Yeah, that would be fine. Has anyone spoken to Radiance yet?" Unique replied, "No, she hasn't called yet and I don't have Charisma's number. But I know that she is coming and Charisma is coming along with her, I believe." Destiny responded, "You're probably right about her bringing Charisma. Hold on, Unique, there is a beep on my other line."

Destiny looked at the number and started thinking to herself, *Who is this? I don't recognize the number.* She answered and asked, "Who is this?" Destiny heard Radiance's voice on the other end. "Dang, you rude! That is no way to great anyone, not even a bill collector." Destiny started laughing on the other end and commented, "You know I don't like answering numbers I don't know, girl! Anyway, what's going on with you?" Radiance replied, "Girl, nothing. Just got home about an hour ago and just got finished taking a shower. I'm putting my clothes on. What time are we getting together?" Destiny responded, "Constance and Unique are already on the other line and they were talking about meeting up at Crab Shack in about an hour. We were waiting on you to call because no one has Charisma's number."

Radiance said, "Well, it must be perfect timing, then. I will meet up with you girls in an hour. Save a spot for me and Charisma."

Destiny clicked over and Unique responded, "Okay! I will tell them now. Hurry up, I'm starving!"

Destiny replied while shaking her head, "Whatever, girl! See you in a moment."

Unique said, "See you soon, lady, and make it quick!"

Radiance hung up the phone, looked in the full length mirror in the living room, and replied, "Damn! I look good!" Charisma walked out of the room and asked, "Girl, you admiring yourself again?" Radiance laughed and commented, "Well, what can I say? If you've got it, flaunt it! If my parents weren't good for anything else, they had good DNA, creating a beauty such as myself!" Radiance giggled and stated, "Just kidding! But look at *you*, Charisma! You look good, girl! You clean up nicely. And look at you in the jeans for the boys, showing off your rump." Charisma smiled and replied, "Well, I try to do what I do. So when are we leaving?"

Radiance answered, "That was my crazy friends on the phone and they're ready now. So grab your keys, lady, and let's get rolling on the freeway." Charisma grabbed her designer bag and stated, "Let's get it, lil' child!"

Unique turned around and looked at Constance. "That was Radiance. She was getting dressed and waiting on Charisma. She said that she would meet us at Crab Shack in a little bit." Constance replied, "Okay!

So let's get on over there. I can't wait to tell you all my news! It's really juicy!"

I woke up today wishing you were near. It didn't dawn on me that you would no longer be here. I miss you so much, remembering all of your advice. You always had great insight. Your heart was always open and your intentions were so sincere. I never had a chance to thank you for being there. When I was going through my struggles, you were always there to redirect me in the right path. Although I was stubborn, you never gave up on me; always reminding me of what being successful could bring. Never becoming impatient. Always reminding me about the importance of living out your dreams. You would always say, "Never let anyone stop you from reaching for the stars." Reminding me that I was a precious gem with unusual shine. Telling me that the world was mine. Now you're gone. Never giving me a clue. Now what is one to do? Many say that you don't miss a good thing until it's gone. For a long time, I tried to prove them wrong. Now I agree. You were truly a blessing to me. Now you are merely a memory. Gone too soon!

Chapter Sixteen: The Naked Truth

◇◇◇

*D*AMON, CHARLES, AND JERMAINE HEADED towards their cars. Charles stopped in the middle of his tracks and said, "Fellas, why don't we go grab something to eat after we go shower and shit? It's the weekend and I don't have shit to do."

Jermaine commented, "You know what, Charles, that doesn't sound like a bad idea at all. Let's do the damn thing!"

Damon replied, "Why not? Fuck it. Let's go get fresh for the females and hit the streets." Charles said, "Sounds like a plan. Let's meet at Crab Shack in about an hour."

The gentlemen agreed, got in their cars, and pulled off. Jermaine got in his car, put his Tupac CD in, and started bumping his head while trying to come up with a good way to tell Radiance that he didn't want a relationship, only friendship. Jermaine really did like Radiance. He thought she was beautiful and smart. He always thought she carried an unusual light within herself and he didn't want to taint it or have her thinking that she got played. He just felt like he was too young for a relationship. Jermaine mumbled, "I'm just going to man up and tell her that I don't want a relationship. Charles was right." Jermaine thought to himself, *I'm going to just have to find a way to tell her, but right now I can't focus on that. Maybe I will figure it out after I finish bumping to Tupac.* Jermaine reached for the radio to blast his music and rolled off.

In the meantime, while Damon was cruising up the block checking out the ladies in their finest spring wear, he noticed the dresses, shorts, leggings and perfectly pedicured feet. Damon said, "All of these females looking all good and shit is making my dick hard! I feel like a kid in a candy store, got damn! This shit is simply amazing. I'm definitely going to get fresh and hit the town tonight. It's a lot to see out here!" Damon pulled up in front of his apartment, parked his car, and went inside to get ready.

Thirty minutes passed since Radiance and Charisma left the apartment. They finally arrived in front of the Crab Shack. As they entered the restaurant, they noticed that Constance, Destiny, and Unique were already seated in the back of the restaurant. Radiance picked up the pep in her step, grabbing Charisma by the hand, and leading the way to the table. When they arrived at the table all eyes were on Charisma. Radiance said, "Hey ladies, this is my girl, Charisma." Suddenly, the stares turned into smiles. "It's so nice meeting you," all of the ladies responded at once. Constance commented, "Girl, have a seat. I heard so much about you. I feel like I already know you." Charisma smirked and said, "Well, I have heard a lot about all of you as well. Radiance speaks very highly of all of you."

"Now that's good stuff," Destiny replied. "Have a seat everybody. I can't speak for everyone, but I can speak for myself when I tell you that I'm starved!" Unique responded, "You never lied about that! Let's eat!" Constance just laughed and said, "Well, let's eat then ladies. I will tell you my big news after we eat." Radiance responded, "Oh, hell no! You need to tell me the news right now. I have been waiting all day for this. You got all up in my head, making me wonder what in the world you had to tell me." Charisma just laughed and said, "Radiance, honey, just be patient. I'm quite sure that Constance will share her wonderful news with all of us in a moment." Destiny yelled out, "Yeah, Radiance, sit your crazy ass down. I like your friend, Charisma. She is all right with me." Radiance crossed her arms, rolled her eyes, and said, "Whatever, you guys!"

When she sat down, the waitress came over and asked the ladies, "What will you all be having?" Constance interrupted her and asked,

"Do you have the special for the crab cakes right now?" The waitress responded, "Why, yes we do." All of the ladies just looked at Constance wondering why she didn't give any of them the chance to select their dishes. Constance then yelled out, "Do you girls like crab cakes?" and they all responded by nodding their heads "yes." "Well, ladies, crab cakes it is." Constance looked over at the waitress and said, "Give us the specials, fry the crab cakes, and give us Coke soda to drink. Thank me later, ladies, I'm treating you all...compliments of me and my fiancé!" Constance reached in her pocket, grabbed her velvet box, and opened it, displaying her beautiful diamond ring inside of it. Everyone's face appeared to be puzzled and Radiance jumped up yelling, "OMG! Bitch, you getting married? Get the fuck out of here!" Questions followed right behind her: how, when, and, where?

Destiny interrupted and said, "Congrats, lady! And as for you, Radiance, does it matter how and when or where? All that matters is that our girl is getting hitched!" Unique said, "Congrats, boo!" Charisma smiled brightly and added, "Constance, that is truly a blessing!" In the back of Charisma's mind, she thought that Constance may have been too young to make such a big commitment, but she didn't feel it was her place to put her opinion in the mix, and didn't want to mess up what could possibly be the beginning of a beautiful new friendship. So, she chose to get out of her seat, walk over to Constance, and give her a proper hug instead of ruining Constance's big day.

When everybody calmed down, they all sat down and waited for their food to come. "Man, I can't wait to eat," Radiance said, while sitting down and looking across a few tables and over at the bar where the television was showing the news. Radiance then commented, "The news is always so damn depressing. There is never anything good on." Charisma replied, "Yeah, that is definitely the case in most situations."

Constance, Unique, and Destiny were still excited, rambling on about the wedding while still looking at Constance's engagement ring. Radiance had not seen the ring up close yet because Unique and Destiny kept blocking her vision and knocking her out of the way. The waitress came out with their food. "Yes," Charisma responded while reaching out for her crab cake. "Honey, a sister is tired, you hear me?" Charisma was astonished when Radiance didn't respond. She looked over at her still looking at the news, and began calling her name but Radiance didn't respond. Across the screen flashed, "Prostitute found dead identified as Lisa Murphy. Suspect of murder victim brought in identified as David Brown." Constance called out Radiance's name and got no response. She noticed Radiance staring at the television with a disturbing look on her face which caused her to look at the television. She saw Lisa's face plastered on the screen. "Oh, shit!" Constance exclaimed and everyone started looking at the television. Destiny said, "That's the woman from Joe's sub shop who is always outside tricking. I spoke to her once or twice and she was really cool." Unique yelled out, "That sure is her."

Charisma reached for Radiance's hand and asked, "Is that a friend of yours, honey? I'm so sorry if it was." Radiance glanced over to Charisma with water in her eyes and responded, "Well, she kind of was a friend to me. I just don't get this life shit!" Radiance added, "You're never promised tomorrow. I can't figure out why bad things always happen to good people. Life is definitely no fairytale."

Charisma replied, "Radiance, life is what you make it. You're right. Life is not always a fairytale. You go through seasons where the sun is not always shining, but then sometimes in a season, everything can appear to be so bright. I know Lisa was a friend of yours, but God called her home for a reason. Her purpose has been fulfilled and no one knows what her purpose was. That's between her and God. Maybe her purpose was to teach you something. Lord only knows that, princess." Constance interrupted to say, "Now that shit was fucked up! That's it. From this point on, I'm going to continue living my life like it's golden." Unique and Destiny both replied, "I think that's a great idea, C."

Radiance continued looking at the news. The murder suspect looked familiar. Suddenly a flashback came of the man who was trying to attack her before Eric scared him away. Radiance yelled, "Shit!" She hopped up from the table and told the girls that she needed a minute. Radiance went to the bathroom, went over to the sink, splashed her face with water, and looked in the mirror. She started remembering how she felt when the man was trying to attack her and how safe she felt when Eric came to her rescue. Flashbacks of Lisa came to Radiance's mind. She remembered her smile. Her image kept coming back over and over in her mind. Radiance shook her head and mumbled, "I sure hope you're in a better place." Radiance wiped her eyes, brushed her hair, and went back out of the bathroom and over to her friends. Constance went over to Radiance and asked, "Are you okay?" Radiance responded, "Yeah, girl, I'm straight now. I can finally see this diamond ring." Radiance grabbed Constance's left hand and stated, "Dang! Girl, somebody loves you!" Unique asked, "Radiance, are you sure that you are okay?" Radiance replied, "For the millionth time, I'm fine, and before you ask me, Charisma, I really am okay! Now let's continue our girl talk. I'm enjoying my friends. Life is too short, so we have to live each day as if it's our last day." The ladies all laughed and continued talking. Constance replied, "I like us hanging out like this. We should do this at least once a month; start a sisterhood. We can call it, 'Diamondz in the Rough.'"

Charisma exclaimed, "I like the sound of that! You ladies should go for it." Destiny replied, "We are going to include you in our group, too. You are a new friend to us." Charisma smiled and replied, "I would like that." Unique commented, "Welcome to the circle!" As the girls continued to enjoy themselves, Constance noticed Virtue and Ambiance walking in and heading in their direction. Constance started thinking to herself, *Here we go, again.* Virtue walked over when she noticed Constance and Radiance. The ladies just stared at Ambiance and Virtue. "Well, don't stare! Show some love," Virtue said, as she went up to Constance and Radiance to hug them. "I have to say we have to stop meeting up like this!" Virtue commented. Constance replied, "Yes, girl, we really do." Ambiance looked at Constance and asked, "How are you doing?"

Constance responded, "I'm well and you?" Constance was thinking to herself, *Virtue might be all right, but there's something shady about her homegirl. I can't put my finger on it, but I can see me busting her ass in the future.*

Virtue commented, "We were going to grab a bite to eat and from the looks of it, so were you. But it doesn't look like you touched any of your food. So with that being said, do you mind if we join you?"

Radiance replied, "Sure we don't. Pull up a chair and by all means join us!" Constance looked at Radiance with her lips twisted and started rolling her eyes. Radiance said, "We were all just sitting here having some girl talk about how life is too short not to live it up to the fullest."

"I can agree with that," Virtue commented.

Ambiance pulled up a chair hesitantly and continued to chew her gum, while looking over at Charisma. "How are you doing? Charisma asked Ambiance, even though she appeared to have a slight attitude. "I'm good," Ambiance replied. Unique, Destiny, Radiance, and Constance started eating their food while Virtue tried to get the waitress's attention.

In the meantime, Jermaine pulled up at the restaurant parking lot next to Damon and Charles. "Damn!" Charles replied, "Nigga, your ass took long enough! I'm hungry as shit! What the hell was you doing all that time? As a matter of fact bro, don't even tell me!" Damon said, "Can you two please stop arguing like schoolgirls and come on so we can get some food? Can you two do that for me, please?"

Jermaine replied, "On the real, Damon, you going to stop trying to son me. I'm not anyone's bitch, homeboy!"

Damon chuckled and responded, "Jermaine, get out of here with that shit! I'm just hungry, nigga, and I want to eat!" Charles interrupted, "Me, too, and if that means I'm trying to son you, consider your ass my son then!"

Jermaine laughed and yelled out, "Whatever, man!" They went into the restaurant and headed over to the bar. Charles said, "It's a group of fine-ass ladies sitting over there. Maybe we should introduce ourselves after we eat."

"Sounds like plan! Let's see who can book the finest one." Charles replied, "That's a no-brainer! I would all day."

Damon laughed and said, "Not while you're in my presence."

Jermaine responded, "You both are wrong. I'm a sexy-ass dude. It might be hard to book a chick with me around!"

As the gentlemen approached the bar while walking over to the nearest table, Damon said, "Shit! That's my girl over there in that group of women!" Jermaine laughed at Damon and when he turned around, he replied, "Oh, shit, homeboy! You not by yourself. That's the girl I was telling you two about. That's Radiance, and I have not returned her phone calls since I hit that. Let's get out of here before they notice." Charles chuckled and replied, "Come on, fellas. Let's try to get out of here, but I don't think that we will be all that successful because your girl has already spotted you, Damon, and she is on her way over here right now as we speak."

"That's just great," Damon replied, as he watched Constance walk in his direction.

"Hey, baby!" Constance commented, as she walked up on Damon and kissed his lips. "What are you doing here?!" Constance exclaimed.

Damon replied, "Baby, I just decided to grab a bite with the fellas. You know how it is. Just fellowship amongst friends."

Constance responded, "I definitely do. I was just doing the same thing with my girlfriends over there. Come on over and let me introduce you to my friends that you don't know already." She grabbed Damon by the hand and dragged him to the table full of females. Jermaine and Charles hesitantly followed behind. Charles paused for a second and mumbled to Jermaine, "You think you in the dog house with that young lady over at the table staring you down with anger in her eyes? Look to the left of her. That's shorty from the basketball court from earlier. Damon just booked that female and got her number." Jermaine stopped thinking about the trouble that he was getting ready to face with Radiance and looked straight ahead. He noticed the girl from the basketball court from earlier and replied, "Damn, that is the female from earlier." Charles responded, "We can't let shit get ugly."

As Constance got to the table, she introduced Damon as her fiancé. A disturbing look came upon Ambiance's face, but she never uttered a word about Damon and her encounter from earlier. Instead, she responded, "Congrats to you both! I hope that it leads to much happiness for you two." Damon was trying not to show the look of nervousness on his face. Charisma and Unique looked at each other and shook their heads, and Radiance tried not to stare at Jermaine but couldn't help it. Radiance started to get irritated, and excused herself from the table and went outside. Charles introduced himself to everyone and asked Charisma was it okay if he sat down. Charisma displayed a pleasant smile and responded, "Sure, you can take a seat."

Charisma noticed his eyes and she admired his chocolate, smooth skin. His sense of style turned her on in so many ways. His smile was captivating and his hair was cold black and curly. She loved everything about him, but in the back of her mind, she felt like she had seen him before, but she couldn't remember from where. Charisma thought to herself, *It will come to me later where I know this man from.*

Everyone else continued to talk amongst themselves and Ambiance continued to watch Constance and Damon interact. She wondered if it was possible for Damon to interact the same way towards her. Ambiance's eyes continued to study Damon's body. Everything appeared to be so perfect. She envisioned him naked and she imagined her tongue licking him from head to toe. She envisioned his dick in her mouth, as she licked it like a tasty dessert. Ambiance closed her eyes for a second and imagined riding Damon's dick as if it were the last ride that she would ever take in her life. She opened her eyes up and she felt her pussy getting moist. She licked her lips and whispered to herself, "Damon, you will be mine sooner then you will ever know."

Twenty minutes passed since Radiance went outside and sat on the bench that was located on the side of the restaurant. She gazed at the stars and started thinking about Lisa and how she was no longer there. Suddenly, she heard a deep voice call her name. She knew instantly that it was Jermaine. "Is it all right if I join you? Jermaine asked and Radiance turned around and looked at Jermaine in complete disgust. "Sure, help yourself."

Jermaine replied, "Listen, beautiful, I know that you don't have a lot of rap for me and I can't blame you. I know that you have been calling and trying to get in contact with me, and I haven't yet taken the time or consideration to call you back. It was because when I was with you Radiance and we made love, I felt something that I never felt before and it was way too scary." Radiance looked over at Jermaine and replied, "Listen, J, cut the shit! I don't have time for it. You don't need to explain anything to me. You wanted to fuck me and you did, and now you don't want me anymore because you got the pussy."

Jermaine responded, "Damn, Radiance! That's real cold. I deserve that, but baby, it was never just pussy for me. I meant everything that I said to you and I will even go so far as to say that I love you but, baby, I'm not ready to be in a serious relationship. I'm still young and working on being a better man. There is no way that I could possibly do that right now, but it would mean so much to me if we could keep it like it is--continue learning each other and developing a stronger connection and friendship. Because you are one of the realest people that I know and that's hard to find in a person, especially a woman. So what do you say? Can we give it a try?"

Radiance stood up, looked Jermaine in the eyes, replied, "Fuck you," smacked him in the face, and walked back inside of the restaurant. Jermaine stayed outside on the bench and thought to himself, "Maybe I had that one coming." He giggled and continued looking at the stars above in the sky. He said, "Lord, please show me the way. I never wanted to hurt her and I do love her, but I can't commit to her right now. God, you know my heart. Show me what to do to make it better. Please take the pain that she is experiencing away. Please put it in her heart to forgive me, and please fix what I feel is broken. Amen." Jermaine held his head down and cried alone on the bench, as he thought about the love he just lost. Radiance stormed in the restaurant door and ran into the bathroom, leaned against the wall, and cried. Her heart was pounding and she quickly wiped away her tears. She mumbled to herself, "Fuck that dude. It's his loss. I'm a great catch and he will soon realize that. I can't believe that I trusted him. I was such a fool, but I will never be anyone's fool again, that's for sure." Radiance brushed her hair in the mirror, went in her bag, grabbed her mascara, and applied it to her eyes. She thought to herself, *The least I can do is fix myself up. Just because my heart is hurting doesn't give me a reason to look a mess in front of my friends. It's Constance's engagement dinner and I have to be supportive of her on her big day. She deserves to be happy on her big day.*

Radiance finished fixing herself up, threw her mascara in her bag, left out the bathroom, and went back to the table where she found everyone talking and hugging goodbye. Radiance replied, "Did I miss all of the action?" Destiny turned around and asked, "Girl, where you been? It's time to go now." Unique commented, "I seen that fine ass man follow you outside. What was that all about?" Radiance responded back, "Absolutely nothing. He is just a guy from school that I know. No big deal." Destiny replied, "Well his ass was fine." She grabbed her spring jacket off the back of her chair and made an announcement, "Well, ladies, it's been real. I'm getting ready to take it inside." Unique interrupted and asked, "Destiny, can you please give me a ride home? I rode with Constance and from the looks of it, she does not want to leave her man's side, and who could blame her on such a special day." Destiny looked over at Constance and told Unique, "You're right. Come on, girl. Let's get out of here. We're gone, Radiance," Unique and Destiny said. "Call us later." Radiance waved to them both and replied, "I will."

Virtue commented, "Radiance, girl, me and Ambiance are getting ready to go too. We're going to go say goodbye to Constance and we're out of here."

"Okay, Virtue!" Radiance responded. "It was good seeing you again, girl, and it was nice meeting you too, Ambiance."

"The feeling is mutual, dear," Ambiance said, as she got up, popped her gum, and walked away.

Virtue followed Radiance, turned around, and saw Charisma saying her goodbyes to a gentleman that she didn't know. Radiance stood and watched Charisma in action. Virtue walked up to Damon and Constance. "Congratulations to you two," she said, "I certainly hope that your marriage will bring you much joy and happiness." Constance blushed and replied, "It will, Virtue. He is so awesome to me and our love is true. I trust him and I know that he will love me unconditionally." She then asked Damon, "Isn't that right, baby?" Damon answered yes with sweat forming on his forehead and his heart in the pit of his stomach. He glanced over at Ambiance and then diverted his attention to Constance. Ambiance smirked at Damon and then looked over at Constance and added, "Yeah, girl! I hope that you remain happy. It's good to know that love still exists. I believe that I will find it one day soon. I certainly hope to see you again. I think that we could be great friends. I have a feeling that we have more in common than you realize." Constance looked over at Ambiance and rolled her eyes. She replied, "I'm looking forward to developing a friendship with you, too." She then thought to herself, *Yeah, bitch! My mother always told me to keep friends close and your enemies even closer.* There was something about Ambiance that Constance was not feeling. Ambiance smiled maliciously at Constance and walked away.

Virtue commented, "Okay, girl! I will see you again soon, I'm sure. We always run into each other at the weirdest places. Constance replied while laughing, "We sure do. Talk to you soon, Virtue." Charisma finally left the gentleman and walked over to Radiance and asked, "You ready to go, girl?!" Radiance responded, "Sure I am, but not so fast, miss!

Who was that fine chocolate man that you were talking to?" Charisma answered, "His name was Charles and he wants to take me out. He was fine, wasn't he?" Radiance responded, "Fine was an understatement! Get them, Miss Charisma, it's good to see you step out of your shell and let your hair down a little." Charisma responded, "Yeah, girl, it's been a while since I have, but it felt good to do it. Do you want to go and say goodbye to Constance?" Radiance turned around and saw Constance gazing into Damon's eyes. It seemed like in her world, no one else was even in the room. It was just Damon and Constance, all alone in their own universe. Radiance replied, "No, girl, Constance is in her own fairytale land now. Let's go. I will call her tomorrow. Let me yell out to her and let her know that we are gone." Radiance yelled out loudly, "C," and Constance's head turned in her direction. "What's up?" Constance replied. "I'm gone, girl. Hit me up later." Constance responded, "Okay!" Radiance laughed and turned to Charisma and said, "See, I told you that she was in fairytale land. I know my girls." Charisma laughed loudly and replied, "I guess you do," and they headed out of the restaurant and straight to the car to head home.

Jermaine finally got up off the bench and headed to his car. The thought of losing Radiance's friendship kept crossing his mind. He really hoped that they could work out their differences. On his way to the car he saw Charles getting ready to pull off in his car. Jermaine yelled out Charles's name but he didn't hear him. Charles pulled off and Jermaine entered his car and said, "That nigga was in his own world. He must have met a female because his mind was somewhere else." Jermaine started his car, turned up his music, and pulled off.

Constance and Damon were in the restaurant. They had just finished paying the bill. Damon came up from behind Constance and smacked her plump ass and said, "I'm going to fuck the shit out of you tonight! It must have been a reason that I ran into your ass here and not at home." Damon then asked, "What made you choose this place anyway, boo?" Constance replied, "It was inexpensive and my girl, Unique, suggested that we come. She said the food was great and baby she never told a story. I'm sorry that I didn't introduce everyone to you one by one. How rude. It's just that I was too excited to see you here. So, I forgot. But the next time, I promise I will. The only friends that I truly have are Radiance, Unique, Charisma, and Destiny. I just met Charisma, but I feel like I've known her forever. Virtue and Ambiance are new to the circle, too. Virtue seems cool. I didn't like her at first, but she's growing on me. It's that one, Ambiance, that I'm not feeling. It's something about her that I don't like." Constance asked Damon, "Have you ever felt that way before?" Damon was speechless. He had a flashback of Ambiance at the ball court in those little shorts. He felt his dick getting hard and at the same time he felt guilty and nervous. He then thought to himself, *Shit could have gotten real ugly if Ambiance had mentioned their encounter from earlier to Constance. It's nice to know that Ambiance is a down-ass chic that wouldn't snitch.* Damon wondered if they could still fuck and if she could be content with being his side piece, if he blessed her with cash every now and then. Constance yelled out, "Damon, I asked you a question! Have you ever felt that way before?" Damon responded, "I'm sorry, baby, no I haven't. Can we not talk about this anymore? You're ruining my fantasy of how I'm going to fuck the shit out of you in a minute, with your back up against the wall. I need my practice if I'm going to bless you properly on our wedding day. I'm so excited, baby." Constance smiled and said, "Yeah, baby! Let's get some practice." They walked out of the door and straight to their vehicles. Damon said, "Come on, girl, I will race you home. First one there should be naked and waiting at the door on their knees, ready to surrender to being their significant other's love slave for the night." Constance responded, "Cool," as she opened her car door and yelled over to Damon, "see you at home and make sure that you are on all fours when I get there, Daddy!" Damon smiled and replied, "I got you, baby! But trust me when I say that it will not be me on all fours this evening. It will be your ass, so get ready quickly!"

How could the one that I trust the most hurt me so? Tell me lies and corrupt my soul. I thought you were my prince and I was your princess. Now I feel like a victim in a horror story. I entrusted you with my heart and you shredded it into pieces. My dreams have become nightmares and inside I'm empty. My days are longer and full of sorrow. No longer am I looking forward to tomorrow. My faith is gone and my will is weak. No longer am I able to sleep. My light is dim. No longer am I shining. Now I walk around with a shield of armor, trying to protect what's left of my heart. Picking up bits and pieces along the way. Every day I pray, but many prayers remain unanswered. Suddenly I'm feeling abandoned. Now I consider myself damaged. No longer able to love or trust. Wanting to protect myself, so I walk alone. No longer do I desire to keep holding on. I have given up on everything and everybody. The world is cruel and my heart is cold. I no longer know how to move on. I'm empty and full of rage. I have become my own nightmare.

Chapter Seventeen: The Million Dollar Man

◇◇

*W*HEN RADIANCE AND CHARISMA AR-
rived home, Radiance walked straight into the guest room
and told Charisma, "Good night!" Charisma responded, "It's not that
late, Radiance. You still have time to do something else if you wanted to,
silly." Radiance smiled and replied, "I know, but it has been a long day
and I want to just call it quits and start off all over again first thing in the
morning. But, I had a great time with you. I'm so happy you decided to
go, Charisma." Charisma responded, "I'm glad I went too. It has been a
while since I went out and kicked it. I even met some new friends and a
man, too." Radiance said, "You sure did! He was hot, too. I got a feeling
that you will talk to him real soon. It would be good for you, Charisma.
You need a little action in your life right now." Charisma responded,
"Not too much action. I'm trying to hold out and see what the Lord has
in store for me. A man always seeks his wife. You should never seek a
husband; when a man finds a wife he finds a good thing." Radiance said,
"Well, he certainly found you. Maybe he is the one. Just enjoy yourself.
And by the way, Charisma, I know that you are a saved woman and I am
saved too, but I'm a work in progress. But girl, there is nothing wrong
with a little sex every now and then. It's a great way to relieve stress."
Charisma's mouth dropped open and she laughed loudly at Radiance.
She responded, "I know that's right! And for the record, I'm a work in

progress too, but I have been doing good holding out. Sometimes I wish I could unleash the tigress in me on someone, but I believe that good things come to those who wait." Radiance smiled and continued walking to the guestroom. "Good night, again." Charisma replied, "Good night, girl. I will talk to you in the a.m."

Radiance went in the guest room and noticed Stephen's business card sitting on the dresser. She picked it up and she could smell the scent of his cologne on the card. Radiance was intrigued by Stephen and his theory about love at first sight. Radiance thought that it was a load of crap. She used to feel that way about Jermaine and she thought that the feeling was mutual. That was until she realized that the whole time it was her sex and friendship he desired. Radiance became outraged with the fact that she felt that she got played. She sat down on the edge of the bed and mumbled to herself, "But even after I discovered the truth, I still love him. The nerve of him, telling me that he loved me too! I can't believe that he looked me in the eyes and lied to me! After telling me that my eyes were the mirror of my soul and if you look deep inside them you can find out everything you wanted to know about a person. I have to get it together quickly. I'm too fly to be going through this nonsense. My name is Radiance and I need to start acting like the woman that I'm becoming, and not some lovesick schoolgirl. Damn! I'm better than this."

Radiance looked at Stephen's business card and decided to call him. "Maybe he can help me get over Jermaine. I need to talk to someone else and have him occupy my time, because Jermaine is in my heart and the shit won't go away." Radiance picked up the phone and called Stephen. "So fate had you call me," Stephen replied on the other end. Radiance took the phone away from her ear and stared at it. She immediately heard Stephen's voice on the other end saying, "Hello? Radiance, I have been awaiting your call." Radiance put the phone back up to her ear and responded, "How did you know that it was me?" Stephen said, "Because it was fate and besides, I don't give my number out every day." Stephen then chuckled and asked, "So how was your day today? I must admit I was hoping to hear from you sooner. You left a lasting impression. Your smile was radiant. Now I know why your parents named you Radiance. That name suits you oh, so well." Radiance started blushing on the other end and starting thinking to herself, *This man is definitely a smooth operator. He knows how to stroke my ego and I love it.* Radiance responded in a very sexy voice, "Why, thank you, Stephen. You certainly have a way with words, I see." Stephen said, "I try to expand my selection in words. Having a great vocabulary comes in handy when you're trying to court a beautiful woman such as yourself." Radiance replied, "Well, sir, I'm impressed. There is nothing like an intelligent man who is capable of conducting a real conversation. I will let you in on a little secret," Radiance's voice turned into a soft whisper, "it's actually a turn-on for me." Stephen responded, "Thanks for that information. I'm making a mental note right now as we speak." Stephen then commented, "Now listen, Radiance, I'm a man who knows exactly what he wants and when I see something that I want, my mentality is to go out and get it. Life's too short for bullshit! So, Miss Radiance, let's cut out the small talk and get right down to business. I'm interested in getting to know you better. I'm a man who believes in fate and when I saw you there was something about you that caused my energy to shift in your direction. Things like that don't happen often. So, with that being said, when is the best time to send my limousine driver over to pick you up so that we can dine in a fine restaurant? Or go to an art exhibit; dancing, or whatever your preference may be? Anything that your heart desires, I'm able to accommodate and make it happen. Hell, we can even take a quick trip to Paris if you like. I own a jet and it is always filled up and ready to go. I have two pilots on call twenty-four hours a day."

Radiance was lost in her choice of words for Stephen. She knew that he appeared to be a successful man, but Radiance had no idea that this man was a millionaire. Or was he just a person who talked a good game and had absolutely nothing? Radiance responded, "You're kidding, right?" Stephen answered, "No, dear. I'm not. I don't have time for games. Time is of the essence and trust me when I say time stands still for no one; not even human beings. So with that being said, let's try to keep up with the time, dear. So let me ask you again, 'What will be the best time for us to link up?'" Radiance responded, "You really don't play around. I like that quality in a man. Well, Stephen, my schedule is open. So when would you like to see me?" Stephen said, "I would like to see you as soon as possible. I told you that time is of the essence. So, I have an idea. I will send a limousine over to you within forty- five minutes. It is still a decent hour; not too late. The weather is perfect and the moonlight is shining brightly. I would like to see how it beams upon your skin on such a lovely night. So you should go and clean yourself up for me, and just put on a nice dress. I will take you shopping tomorrow if you like. My stylist has a great eye for fashion."

Radiance giggled and responded, "That sounds like a plan. But, I have to find something to wear. I feel like Cinderella. Stephen said, "I have no problem being Prince Charming, precious. Let me call my driver and tell him to pick up my princess in forty-five minutes." Radiance smiled and responded, "Okay! Let me go and get dressed. Prince Charming, will you be with your driver when he comes to pick me up?" Stephen just replied, "Wait and see. Sometimes it's good to have a pleasant surprise. You don't need to know every move that you make. Sometimes it's good to live in the moment and do whatever comes naturally to you. I will see you soon, either way. Now go and get ready. I told you, time is of the essence." Radiance said, "Yes, you did. I shall see you soon."

Radiance hung up the phone and started to wonder what on Earth she should wear. She mumbled to herself, "I don't have anything to wear." She went through her bag of clothes and spotted a sexy little red dress. Radiance stopped and stared at the dress for a moment and thought to herself, *I'm feeling sexy... why not go for it?* She grabbed her towel and rag, and went into the bathroom to wash up. Fifteen minutes passed and Radiance went back to the guest room, grabbed some oil, and started rubbing her legs down. She wanted them to be perfect for Stephen. Radiance felt like she was in the middle of a dream. She felt like a Disney princess and wondered if she had finally met her prince. Radiance started whispering to herself, "After all of the hell that I encountered, a Prince is due to come and slay demons, climb on mountains, confess his love to me, and whistle for his magical unicorn to come and fly us away into the gates of heaven and live happily ever after."

The phone rang, Radiance picked up, and Stephen responded on the other end, "It has been about thirty minutes, dear, and my driver is outside waiting for you." Radiance said, "Wow, how did you get your driver here so quickly? And how do you know the address to where I'm residing? I haven't even given that to you yet!" Stephen laughed on the other end and replied, "Gorgeous, don't be alarmed. I can assure you that I'm no psycho fixing to take you some place and eat you or something. I'm simply a man who knows what it is that he wants, and so far I want you. And besides, if you call information and give them a number, they can give you the address as long as it is public information."

Radiance put her hand on her chest, began laughing, and responded, "I was starting to get scared, but I'm over it now!" Stephen laughed and said, "I'm so glad you are. Please don't ever feel threatened by me. I would never hurt a fly." Radiance smiled as she slid her feet into her pumps and replied, "I will be down in one second." Stephen replied, "Sure thing, beautiful. I will alert my driver and let him know."

Radiance hung up the phone, grabbed a sheet of paper, and wrote Charisma a note stating that she was going out and don't wait up. She placed the note on the living room table and walked out. She didn't want to distract Charisma in her room. Radiance raced down the flight of apartment stairs and noticed the pearl white limousine shining and waiting for her. A chauffeur was standing along the side as if he were waiting to open up the door. Radiance's eyes enlarged as she proceeded to walk over to the limo. The chauffeur greeted her as she approached the limo and simply said, "Good evening, fair lady. May I do you the honor of opening up the door for you as it is my job." The chauffer chuckled and added, "Sir Stephen told me to handle you with great care, as you are as delicate as a flower." Radiance felt like she was in one of those fairytale movies where she was considered to be royalty with real life servants that catered to her every need. Radiance responded to the chauffeur, "Thanks for being so kind by opening up the door for me, but for future reference, I could really do that myself. I'm not handicapped."

Radiance flashed her radiant smile and the chauffeur smiled back at her. He replied, "By no circumstances should you ever have to open up a door all on your own. What kind of man would allow a lovely lady to do such a thing? I will let you in on a little secret...if you go out with someone and he doesn't open the door for you, kick his butt to the curb!"

Radiance entered the limousine and saw all of the fancy contraptions, wine, television, snacks, and many other beverages. The chauffeur cracked his window lightly and said, "Help yourself to anything that you like. I'm quite sure that Sir Stephen will not mind." The chauffeur rolled his window back up and Radiance turned into a kid in a candy store, grabbing a few snacks and an orange soda. Radiance started thinking to herself, *This shit is dope! A girl could get used to something like this!* Radiance sat back in the limousine, opened up her snacks, and began munching on them. "I'm going to enjoy this ride," she whispered, as she rolled down the window and started enjoying the view of the city.

Meanwhile, Charisma left her room and started calling out Radiance's name. She heard no response back, so she walked into the guestroom and saw that Radiance left her clothes that she had on from earlier, on the bed. Charisma scratched her head and called out her name again, only to get no response. Once again, she went into the living room. She saw that Radiance left a note on the living room table that read,

Hey, Charisma! I didn't want to disturb you. I decided to take your advice and go out and live a little. I have a hot date with a very classy guy and I will not be home tonight. He is having his driver pick me up and we are going to hang out for the rest of the night. Don't wait up and I promise I will be a good girl. Love you, girl. I will see you tomorrow.

~Radiance.

Charisma looked at the note and said, "Dammit! Radiance going out with some guy was not exactly what I had in mind when I said enjoy the night." She laughed as she put down the note and went over to her purse. She started thinking, *Maybe having a little fun is exactly what I could use at this time in my life. Just because I love the Lord doesn't mean that I should be alone.* Charisma went in her purse and grabbed Charles's business card. She stared at it and said, "I'm going to go for it. No longer am I going to stay in a shell. It's time for me to crack open!"

Charisma picked up the phone and called Charles. Her hands trembled as she listened. Each time the phone rang, she jumped up nervously. Finally, Charles picked up on the other end. "Hello?" he responded. Charisma's heart started beating fast as she replied, "Hello," attempting to try to sound sexy and seductive on the other end. "May I speak to Charles?" Charisma asked. There was a slight pause and Charles responded, "This is he."

"Hello, Charles. This is Charisma. I met you at the restaurant earlier today and I wanted to reach out to you to say hello. I really enjoyed our conversation and I wanted to see if you were up to finishing it." Charles responded with excitement in his voice, "Sure, I would love to continue our conversation. When I was talking to you earlier, I must admit that I didn't hear you much. I couldn't get past your beauty and there was something different about your aura. It was like you possessed some light in you. I don't know how religious you are, but I could feel the God in you."

Charisma was silent on the other end as she looked up towards the ceiling and whispered, "Thank you, Lord! I think that my prayer must have been answered!" Charisma responded to Charles, "I felt that way, too. I'm so curious to learn all about you. Like, do you acknowledge God and put him before all others?" Charles said, "Why, yes I do. It's very rare that a woman asks that question. That says a lot about your character."

Charisma began smiling as bright as the sun on the other end and said to Charles, "You have to ask these questions. It's so important to know them, along with, 'what are your dreams, are you saved, do you work, have Children, are you married, and are you able to vision?'" Charles responded, "I certainly understand that and the answers to your questions are, my dreams are larger than this world and I have been saved for seven years; however I'm a work in progress, the furthest thing from a saint. I do work, but I can't tell you a lot of information on that at this time. My work is a little complicated and I'm trying to find another source of work. No longer am I fulfilled with what I do. I don't have any children that I know of, and I have never been married because I have never met the right woman to keep me balanced. Last but not least, Charisma, of course I have vision, because that is the key to happiness and success. You have to be able to envision things as if they already are."

Charisma took a deep breath on the other end. She couldn't believe that Charles had all of the qualities that she had prayed for in a man. Charisma started to wonder, *Is it possible that my prayers have been answered? I'm so tired of being lonely*, she thought to herself, *and I want to commit and give myself to another. My body is yearning to be touched and I don't know how long I will be able to battle this demon of lust and desire.*

Charles then asked, "Are you still there?" Charisma responded, "Yes, Charles, I'm still here. I just got choked up in words, that's all." Charles then asked, "Where do you reside?" Charisma responded, "I stay at Strawberry Hill Apartments, right off of Gwynn Oak."

Charles exploded in laughter. "Get out of here! I stay over here, too. I just moved in the neighborhood about two weeks ago." Charisma giggled on the other end and responded, "Are you serious?" Charles continued to laugh and said, "I couldn't make it up if I tried. I live on 401 Strawberry Court, Apartment D." Charisma's mouth dropped and replied, "I live over at 403 Strawberry Court, Apartment D." Suddenly, Charisma had a flashback of the other day when she saw the guy taking out the trash. *It was Charles,* she thought to herself. *I knew I saw him somewhere before. He is the one that made my pussy moist from watching his every move.*

Charles then said, "Well, nice to meet you, neighbor. I know that this is a little forward, but why don't you come over for a cup of coffee? I feel like I have known you forever and I would love to continue our conversation in person." Charisma thought about it for a second and decided to take Charles up on his offer. She soon replied back to Charles, "Sure, why not? I think that it would be a great idea. I love coffee and conversation, and I can save gas money because I can walk right to you."

Charles responded, "Okay! I would love that. How long before you can get to me?"

Charisma said, "Let me grab my sweats and tennis shoes, and I will walk right over. I will see you in about fifteen minutes." Charles laughed and hung up the phone. He instantly started picking up everything off the floor and placing it in the closet. Charles went over to the kitchen to put all of the dishes in the dishwasher and went to his room to quickly make his bed. Charles lit all of his scented candles. He wanted to impress Charisma. He felt that they had a great connection that he wanted to explore and see what was coming next. She appeared to be a woman of great substance and he wanted to have a chance to get to know her better.

Charles went into his bedroom and grabbed some clean basketball shorts and a tank top. Charisma grabbed her keys and headed over to Charles's apartment. She was nervous. *It has been a long time since I have been alone with a man,* Charisma thought to herself. She shook her head and whispered, "Girl, don't mess this one up." As Charisma walked, she tried to come up with creative ways to appear both sexy and classy. Charles sprayed on some cologne and rushed to the living room. He turned on a movie. He didn't want to make it seem like he was pressed. Before Charisma arrived, he opened a glass of wine and had coffee brewing in the kitchen. Charles sighed as he commented, "I can't believe I'm going through so much for a female. She has to be a special."

Charles walked towards the couch and as he was walking, he heard a knock at the door. He peeped through the peep hole and saw Charisma fixing her hair. Charles smiled and opened up the door. "Glad you could make it over," he said, as he instructed Charisma to come inside and make herself feel at home. Charisma walked over to the couch while looking at Charles in his tank top and shorts. Her pussy instantly became wet as she looked at his defined calf muscles and his strong back. Charisma attempted to divert her attention to something else, but every now and again, her attention was brought right back to Charles.

Charisma commented, "This is a pretty nice place that you have here." Charles responded, "I try. So it's not too bad for a bachelor pad?" Charisma replied, "Not at all! I love the artwork on the walls. Very modern-like in here." Charles laughed while in the kitchen reaching for wine glasses and mugs. He said, "Now, Charisma, I have coffee and wine in here. Which one do you prefer?" Charisma replied, "I will take the wine. It will help me relax. It has been a long day."

"Wine it is," Charles replied, as he poured wine in the glasses. I selected a movie. I hope that it is okay. If you don't like it, there are many under the television stand. Feel free to select one. It's kind of cool having company. I get so lonely at times, and I'm really a romantic guy. I would love to have a lady to spend time with."

The sound of Charles's voice sounded like music to Charisma's ears. Charles went over to Charisma and sat right beside her. The aroma of Charles's cologne was driving Charisma crazy. Charisma tried to maintain her composure, but her pussy was not behaving. It was jumping and had a mind of its own. Charles looked over at Charisma and asked, "Are you comfortable?" Charisma commented, "Yes, I'm good," with her legs crossed, waving back and forth with the glass of wine in her hand. Charles laughed and asked, "Are you sure? Because you appear to be nervous. Let me give you a quick neck massage.'

"I won't bite! exclaimed Charles. "Trust me, I can be a good boy and I'm always on my best behavior. Unless you want me to be naughty, and

I'm sure that isn't what you want. So, Charisma, just sit back and let me help you relax a little. I will take good care of you."

Charisma responded, "I would love that. It has been a really long time since I have relaxed." She placed her empty wine glass on the living room table, kept her legs crossed, and prayed that her pussy muscles would stop jumping. Instead, her pussy became moist. Charles's hands were full of strength. Her eyes closed as she bit the bottom of her full lips. Her legs continued to swing back and forth, as they were crossed. She was horny and relaxed. *This is a deadly combination*, Charisma thought to herself. Charles then asked, "Are you feeling a little more relaxed right now? I want you to feel like you're at home, and it is impossible to do that if you're tense." Charisma responded, "I agree. Your hands are like magic. You really have a way of making a girl feel special. You should give some of these other brothers lessons." Charles laughed and replied, "There is really nothing to teach. I don't run game or any of that nonsense. I just treat a woman the way that I would want to be treated, and I add a little extra tender love and care in the mix." Charles smirked as he moved Charisma's hair off of her shoulder and he noticed her rose tattoo. It was a turn-on and Charles began thinking to himself, *This woman has a wild side to her.* His dick enlarged in his basketball shorts and he placed his smooth soft lips on Charisma's shoulder. He then caught himself and responded, "I'm so sorry, Charisma. I would never want to offend you. This is not appropriate." Charisma stood up and exclaimed, "Damn right, it's not appropriate!" as she walked over to his balcony and opened the door. Charles felt embarrassed and he closed his eyes and shook his head. He began thinking, *I really messed up now.* Charisma took a seat on Charles's chair outside, removed her sweats and panties, and thought to herself, *Lord, please forgive me, but I'm only human.*

Charisma yelled out Charles's name and when he opened his eyes, Charisma's pussy was flashing him from the balcony. Charisma then replied, "The appropriate thing for you to do right now is to come and eat my pussy while my hair blows in the wind. Drop down to your knees and crawl your ass over here right now. Don't make me wait too long. That is a direct order. Do you understand the words that are coming out of my mouth?" Charles's mouth dropped open and he responded, "Yes, I understand," as he thought to himself, *I would have never imagined this happening. Normally this shit would turn me off, but at this moment I have never been this turned on in all my life.*

Charles dropped to his knees and crawled towards Charisma, watching her legs rock back and forth. His dick was as hard as a brick. He paused for a second and pulled his shorts and tank top off. Charisma watched his dick and continued rocking her legs back and forth. She exclaimed, "Come on, baby! My pussy is expecting you." Charles finally reached his destination of being right in between Charisma's legs. She then responded, "Good job," while rubbing Charles's head. "Let me see your tongue," she ordered, and Charles stuck out his long, slender, and narrow tongue. Charisma pointed to her pussy and instructed Charles to lick away, and that is exactly what he did. Charisma gapped open her legs as wide as she could, grabbed the balcony railing, and started yelling out, "Lord, have mercy on me!" Charles continued to tongue the center of her pussy. His motto was to not leave one spot untouched. The wind started blowing, causing Charisma's hair to blow in different directions. Charles stopped feasting on Charisma's pussy and he grabbed her by the wrist, pulling her off the chair. He then instructed her to arch her back and place one foot on the chair, and Charisma did exactly what was told to her. Charles smacked her ass, causing Charisma to feel a sting that was pleasing to her.

"Oh, Charles!" Charisma responded and Charles remained silent as he attempted to put his brick hard dick into Charisma's tight pussy. He noticed that he was not successful. Charisma screamed from the top of her lungs and Charles rubbed her back gently and whispered, "It will be okay! I can tell it has been a while, but you are in safe hands."

As he rubbed her back, he eased his dick in slowly, and Charisma's pussy became wet. Her yelling turned into heavy breathing. "That's my girl," Charles said, "take all of this dick, boo. It now belongs to you, and if you want it, tell me you do." Charisma replied, "Charles, please give me the dick! I'm in need of every inch of it!" Charles pumped slow and then hard, moving in and out. He started licking her back and he noticed Charisma's breasts moving from side to side. Charles started moaning and then he said, "Baby, I'm about to bust! Where do you want me to bust?" Charisma then responded, "I want you to bust right inside of me!" Charles's body began shivering and he exclaimed, "Your wish is my command!" Charisma yelled out as if she were a wolf howling at a full moon. Charles and Charisma soon collapsed to the ground, and Charles grabbed her tightly and said, "I think that I might have just met my soul mate."

Charisma looked and smiled. Charles glanced at her and said, "You are the one for me."

My body has been yearning for your touch. With you, I can never get enough. Every day, I crave the sweetness of your love. Our bodies fit together like matching gloves. When we're not together, I close my eyes and think about you, touching myself with my hands, pretending that it is you. The very thought of you makes my knees quiver and then my body starts to shiver. I feel like a drug addict with an addiction and when I'm with you, I can get my fix. My body explodes when I think about your good love. The thought of your touch drives me wild. I find myself envisioning your smile, kissing your tender lips. While your eyes hypnotize me, making me the love slave you want me to be. At this moment, your every wish is my command

The definition of your body has me in a trance. At this time, love is all that is on my mind. Don't keep me waiting. We are running out of time. My body needs to be taken care of, so come and give me some of your good love.

Chapter Eighteen: What's Done in the Dark Must Come to the Light

◇◇

*D*AMON GOT HOME TO FIND CONSTANCE ON all fours. "Now that's what I'm talking about!" Damon responded. "I like to find you in that position, on all fours, naked, ready to intake this monster right in your mouth!" Damon walked over to Constance and stood right in front of her face. He unfastened his pants and pulled his dick out. He hit Constance in the face with his dick lightly and commented, "Put the monster in your mouth. Imagine it being a new, flavored lollipop that you are anxious to taste." Constance licked her lips and responded, "If that's what you desire, baby, then that's exactly what I will give you." She grabbed Damon's semi hard penis and stuck it in her mouth, first licking it up and down in slow strokes. Damon moaned as his penis expanded. Constance then started taking her tongue and twirling it in circular motions on the head of his penis. Damon grabbed Constance's head and attempted to feed her more of his dick. "That's right, baby! Suck the monster!" Damon yelled out, with his eyes looking towards the ceiling. He was forcing his dick in her mouth, pushing her head by force harder and harder on his penis. "Deep throat that shit!" Damon exclaimed. Constance continued sucking his dick. "I'm about to bust," Damon screamed out, as he released his secretions in Constance's mouth. He then responded, "Now swallow it, baby! Does it go down your throat smoothly?" Constance swallowed and responded, "Yes, it went down just fine, baby!" Damon dropped to his knees and fell out on the floor. "You're just too good to me". Constance smiled and commented, "Anything for my Daddy!" Damon smiled, as he looked over and saw Constance putting on her clothes. "Where do you think you're going?" Damon asked. Constance replied, "Baby, I have to go home and start packing up some things. I never got a chance to do that earlier because I had to meet up with my girlfriends. It's probably going to be too late after I'm done packing, so I will probably stay at my mother's house for the night." Damon responded, "I don't like the way that sounds.

I miss my baby whenever she isn't around, but I understand that you have to go and get your stuff. Besides, I will have the rest of my life to make you happy." Damon walked over and kissed Constance on her forehead and said, "You might want to brush your teeth before you go. Get the taste of my dick out of your mouth, although I know that you find it to be delicious!" Constance laughed and punched Damon in his chest. She exclaimed, "That is not a bad idea!" and walked towards the bathroom to brush her teeth. Damon watched Constance walk in the bathroom and he then reached in his jean pocket and pulled out Ambiance's number. "I can't wait to call her sexy ass," he whispered to himself. He quickly put the number back in his pocket when he heard Constance leaving the bathroom. Constance yelled out to Damon, "Baby! Did you see my keys?" Damon said, "Yes, baby! Your keys are on the floor right next to me." Constance left the bathroom and walked over to Damon, grabbed her keys off the ground, and kissed him on the cheek. She commented, "I will be back first thing in the morning." Damon pouted as he watched Constance put her shoes on. "Baby! Do you have to go?!" Damon exclaimed. Constance responded, "Yes, baby! But I promise I will be back in the morning." She took her keys and dangled them and asked Damon, "Do you hear that?" Damon smirked and responded, "Yes, I do." Constance laughed and replied, "That is the sound of the keys to our new home. So with that being said, I have to come back."

Constance proceeded to walk over to the door and said,"I will see your ass when you get back." Constance winked her eye and added, "I will see you soon," and she walked out of the house, closed the door, and headed towards her car. Damon had the biggest smile appear on his face as he heard the door close. He rushed over to the window to make sure that Constance got in her car safely. When he saw Constance enter the car, he said, "It's showtime. I have this house to myself until the morning." He ran to his jeans, grabbed Ambiance's phone number, and decided to call her. He anxiously dialed her number and heard her pick up instantly. "Hello," Ambiance replied. "Well, hello," Damon responded back. Ambiance giggled and said, "Well it took you long enough to call, Damon."

In the meantime, Radiance pulled up in front of a mansion and noticed white Christmas lights. The limousine stopped and Radiance started thinking to herself, *This man has Christmas lights up in the middle of the Spring. Must be nice.* The door soon opened and the chauffeur extended his hand to help Radiance get out of the car. She took his hand and got out of the limousine. She pulled her dress down and continued staring at the white lights. She looked ahead and saw what appeared to be a doorman straight ahead waiting for her to make her way to the door. As she walked, the only sound that she heard was the sound of her stilettos walking towards the door. The doorman opened the door and said, "Sir Stephen has been waiting for you to arrive. Let me show you the way." Radiance looked around at all of the fine art and flower arrangements. The doorman took a red rose and asked, "Mademoiselle, can I please put this in your hair? It compliments your outfit and I will let you in on a little secret between you and I: Stephen loves flowers on a beautiful woman such as yourself." Radiance laughed and replied, "Thank you for the heads up." The doorman put the flower in Radiance's hair and she headed towards an entertainment room where she saw rose petals on the floor and Stephen standing in a gray suit. He looked like something from a magazine cover.

"Damn! You look great," Radiance commented, as she headed towards him. She heard music coming from outside, near the pool area of the entertainment room. When she got closer, she heard the sound of a saxophone playing and saw a really well-dressed man. When she looked on the opposite side, she saw a woman playing a guitar. "This is amazing!" Radiance exclaimed. Stephen stated, "The only thing that is amazing is you." He took his finger and lifted up her chin. He then took her hand and kissed it, and asked Radiance, "May you please do me the honor of dancing with me?"

"I'm no dancer," Radiance responded while laughing. Stephen then commented, "That's okay! Just follow my lead and we will dance to one beat, one sound. And the only noise that we will hear is the one that we create." Radiance smiled and agreed to the dance. She kept thinking to herself that she heard that one beat, one sound statement from someone else and couldn't think of who. Stephen continued to lead and Radiance followed. As she looked at his eyes, she felt like he was captivating her. Eventually the music stopped and Stephen led Radiance to the table. He already had red wine in the glasses, waiting for her arrival. "Drink up, Miss Radiance. Remember that one glass of red wine a day can help keep the doctor away." Radiance chuckled as she took a sip of the wine. Stephen kept staring at Radiance and commented, "You are as beautiful as it gets. You look so lovely tonight, fair lady. My heart can't take your beauty. You are what I have been searching for all my life. I'm a very successful man that can give you anything that money can buy. Material things mean nothing to me. What good is having all of these wonderful things if I have no one to share them with?" Radiance responded, "I don't know, Stephen. I imagine it is tough being as successful as you are and not having anyone to love unconditionally. All that I ever really wanted in life was to be loved properly. I never encountered anything like that. All that has ever happened to me is disappointment and pain."

Stephen gazed into Radiance's hazel eyes and responded, "Let me ask you something again." Radiance looked at Stephen with a concerned look. "Okay! Sure. Go for it."

Stephen then asked, "Do you believe in love at first sight?" Radiance looked at Stephen and responded, "I didn't used to think so before, but now I'm starting to view everything different because my heart has not skipped one beat since I have been here with you, and I find myself being so intrigued with you at this very moment." Stephen smiled at Radiance and replied, "I feel the same way. It's a feeling of déjà vu." Stephen continued, "I told you from the beginning that I'm a man who knows exactly what he wants, and Radiance, I want you. The way that you make me feel is unreal and I feel like I have known you forever. It's like a romantic movie that I never want to end." Radiance smiled and replied, "You hardly even know me. How do you know that I'm the one that you desire?" Stephen answered, "Because I believe in fate." Stephen rose from his seat, went over to Radiance, leaned over, and kissed her lips lightly. He took her by the hand, helped her get up, and led her to a flight of stairs in the hallway. Radiance looked over at the flight of stairs and turned to Stephen and asked, "What does these stairs lead to?" Stephen responded, "You will soon find out." Stephen grabbed Radiance closely and picked her up, and carried her up the flight of stairs.

Chapter Nineteen: All Good Things Come to an End

◇◇

CHARISMA CONTINUED PUTTING HER CLOTHES on, feeling ashamed and pleased at the same time. Charles watched her every move. He was still amazed at what had just taken place. Charles responded, "I hope that I can see you again, Charisma, and that you didn't just use me for my goods." Charisma looked up with a puzzled look on her face. She then exclaimed, "Charles, please! Don't get the wrong idea about me. I don't do this all of the time." Charles exclaimed, "Calm down, Charisma! I know that you're not a loose woman. I think that you are looking too much into this. It's okay to live a little and let your hair down. You will not be judged for that." Charisma responded, "It makes me happy to know that you have an open mind about this type of thing." Charles exclaimed, "Of course I do!" as he walked back inside of his apartment, exposing his naked body.

Charisma watched his tight ass as he went inside. She licked her lips and watched him bend down in the living room, reaching for his basketball shorts. "We have to get together again real soon!" Charisma exclaimed. Charles chuckled and responded, "Yes, we do," as he kept staring at his cell phone on the table. "I'm not trying to be rude, Charisma, but I have to get ready to go to work." Charisma looked over at Charles with an irritated look on her face and replied, "It's one o'clock on a Saturday morning. I thought you were off. What is it that you do again?" Charles responded, "I told you that I'm not happy with my current position and that I'm seeking other employment, but the bills still have to get paid until then. That's about all that I can tell you about my work. I don't care to discuss it anymore. Please don't take it personal. Charisma, I like you and I don't want to make things tense between us." Charisma exclaimed, "It's okay! Charles, we don't have to talk about your work anymore. You can keep your top secret," Charisma giggled, as she opened up the apartment door and proceeded to exit. Charles jumped in front of Charisma with a smile on his face and replied, "I really want to see you again, Charisma. It has been such a pleasure spending time with you." Charisma smirked and said, "You will see me again." She pushed Charles out of the way playfully and walked away. Charles smacked her on the ass as she left and neither one of them uttered a word. Charles continued to stare until Charisma walked down the stairs and exited the apartment's main entrance door. Charles sighed and exclaimed out loud to himself, "Time sure does fly past fast when you're having fun!"

Constance finished packing up all of her items and started loading up the car so that she could hurry back to her precious Damon. As she was putting boxes in the car, she noticed Walter over at Radiance's house, sitting on the step. She called out his name, "Walter!" and he turned around and noticed Constance. He ran across the grass over to Constance and exclaimed, "Hey, C! I missed you!" He hugged Constance tightly and smiled brightly. "Hey, baby!" Constance replied, "What are you doing here?" Walter responded, "Miguel left something over Mom's house when he moved out and he needed to get it back, so we had to get it while Mom was not home because she told us that she no longer wanted us here." Walter asked Constance, "Where is my sister, Constance? Miguel and I have been unable to reach her and she is not living with Mom anymore. From the looks of things, her room is empty." Constance replied, "Your sister is over a friend of ours' house and she didn't have Miguel's new number to reach out to you. She has been worried sick about you, so go on the porch and grab that pen on the table and write down Miguel's number so that I can make sure that Radiance gets it." Walter replied, "Okay," and raced up the porch steps to write down the number. Constance continued to load the car and looked up and saw Miguel walking in her direction. "Hey, baby girl! How have you been?" Miguel asked, and Constance replied, "I'm good. What about yourself?" Miguel shook his head and replied, "I'm sure you heard about my mother kicking me and Walter out." Constance interrupted and exclaimed, "Radiance, too!" Miguel yelled out, "Get the fuck out of here! I noticed that there were things missing out of her room." Constance replied, "She has been trying to get in contact with you, but didn't have a cell phone number for you. Walter is writing it down now for me."

"Make sure you have my sister call me as soon as possible. I'm leaving for California in the morning and Walter is coming with me." Constance looked at Miguel with a disturbing look on her face and replied, "Excuse me? You're going to California for what reason?" Miguel laughed and responded, "To live. I have some homeys down there and I just applied for a job down that way, and they just offered it to me. It's a great opportunity for Walter and me to get a clean start. I'm going to raise him now and teach him how to be a man, and live out all of his dreams. I want that for his future. My mother doesn't give a fuck! I spoke to her briefly and she is all good with the idea." Walter ran down the steps and handed Constance Miguel's number and noticed his brother standing right there. He exclaimed, "Miguel, you could have given Constance your number!" Miguel smacked Walter in the head gently and replied, "That's okay! That's what you are here for!" Walter laughed and responded, "Whatever." He turned to Constance and said, "Please have my sister call me. I miss her and I want to go over and stay with her, wherever she is." Miguel turned around, looked at Walter, and said, "We had this conversation already. We are leaving for California in the morning and we will build something new down there. Radiance is welcome to come, Walter, but you are my responsibility. Now go get in the car. I will be there in a minute." Walter responded, "Okay, Miguel, whatever you say. But I'm tired of you bossing me around." Miguel replied, "You just do what I say."

Walter turned around and walked across the grass, heading towards the car. Miguel continued speaking to Constance, "Make sure you take care and whatever you do, give my sister my number so that she can call me. Okay, baby girl?" Constance replied, "Okay! I got you!" Miguel gave her a hug and a kiss on the cheek, and said, "I don't know when I will see you again, but I want you to know that I appreciate you being a good friend to my sister. She needs a true friend right now. It's going to seem like she is living in a world all alone and I don't want her to ever feel that way. Take care of yourself, Constance." Miguel turned around and headed towards the car. Constance just waved goodbye and watched him get in the car. She started thinking to herself, *I will let Radiance know in the morning.* She put her last bag in the car and then she went in the house to shower and get ready to surprise her man.

It was two in the morning when Ambiance arrived at Damon's house. She walked up the stairs of the duplex porch and knocked on the door. Damon peeked through the peep hole and saw Ambiance with nothing but a trench coat on. Damon whispered, "Damn! That bitch really is about her business!" He looked out the peep hole again and noticed that Ambiance had on red pumps as well. He looked down at his dick and said, "Monster, we getting ready to wear that bitch's ass out, and she can't be ready for all of that!" He stroked his penis and opened up the door. Ambiance walked in and exclaimed, "Don't ever have me waiting at the door for so long!" She walked right up to Damon, grabbed his dick, and stuck her tongue down his throat. She pulled away from his lips and started talking shit. "So, Damon, is your dick ready for our play date?" She let go of his dick and took off her trench coat, allowing it to hit the floor. Underneath she had nothing on, but when Damon looked down, at the bottom of her stomach just above her pussy, he noticed that it had *Desire* spelled out with an arrow pointing to her pussy. His mouth dropped and Ambiance replied, "If your mouth has to remain open, I want you to use it to tell me that you desire my pussy." Damon's dick expanded instantly and he replied, "Damn! I never had any shit like this ever happen to me, and yes, baby, I desire your pussy!" He continued looking down and noticed Ambiance's red pumps and fat beautiful legs. His dick started dripping pre-cum. Ambiance noticed it, dropped down to her knees, and started licking the pre-cum from the tip of his dick. She replied, "Now we can't allow perfectly good nut to go to waste now can we?" Damon was speechless as Ambiance wrapped her tongue around his dick and started deep-throating him, causing him to yell out for mercy. Ambiance removed her tongue and told him to lie down on the floor. Damon did it with no questions asked. Ambiance stood up and Damon's eyes looked at her curvy, beautiful body and her full breasts that were as perky as they could get. His eyes traveled back down to her smooth legs and he began staring at her red pumps. Ambiance exclaimed, "Now let me put my warm, moist pussy on your fucking sliding board!" Damon bit the bottom of his lip and replied, "Please do, but let me grab a condom." Ambiance replied, "There is no need for a condom, sweetness. I'm on the Pill and trust me, I'm disease-free. And besides, my pussy needs your undivided attention right now." Damon began thinking to himself, *I don't know about fucking this bitch raw, but anything that fine can't possibly be infected.* And *she did say she was on the Pill.* Damon then replied, "It's all good, girl. Now just come and give me that good pussy." Ambiance exclaimed, "Good pussy is right! I'm about to allow you to sample it." She knelt down slightly, grabbed Damon's dick, and did a slight split that landed her right on Damon's dick. They both yelled out in unison, "Oh, shit!" Damon yelled out, "Damn, bitch! Where did you learn those moves?" Ambiance replied, "Shut up and stop asking questions! Too much talking and not enough fucking! Now smack my ass! I love the sensation of it." Damon begged for mercy as Ambiance rode him like she was in a rodeo competition. Damon gripped her ass and pulled her harder and harder on his dick. Ambiance moaned loudly and started grabbing on her own breasts. She yelled, "Damn, this dick is great! Oh, shit! I can't take it!" Damon exclaimed, "Take it! Every bit of it!" They continued to fuck like wild animals.

Constance sprayed on her fragrance and headed towards the mirror to make sure her lingerie was perfect. She turned to the front and to the side, was pleased with all that she saw, and headed out the door. She grabbed her slow jam CD and her keys, got in the car, and started driving to her new place. Constance put on her CD to get herself in a sexy mood. She began talking to herself, "Damon, baby, I hope you are ready for all of this good love. I'm ready for a really special night."

In the meantime, Jermaine was lying in his bed with his basketball in his hand. He started thinking about Radiance and what she was up to. He missed their long talks and friendship. It was never just sex with her, although the sex part was a big part of it. He missed her jokes, gentle kisses, and the way she called his name. He loved when she did that. Jermaine whispered to himself, "I'm not going to call her, but I'm going to go to the court to help me get my mind off her." Jermaine jumped up, put on his tennis, and walked across the street to the middle school basketball court to clear his mind.

Meanwhile, Ambiance continued to show Damon her many sex tricks, driving him wild. Damon exclaimed, "I don't know how much more I can take! My battery is getting low!" Ambiance giggled and responded, "Don't worry! I know how to recharge it!" Constance pulled up in front of her house and looked in the rearview mirror to make sure she was perfect. She went in her purse to grab her lotion. She rubbed her legs down and reached for her red pumps. She put them on and headed towards the door. She grabbed her keys, put them in the door, and opened the door. When she opened the door, she walked in, smiling brightly. When she got in the living room, she discovered Ambiance's ass naked, with her breasts jiggling loosely. Her heart dropped and tears filled her eyes, as she yelled out, "What the fuck is going on in here!?" She went over to Ambiance, grabbed her by her hair, and pulled her off of Damon's dick. She started banging her in the face and Ambiance started swinging, trying to defend herself, but didn't stand a chance because it appeared as if Constance had the strength of ten grown men. "Get the fuck off of me!" Ambiance screamed, but Constance paid her screams no mind. She grabbed her by her head and began banging it against the hardwood floor. Damon got off the floor, completely naked, and tried to get Constance off of Ambiance. Constance took her elbow and attempted to elbow him in the dick, but hit him in the stomach instead. She then reached for Ambiance's neck and exclaimed, "Bitch, I'm going to kill you tonight! You disrespectful bitch! How dare you come in my house and fuck my man! I know your ass knew he had a girl!"

Ambiance scratched Constance in the face. She then grabbed her heel and hit Constance. Ambiance yelled out, "Fuck you! If you were doing your fucking job, none of this would have happened, you fat, pathetic bitch!" Ambiance managed to get Constance on the floor and started hitting her. Constance took her fist and hit Ambiance in the nose, causing her to bleed everywhere. Damon finally went back over to Ambiance and pulled her off of Constance. "How could you do this to me, Damon?!" Constance screamed out at the top of her lungs. "You said that you loved me and I leave for one minute, and you bring this nasty bitch in our house, where we make love every day. You were untrue! You said you loved me!" Constance then grabbed the lamp off the floor, which was the only piece of furniture in the house, and she threw it at Ambiance and Damon. She ran in the kitchen to find a knife and noticed that there was nothing there. Damon ran over to Constance while still naked, and reached for her with tears coming down his face. "Baby, I'm sorry!" Damon exclaimed. Constance pushed him as hard as she could, causing him to fall down on his back. She took her ring off and threw it at Damon. "I won't be needing this!" Constance went back over to Ambiance, and noticed that she was backing up against the wall. She hit her in the face as hard as she could, causing Ambiance to grab her face and ball up in a fetal position. Damon got up off the floor and went back to Constance. "Baby, please let me explain!" Constance replied, "Just save it," with tears streaming down her eyes. Constance exclaimed, "I never want to see you again!" Damon reached for her wrist and responded, "You think that you can leave me just like that?" with bass in his voice. "That's not how it goes, Sunshine! You are here with me forever. Until death do us part, bitch!" "You got the game fucked up." Constance replied, "Fuck you!" and punched Damon in his dick. She replied, "Don't ever fucking contact me again in life! If you do, I swear to God that I will fucking kill you and that's a promise!" Constance stormed out the door with endless tears. She went to the car and pulled off, driving as fast as she could. She couldn't get herself together. Her heart was shredded into pieces and her eyes were still filled with tears. Other cars were honking at her. She ran every stop sign. Her mind traveled to every bad moment she ever encountered. Suddenly, she had flashbacks of every time her stepfather raped her, causing her so much pain. Rage filled her heart and Constance started screaming in the car as loud as she could, banging the steering wheel. "I fucking hate men! They're so fucking disappointing to me!" Constance finally pulled up in front of her mother's house and took what appeared to be the longest walk of her life. She got to the porch, sat down, and cried by herself alone in the dark.

My heart is shattered in a million pieces. No longer am I willing to take a journey known as love. All of my fairytale stories have turned into nightmares. No longer do I trust. Everything that you say to me is in question. I don't want to walk in fear. I shut everyone down before I allow them to get near. My new way of thinking is get them before they get you. Everyone is untrue with a hidden agenda to hurt and cause pain; drain my energy. Bring misery and suffering. Trying to steal my shine. Not knowing that the world is still mine. I'm too strong for this. It's time for me to flip the script and become the thing that you create. Either you will love it or hate it. No longer will I play the fool. Instead my mission is to rule and make people feel the emotions that I feel every day of my life. I'm tired of holding everything in. No longer will I pretend to be something that I'm not. It's time to meet the one you created. Either you love it or hate it.

Chapter Twenty: The Drama in My Life

◇◇

*J*ERMAINE WENT OVER TO THE BASKETBALL court and started shooting hoops all by himself, thinking about Radiance and what she was up to. Jermaine thought to himself, *I have got to shake this girl. I can't keep having her on my mind, especially when I know that nothing will ever come out of this relationship. I'm too young for this shit! But, I can't shake this feeling that I have for her. The shit just won't go away!* Jermaine started dribbling the ball harder, ran up to the basketball goal, and slam-dunked the ball. Suddenly he heard two male voices from across the street yelling, "Good shot, homey!" The gentlemen appeared to be walking in his direction. Jermaine turned around and noticed Lamont coming in his direction. "You have a serious game, homeboy!" Jermaine chuckled and replied, "Thanks, Slim," while giving Lamont a handshake. Lamont replied, "The streets is watching, nigga, even when you don't have a clue. Let me introduce you to my man, Mark. He is a scout for college basketball." Jermaine laughed while giving Mark a handshake. "What's up, big homey!" Jermaine exclaimed. Mark responded, "Nothing much, Jermaine. I have been watching you for the last few weeks from afar and I think you got the skills that are required to make it in the pros. We have a summer program that we offer to a selective few like yourself, to go and enhance your skills, and get educated while doing it. I know school is letting out in the next few weeks and I wanted to come and speak to you personally to offer you a spot on our winning team. You can get trained properly and get paid while you play." Mark added, "My man Lamont over here went to school with me back in the day and he had some skills, too. I thought this dude would go pro, but he dropped out and made a living out here on the streets instead." Lamont interrupted Mark and said, "Nigga, I still got skills, but that school shit was never for me! I'm an entrepreneur, but homeboy over here got what it takes and we need someone from the hood representing for the fellas." Jermaine laughed and responded, "I'm always willing to upgrade myself. Mark, this sounds like a great opportunity." Mark responded, "Jermaine, it is the best opportunity for you and you came highly recommended by Lamont. I know he would never recommend a slouch and man, I seen your skills too." Lamont interrupted, "Come on, homeboy. Let's go to the twenty-four hour breakfast spot and talk about your future with my man over there. You're bigger than this street shit! Shorty, you need to become a superstar." Jermaine replied, "Sounds like a plan. Let's go."

Lamont, Jermaine, and Mark headed towards Lamont's car and over to the breakfast spot.

Ambiance got home, applied ice to her face, and started yelling out loud, "I can't believe that big bitch hit me and I damn sure can't believe that Damon put me out so that he can be alone and cry about that fat bitch! It's a fucking disgrace to me that he would have something this damn fine and be thinking about a fat bitch! That bitch ass nigga got the game fucked up. I look so goddamn good that I can barely resist myself. The nerve of that bastard playing me!" Ambiance picked up the phone and called Virtue. She picked up, asking Ambiance, "It's two in the damn morning. Why are you calling me when you know I'm out of town for a month on this acting shit?! It's my big break and you're trying to mess it up by interrupting my beauty rest." Ambiance exclaimed, "Girl, I'm coming to Atlanta with you while you're on your acting stuff! I need a break from this town, so I'm going online right now to book a flight and I'm heading in your direction. I have an older cousin down there and she has been trying to get me down there for a while, so I'm going to take her up on her offer. So Atlanta, here I come! The sky is the limit, baby!" Virtue interrupted Ambiance and replied, "You woke me up out of my sleep to tell me some bullshit like that?! You could have waited for later on in the day to tell me that. So let's stop playing this juvenile game, Ambiance. What is your real reason for contacting me about some bullshit?!" Ambiance laughed and replied, "Virtue, you're so crazy! Why can't I just want to talk to my girl?" Virtue responded, "Because it's two in the morning and if you don't tell me the real deal, I'm hanging up and I will see you when you land in the morning." Ambiance replied, "Fine, Virtue, I will tell you. I got into a fight with your fat ass new girlfriend. I knew it was a reason that I didn't like her big ass." Virtue responded, "Ambiance, what the hell did your disrespectful ass do now? Did you call her fat or something?" Ambiance replied, "Hell no! I just fucked her dude, that's all... In their new apartment." Virtue raised her voice on the other end and yelled out, "What the fuck did you just say to me? Ambiance, I know I didn't hear that shit clear!" Ambiance said, "You heard me. All I did was have sex with Damon." Virtue interrupted, "That's her fiancé, Ambiance. You just saw them together the other day at the restaurant. They were getting married. Ambiance, that's fucked up on your end. Why would you do such a horrible thing?" Ambiance replied, "Please, girl. I'm better than that big bitch! Damon asked for my number and I gave it to him. He wanted to fuck and so did I. What's the big fucking deal?" Virtue responded, "The big deal is he belongs to another person and your nasty ass felt the need to break that union up and that shit isn't cool!" Ambiance exclaimed, "Yes it is, because we both wanted the shit! And we were just bold enough to get it." Virtue exclaimed, "At another person's expense of heartache and pain! Ambiance, that's it for you and me. If you did that to someone else, then you would do the same shit to me. I can't roll with people like you. It's not a real good look. Lose my number and when you get to Atlanta tomorrow, don't seek me. This friendship is over."

Virtue hung up the phone in Ambiance's ear. "Hello?!" Ambiance exclaimed, and all she heard was the dial tone. "No, that bitch didn't hang up on me! That's why I don't do bitches. They're so emotional. I will just hit her up tomorrow when I land in Atlanta. Maybe she can pick me up from the airport." Ambiance lay down in the bed and put the ice on her nose. As she closed her eyes, she started thinking about Damon. While she masturbated, she whispered to herself, "I don't know what it's going to take, but Damon, one day you will be all mine."

Damon called Constance over and over again, just to get the answering machine. He called once more and Constance picked up. She replied, "Damon, please stop calling me. I never want to see you again!" Damon interrupted, "Please, Constance, don't be like that. Baby, let me explain." Constance exclaimed, "There is nothing left to explain! Just let me be, Damon. You're a cheating bastard that never told the truth and you are the very reason that I never want to deal with another man in all my life. You all are insensitive creatures and I don't want any parts of your foolish ways." Damon responded, "Baby! You don't mean that. You're just a little upset right now. Please come back home and I promise you that I will make it better." Constance interrupted, "How, Damon? By fucking me? I wouldn't fuck you with someone else's pussy, you cheating bastard! Go and reach out to the bitch that you were fucking, the one that has taken my place!" Constance hung up the phone. Damon replied, "I fucked this one up big time," as he stretched out down on the floor and cried silently. Constance continued sitting on the steps upset.

She called Unique and Unique picked up with a cracking sound in her voice. "Hello!" Unique exclaimed and Constance responded upset, "My world is upside down, Unique, and I need to talk to you right now. I will explain everything when I get there. Just crack your bedroom window open on the side, and I will come in that way. I know that your grandmother is sleeping and besides she wouldn't allow you to come out, it's late. So I'm coming to you. Wake your ass up. I really need you right now."

Destiny was lying on her bed when she heard a knock at her door. "Who the hell is it at my door at this hour?" she whispered to herself. When she arrived at the door and looked out the peep hole, she noticed Mr. Officer. But this time, he was dressed in normal clothing. His tee shirt was fitted and showing off the definition of his body. Destiny opened up the door and said, "This shit has got to stop, dude. You are borderline stalking me and that shit isn't cool." Mr. Officer responded, "Just remain silent." He forced his way into Destiny's house, closed the door behind him, picked her up, and took her to the kitchen counter. He sat her on top of it and he lifted up her tee shirt. He started nibbling on Destiny's breast. He unbuttoned his pants, allowing them to hit the floor. He pulled Destiny closer to the edge of the kitchen counter and said, "You're my addiction. I can't function without your pussy." Destiny's eyes enlarged as he nibbled on her breast. Her pussy started overflowing in juices. The heavy breathing started. Mr. Officer pulled out his big black dick and began giving Destiny the fuck of her life. Her nipples became hard and perky as he pumped in and out of her pussy. Mr. Officer exclaimed, "Your pussy is warm and soothing. It feels as wet as the river on a summer day and I'm about to explode inside your walls." Destiny replied, "Let's climax together," and together they did. "You're amazing," they said in unison.

I feel so cold inside, but you're melting the ice from my heart. You are always in my thoughts. I include you in my dreams. I'm attracted to your inner mystery. The energy that you bring feels so good to me. I'm addicted to you, wanting you in the morning and at night. Without you, I can't get right. You send chills all over my body. I find myself trembling when I think of you. Every night you're featured in my dreams. You impact me like no other, but I don't even know your name. You're a stranger, but you seem so familiar to me. The way that you walk and talk is instilled in my memory bank. How could a complete stranger connect to me? Steal my heart and run away with my soul? Create emotional tides and cause me to get lost in his eyes? You make feel warm inside. A feeling I can't explain. I find myself trying not to allow emotions to take over me.

Chapter Twenty-one: Curious

◇◇◇

*U*NIQUE GOT UP TO MAKE SURE THAT HER bedroom window was open for Constance. She had no idea what she needed to talk about, but she knew that it had to be important for her to travel in the middle of the night. Unique grabbed her tee shirt and put it on. She then went back over to the bed and bundled back in her sheets. Unique started thinking to herself, *I hope whatever Constance has to tell me is good, because it's late as hell and I want to go back to bed. People are so inconsiderate with your time, always wanting to meet you on their terms.* Unique lay down, closed her eyes, and was on her way to sleep. Suddenly, a sound came from the window and Unique looked over and noticed Constance climbing through the window. "Hey, lady!" Constance exclaimed, with tears streaming down her face. Unique jumped out of the bed and exclaimed, "Constance, what's wrong? You look like shit! And that's not like you at all. I don't like seeing you this way." Constance went over to Unique and placed her head on her shoulder and told her about Damon and Ambiance sleeping together in their new place. Unique's mouth dropped open as Constance continued telling the story with tears rolling down her face. Unique exclaimed, "Get the fuck out of here, Constance! I'm so sorry that you had to go through that." Unique grabbed Constance closely, gave her a hug, and kissed her on her head. "Don't worry, you will be okay! Fuck that nigga. You are a great lady and it's his loss. You should go and pawn your engagement ring, and go buy that car his ass promised you." Constance managed to crack a smile and said, "That doesn't sound like a bad idea, but I took that ring and threw it at his ass just before I beat that bitch's ass." Unique yelled out, "You did what?! I hope you didn't tell me what I think I heard. You never give a nigga back the ring. You keep that shit as collateral for pain and suffering!" Constance interrupted Unique while smiling slightly and water still flowing from her eyes, "Unique, some shit just isn't worth it! And besides, I'm never fucking with another nigga in life." Unique looked at Constance with a concerned look on her face and replied, "Girl, you don't mean that. You're just going through something right now but it will get better." Unique grabbed Constance's hand and took her free hand and started wiping away her tears. "Just let it go, girl. Tears can help you cleanse your heart when it's wounded."

Constance continued crying and looked up at Unique. She exclaimed, "I mean it, Unique! I'm never fucking with another man." She pulled Unique closer and tongue kissed her. Unique pushed Constance away and replied, "Oh, hell no, Constance! I know that you're hurt and all that shit, but you know that I don't do women." Constance moved in closer to Unique and responded, "How do you know if you never even tried?" Unique exclaimed, "Chill out, C! You're taking this hurt shit too far!" Constance responded back, "Let me ask you a question. Do you trust me?" Unique exclaimed, "Sure I did, until you kissed my lips!" Constance laughed and whispered, "They were soft and full, too. Let me ask you another question. Do you love me?" Unique exclaimed, "Of course, bitch, you know I love you! We have been friends for years." Constance interrupted and said, "I know you don't do females, but my heart is hurting right now and I just want to step out of my box for a minute and be someone else. So with that being said, Unique, let me eat your pussy." Unique moved towards the bedroom wall and exclaimed, "Now you're scaring me, Constance! I don't want to experiment with that shit!" Constance walked over to Unique and replied, "It will be our secret. No one will ever know and we will never look back on this shit again ever in life!" Constance grabbed Unique's breast through her shirt and watched her nipples perk up. Unique replied, "Stop this shit right now!" Constance ignored her as she pulled Unique closer, removing her shirt. "Stop it!" Unique replied, but didn't put up much of a fight. Constance exclaimed, "Bitch, just cut it out. You know that you like it." She pulled Unique closer and then pushed her on the bed. She instructed her to gap her legs open. Unique started thinking to herself, *What in the hell am I about to get myself involved in?* Unique followed the instructions and gapped her legs open. Constance responded, "Now that's my girl," as she stuck her whole face in Unique's pussy, while blowing on her clit. Unique grabbed Constance by her hair and began moaning, as Constance continued feasting on her pussy like she was a professional. "Oh, Constance, that feels so good," Unique said, as she climaxed in Constance's mouth while pulling her hair, and tossing and turning. "Damn, C! I didn't know it was like that. Your head game is like no other's." Constance continued blowing in Unique's pussy, as if she had mastered the skills of eating pussy. For a while, Unique squirted secretions in Constance's mouth. Unique instantly felt embarrassed, and pushed away from Constance after she realized what had just taken place. Constance exclaimed, "Don't be ashamed, Unique, this is our secret and I will take it to the grave. Thank you for being there for me in my time of need." Constance licked her lips, tasting Unique's secretions, and lay across her bed. She looked at Unique and told her, "If no one ever tells you this, remember me telling you, baby... You are beautiful and I appreciate you." She moved in closer to Unique and began stroking her hair. Unique exclaimed, "Thanks, Constance! But I have to ask you...what is going on with you?" Constance replied, "The only thing that is going on with me is life, but from here on out I will be different, and I'm never dealing with another man. I'm done with them." Unique's eyes enlarged and she replied, "You keep on saying that." Constance exclaimed, "I mean it! Just wait and see." Unique looked at Constance with a blank expression on her face. As Constance moved in close to Unique, she whispered, "Enough of that for now, Unique. But don't worry, your secret is safe with me." Constance hopped out of the bed and headed towards the bedroom window. Unique yelled out to Constance, "Where are you going?" Constance responded back, "I'm just going back to my world. The streets are looking for me." Constance smiled and exited the window. Unique watched her leave and she began traveling back in her mind, remembering the way Constance made her feel in just a short period of time. How could something so wrong feel so right? Unique whispered to herself, "If I enjoyed it, what does that mean to me?"

Must be a full moon out. I'm feeling sexy and free. Feeling like I'm no longer me. Ready for a change in the atmosphere. Ready to forget about what I'm used to. I'm going to do me and boo, you can do you! No longer playing the fool. You better watch out for my new attitude. I'm coming at you with full force and I'm taking no prisoners. The world is not prepared for my mischief. Striking down anything and anybody that gets in my way. I'm currently seeking my new prey. You can refer to me as a natural disaster, as I knock down buildings. Trying to mend my wounds that I received doing many battles. Many said, "Fuck me!" Well, I say, "Fuck you!" Tried being nice and at the end, many thought I was a fool. Taking my kindness for a weakness and playing with my heart. Well, today, I declare that I'm getting a new start. Hurting everyone the way that they hurt me. I want them to feel what I felt when I was living in misery. Maybe I will use the word love in vain. Get in good and then cause them pain. Or maybe, I can get in their mind, make them like me. Get what I want and then tell them that they're wasting my time. I'm a good girl gone bad. World, please get ready to feel my wrath.

Chapter Twenty-two: Life's No Fairytale

RADIANCE WOKE UP AND FOUND STEPHEN staring at her. He was gently stroking her hand. "Did you sleep well?" Stephen asked and Radiance responded, "Well, yes sir, I did. It was so peaceful. I felt like I haven't rested in forever. Maybe it's because I have so much going on." Stephen responded, "Well, we have to find a way to simplify your complicated life. No woman of mine should have a worry in the world. You're so precious and your only worry in the world should be for you to look beautiful and get anything that your heart desires. I have taken the liberty of having my servant run your shower water for you. Everything that you need is in the bathroom, including your clothes. Please go and get yourself together. The driver will be taking us shopping shortly. There are certain things that I have to get you if we're going to be together." Radiance replied, "You're doing too much, Stephen. How does either of us know if we should be in a committed relationship? Did you forget that we just met?" Stephen exclaimed, "I'm aware of that, but this is fate and dear, you are a part of my destiny! Just sit back and enjoy what blessings God has in store for you. I'm a part of your life and I might even be your husband." Radiance smiled and agreed to get dressed. "Only time will tell!" she exclaimed, as she went in the bathroom. Stephen watched her every move and thought to himself, *I'm in love with that woman and she has no idea. I have prayed for her and God finally answered my prayers.*

She will be my wife. I have found a great thing, and I'm going to declare my love for her on this day.

It was morning already and Jermaine woke up and stretched. He had been thinking about what Mark and Lamont were proposing last night at the breakfast spot, and he felt in his spirit that he was going to go for it. He was excited about how bright his future was looking and wanted to share it with someone special. He instantly thought about Radiance and how she was so supportive of all of his dreams. Jermaine started second-guessing himself and began thinking about the possibility of being in a relationship at an early age. He started talking to himself, "I wonder if I will be missing something if I choose to go after my dream versus following my heart. I guess I will never know because I'm going to follow my dreams and go to the basketball camp in two weeks. But I will attempt to catch one last glimpse of Radiance's face so that I can at least have a sweet memory embedded in my brain."

Charles parked his car in front of Druid Hill Park, waiting on his boss. He was glad to see that he just arrived in his Cadillac and told him through the window to park and come to his car. Charles parked and went right over to the passenger seat, and greeted him. "What's up, Lamont?"

"What's up, homeboy? You got my money from last night?"

Charles exclaimed, "Yeah, I got it!"

Lamont nodded and responded, "That's what's up, big homey! Did it take you long to get it?" Charles responded, "No, it didn't. Eric was right where he said he would be, on time."

Lamont laughed and responded, "He is a cool-ass little nigga, but his ass has got to go because his money is becoming too long and it's only one nigga that can run this city and that's me." Lamont chuckled and exclaimed, "You heard?!"

Charles looked at Lamont said, "Yeah man, I feel you."

Lamont responded, "My man! I saw your boy last night, the one you were hooping with the other day and I had Mark with me. We are getting ready to send his ass to camp. Shorty has some serious game and we need to have a nigga like that representing our hood. *And,* I like homeboy's attitude. He is humble and I like that. I told you that I was going to look out for your boy." Charles smirked as he nodded his head and replied, "Good looking, Lamont. You always looking out for people." Lamont laughed and responded, "Anytime. I'm about to look out for you, too. I know your ass has been wanting to get out the game real heavy, and you been one of my best employees for the last couple years. I don't knock anybody's hustle when they want to walk a straight path, so I have one last job for you and then I'm going to break you off with three hundred thousand to go and get a fresh start. Open up a business and shit! Get you a shorty. Travel and live life real big!" Charles responded, "That sounds real good, Lamont. I'm in, but what is the assignment?" Lamont exclaimed, "I'm glad you asked! I need Eric killed tonight. Try to catch him alone, but if he is with someone else, kill their asses too and walk away. You done this shit a million times, so you don't need instructions. When you're done, hit me and I will meet you so you can get your paper."

Charles's heart began to race and he thought to himself, *I will do this shit one last time and then I'm out the game forever*! He turned around, looked Lamont in the eyes, and replied, "Consider the shit done! He shook his hand, left the car, and as he was walking, Lamont yelled out the window and replied, "Remember anyone he's with has to go, too. And remember, homeboy, the streets is always watching."

Constance arrived at her mother's house after roaming the streets all night until the early morning. She found Damon there. Constance looked and asked Damon, "What the hell are you doing here?" Damon replied, "Baby! I can't live without you. I'm so sorry. I will never hurt you again." Constance chuckled, "You're damn right you won't, because I'm done with men and I'm done with your sorry ass. So, if you excuse me, I would like to go inside." Damon stood up and roared like a furious lion as he yelled, "Sunshine, I told you that we are not over until I say so!" He jumped in front of Constance, trying to block her entrance. Suddenly all of the hate, frustration, anger, and rage surfaced in Constance as she cocked back her fist and punched Damon in the face as hard as she could, causing him to fall on the ground. Constance looked at him and hawked spit in his face. "You are a sorry bastard, and if you come in my path again, I will kill your monkey ass." She went to the door and went inside to find her stepfather sitting in the living room. Constance was still upset with all that just happened with Damon and became even angrier when she saw her stepfather. As she walked past the living room, she could feel his eyes on her ass. Not even a minute passed before her drunk stepfather responded, "I think that you should give me some of that sweet pussy willingly before I take it from your ass!" Constance replied, "Suck my dick and step off! I'm not the one for this shit today, so do yourself and me a favor and shut the fuck up right now, before things get ugly in here!" She proceeded to walk away and her stepfather got up and grabbed her wrist and forced her on the couch. He started ripping her clothing off of her and tears surfaced in her eyes. Constance's stepfather said, "I won't suck your dick, but bitch, you can suck mine! As a matter of fact, here it is!" Her stepfather pulled out his dick and began hitting her with it. Constance replied, "Stop! I will suck your dick, daddy." Her stepfather looked at her dazed face and replied, "Good girl."

Constance opened her mouth, stuck his dick in it, and attempted to suck it. She bit his dick as hard as she could. The taste of his blood filled her mouth as her stepfather screamed out in pain. Constance spit all of his blood in his face, stood up, grabbed the lamp off the nightstand, and hit her stepfather over his head, causing him to go unconscious. Constance went in the bathroom and started yelling from the top of her lungs, "WHY ME?!!" When she looked in the mirror, she cried as she started corn rolling her hair.

Destiny woke up to find that Mr. Officer was no longer there. Beside her was a letter that read:

Dear Destiny, let me first let you know that I enjoyed you like I never enjoyed anyone before. You made all of my wild fantasies reality and I cher-

ish the time that we shared. You made my life truly worth living. The love that we made was as real as it gets and I think I fell in love during the process of our little sexual sessions. You connected to my soul and you're always in my thoughts, invading my mind and forever taking over my heart. It's funny because you don't even know my name, so let me tell you. My name is Leon Harrison and I'm twenty-five years old, with no wife or children. I have been an officer for only two years and I enjoy writing beautiful poetry, traveling to beaches, and spending time with family and friends. One day I would like to marry and treat my wife to the finer things in life. Thank you for letting me know that fantasies can come true. By the time that you receive this letter, I will be gone. I have resigned from my job as an officer and I have enrolled in the military. When you awake, I will be on my way to Africa to serve as a commanding officer. If it is your destiny, we will meet each other again. But before I go, let me leave you with a poem:

My heart is dancing to a different rhythm and now it never skips a beat. I have encountered love for the first time and I didn't even seek it. The way you make me feel is so rare and unique; remembering the softness of your touch and the sensation of your kisses. Mesmerizing me with your smile and stealing my heart; causing me to get addicted to the love that we make. Inspiring me to live each day as if it's my last. Showing me that dreams can come true every day. From here on out, I will remember you. Now you will appear in my dreams and you're the main attraction of my fantasies. Maybe you're my destiny.

Sincerely,
Leon Harrison

Chapter Twenty-three: The Rebel in Me

◇◇◇

*D*AMON ARRIVED HOME AND SAT ON THE floor. He cried all alone. He started thinking to himself about losing the love of his life, and he thought about Ambiance and how she wasn't worth losing the only woman he had ever loved. He was shocked by Constance's reaction towards him. He whispered to himself, "I deserved it." He knew that Constance would never forgive him for all that he had done, but he wanted to apologize. So, he went in his cell phone, called the local florist, ordered five dozen roses, and told the florist to put two simple words on the card: "I'm Sorry." The florist agreed and got his credit card number and Constance's address. She asked him, "Was there anything else you need to add?" Damon exclaimed, "Yes, there is! Put down on the card, 'I love you and you will always be my first love, Damon.'"

As he hung up the cell phone, he thought about all of the happy times that he and Constance shared together, and it made him smile. Damon went into the dip of his pants and grabbed his nine millimeter. He began shining it with his shirt. "Life is what you make it!" he exclaimed. He thought about Constance and knew that life would be nothing without her, so he whispered to himself, "I love you, Constance." He stuck the gun in his mouth and pulled the trigger back. His brains scattered all over the apartment and blood splattered everywhere. Damon's body lay lifeless and no one had a clue.

Ambiance pulled up at the airport and grabbed her bags. She called Damon's cell phone to get no response and began thinking to herself, *Fuck him! That dude was lame anyway, and he didn't have enough money to take care of me in the first place.* She checked in her bags and raced to the terminal. She handed the flight attendant her ticket and took her seat, as she whispered, "Atlanta, here I come."

Radiance and Stephen arrived in front of a jewelry store and Stephen instructed the sales person to get the largest diamond ring in the store. Radiance smiled and said, "You're kidding, right?" Stephen exclaimed, "No, dear, I'm not! I don't have time for games. I told you from the beginning that I'm a man who simply knows what he wants and baby, I want you." Radiance's eyes watered and Stephen reached for her hand and kissed it while they waited for the ring.

Constance looked at herself in the mirror and exclaimed, "Hello, new me!" She had cornrows, a white tee shirt, jeans falling from her ass, and a pair of Timberland boots. She walked out of the bathroom and headed towards the front door. She noticed Eric across the street and headed in that direction. Eric was drinking a forty and exclaimed, "Damn, Constance! What the hell happened to you? What's up with the clothes?" Constance replied, "Life happened to me, Eric, and I have turned over a new leaf. Listen, I didn't come over to discuss my new look. I came over here to discuss business."

"Really!" Eric exclaimed, "what kind of business?"

"I want to work with you and get this paper, and I know that I can do it, too." Eric looked over at Constance and laughed. "Baby girl, I don't think that you want to do any of this shit! The game is a hard field to get into and once you're in it, there is no turning back." Constance responded, "I'm aware of this, and I don't want to turn back. I want this shit to be a lifestyle for me and it would be to your benefit to have a bitch like me on your team. Just give me a chance to show you." Eric said, "Constance,

I don't want to expose you to this world, on the real." Constance yelled out, "Just give me one chance!" Eric responded, "You are serious about this shit!" Constance replied, "What, you thought I was bullshitting?! I'm serious about this shit, Eric! Dead-ass serious." Eric replied, "Well, if that's the case, my mother always said give a lady what she wants. I have a package that has to be delivered at twelve midnight tonight, and I could use the company. So, you can ride with me and I will show you the ropes. Meet me up at Joe's sub shop at 11:30, and we will ride out at that time."

"I'm there!" Constance exclaimed. "See you soon."

Radiance and Stephen waited for the sales person, and she finally came with a beautiful diamond ring that sparkled so brightly. Stephen handed her his credit card and said, "Just charge it." The sales lady asked, "Are you sure?" Stephen said, "I'm positive," without ever looking at the price tag. He took the ring and bended on one knee, asked Radiance to, "Let God guide your heart and do me the honor of being my beautiful bride, angel. Fairytales can come true. Let me be your prince coming to rescue his princess." Radiance responded, "I feel like a girl in one of those fancy movies. I know this sounds crazy but, yes, Stephen, I will marry you!" Suddenly, everyone in the jewelry store started clapping and Stephen got up and hugged Radiance. He replied, "You won't be sorry." He slid the ring on Radiance's finger and added, "Thank you for making me the happiest man in the world."

Charisma woke up and started getting herself ready for her day. She thought about Charles and how good it felt to be in a man's strong arms. She had a great feeling about Charles and felt that her prayers were finally answered, or so she hoped. Charisma whispered to herself, "A man who finds a wife finds a good thing." A smile came upon her face and she continued getting dressed with hopes of seeing Charles again real soon.

Radiance was in a world of her own with Stephen. She couldn't believe that she agreed to marry a man she barely even knew. She thought she was in a fairytale that would never end. Radiance began thinking, *It's good to finally be happy after all of the hell I've been through with my mother and the heartache and pain I endured with Jermaine. Something good has got to happen.* Radiance instantly started thinking about Walter. She missed him so. She had not heard from him since he left with Miguel. "Damn! This is the longest I have been apart from him," Radiance whispered softly to herself.

Walter and Miguel got out of the taxi cab at the airport and headed towards the main entrance door of the terminal for their flight to California. Walter turned towards Miguel and asked, "Did my sister call me?" Miguel responded back, "No, she didn't and I'm surprised." Walter said, "Okay," and turned his head away in an attempt to hold back his tears. He didn't want to go to California and he really missed his sister. Walter whispered, "I hope that you haven't forgotten about me, Radiance." Miguel said, "Come on, little man," as he showed the security guard his identification and raced towards their airplane, because the flight attendant was calling last call for boarding the flight. Walter followed hesitantly and prayed that his sister would come and rescue him.

"Radiance, darling, are you okay?" Stephen asked, while holding her hand tightly, yet delicately. Radiance responded back, "Yes, Stephen, I'm okay! Just thinking, that's all." Stephen asked, "Are you sure that everything is okay?" Radiance responded while looking in his eyes, "I've never been better. Everything is just fine," although in her heart she knew that she was being untrue. She had a feeling that something was wrong, but she had no idea what it was. Instead, Radiance pretended to be enjoying herself with Stephen and she reminded him that she soon had to get back over to Charisma's house to tell her and her friends what her plans were and explain her mystery fiancé. Stephen smiled and replied, "That may not be a bad idea. Maybe you should call them and arrange a meeting. I will have my driver take you ladies to any place you want to go. The cost will be on me. My lovely bride-to-be should have all of the desires of her heart." Radiance giggled and exclaimed, "I love the way that sounds." Stephen handed Radiance his cell phone and instructed her to call her friends. Radiance exclaimed, "I will send a blanket text message instead!

I will tell them to meet me at the harbor at nine." While texting, she indicated that it was an emergency. Radiance leaned over on Stephen's shoulder and asked him, "Is this really happening?" Stephen responded, "Yes it is, because it was fate that brought us together."

I never imagined that there could be anyone like you. So sincere and true. You believe in following your heart, not always going with your mind. Never do I have to question your love for me. You express it over and over again. When we're together I feel like we entered the gates of heaven. Nothing but complete paradise whenever you're near. I know that I'm able to depend on you, you're so sincere. I feel nothing but good vibrations whenever you're near. Which makes it easy for me to trust and it feels so good.

Chapter Twenty-four: The End Is Near

⬦⬦

*C*HARLES WENT HOME AND STARTED GETTING prepared for that night. Everything had to be set up perfectly. There was no room for mistakes. He pulled out his all-black clothing and loaded his gun. "Thank God this is my last job!" Charles exclaimed. "I don't feel real good about this shit. Taking people's lives when they have family and children don't sit real good in my spirit. After tonight, I'm out of the game."

Constance heard her cell phone chirp in her jean pocket and saw a strange number. But when she looked at the text message, she saw that it was signed off at the end as *Radiance*. Constance looked at the message again and read it. She saw the request asking her to meet at the inner harbor at nine. "Emergency now? What the fuck is the emergency?!" Constance exclaimed, while shaking her head and placing her phone back in her pocket. "I will go for a minute," Constance said out loud, while she was sitting in the park trying to gather her thoughts from the series of messed up events that took place in her day. She started strategizing the perfect plan on how to get money with Eric, in her head.

Destiny called Unique and Unique picked up responding, "Talk to me." Destiny responded, "Unique, did you get a text from Radiance asking us to meet up with her?"

"Yeah! I got it," Unique responded. "The shit said that it was an emergency. I wonder what that is all about." Destiny responded, "The hell if I know. I'm looking forward to finding out. Do you need me to pick you up or meet you there?" Destiny asked. Unique responded, "I'm going to meet you there." Destiny exclaimed, "Okay! That sounds like a plan. By the way, did you speak to Constance to see what she is doing?" Complete silence overcame Unique and flashbacks came to her mind about her and Constance's up close and personal encounter. Unique was surprised that her friend enjoyed pussy like a delicious dessert, and she actually liked it, too. *What does that say about me?* Unique asked herself in her mind. "Hello!" Destiny yelled on the other end. "I asked you a question, girl. Did you talk to Constance?" Unique replied, "No, Destiny, I haven't seen her."

"Well, that's all you had to say," Destiny replied while laughing. "I will see you there, okay?" "Yeah, I will see you there," Unique replied. "See you at nine, Destiny. I'm hanging up the phone now." Destiny responded, "See you later, child. I'm about to get ready. You should do the same." Unique giggled and responded, "I'm on it."

Charisma received a text asking her to meet Radiance at the harbor at nine. Charisma giggled when she saw it and exclaimed, "This girl has me going out more than usual these days! I wonder what is so important that we have to meet up. She got me curious about what's going on or where she traveled to in the middle of the night, leaving me only a note. That little girl is too much for me." Charisma shook her head and continued laughing. "I can't wait to hear her dying emergency. Let me go and get myself ready."

Charles placed his gun down and went to the couch. He was tired but didn't want to go to sleep. He often had nightmares when he went to sleep. Charles remembered every face of each of his victims. He could hear their screams. It brought sadness to him when he thought about it. "Life's a bitch and then you die!" Charles said out loud. "I have a lot of explaining to do with God at the end of my crossroad here in life. I just hope He can forgive me. This is the only work I know how to do, but I know that karma is a bitch."

Constance was rolling dice with a few of the goons in the neighborhood. "Snake eyes!" one of the dudes yelled out.

"Man, that's some bullshit right there," Constance replied while looking at her watch. "I can't keep losing my money to you niggas. I'm going to play one more game with this tough ass twenty dollar bill, and then I'm out. I have to meet my homegirls in a few minutes."

Lamont went into his condo with his briefcase. He went into the office, opened it up, and started counting his money. He smiled and said, "It's rewarding being me. This street life is mine and once I take this nigga, Eric out, I will have more. Damn shame, though. He was a cool little nigga, but business is business."

Unique grabbed her keys and headed out the door to go to the inner harbor. She wanted to arrive earlier than everyone so that she could have some time to think about what went on with her and Constance. *Why was she still thinking about it and was it possible for her to like it? What the hell is wrong with me?* she wondered. *I got to get this shit under control and I have to do it quickly.*

Destiny sat inside the kitchen after reading the letter from Mr. Officer, and her heart began to beat faster and faster. She looked at the kitchen counter and had flashbacks of him touching her body in forbidden places and licking on her nipples in circular motions, causing them to rise and making them perk up instantly all over again. Her pussy began leaking like a running faucet. She closed her eyes and exclaimed, "I don't know why I feel the way that I do about this man, but it's like he has become a part of me and now I don't know how I'm going to function without him!" She then left the kitchen and headed towards her room so that she could get dressed to meet Radiance.

Unique arrived at the harbor and headed towards the carousel located in the center of the harbor, overlooking the water. Unique walked over towards it, paid the attendant, and decided to take a ride while she waited for her friends.

Constance yelled out, "Damn! I lost again. That's it. I'm out. I have to go meet my friends. It's been real, fellas. I just want to let you all know that you're some cheating bastards. I lost enough of my money!" The gentlemen yelled out in unison, "Don't punk out now, Constance; the fun is just getting started!" Constance chuckled and replied, "I'm not ever scared but I really have to go and meet my homegirls."

The end is here. No more obstacles or tests. Either I fall down or a natural success. No more misleading or confusion. I'm presently aware of my future. My destiny is right in front of me and everything is crystal clear. In between, I lost some friends and family. They don't understand the new me. Now everyone is into passing judgments on me. It's me against the world, facing this thing called life. No more living in paradise.

Chapter Twenty-five: Life's a Bitch

◇◇◇

*U*NIQUE GOT OFF THE CAROUSEL AND AS soon as she got off, she saw Constance sitting on the bench right in front of her. Unique's heart instantly dropped to the pit of her stomach when she saw Constance dressed in cornrows, baggy jeans, a tee-shirt, and a toothpick. Unique yelled out, "Constance, what's up with you dressing up like a dude? Are you all right?" Constance laughed, as she stood up, went over to Unique, and smacked her on her ass. "Everything is cool, cupcake. Don't worry your pretty head off about that." Unique yelled out, "Stop that shit! Constance, I don't feel comfortable with you touching my ass like that, so please just stop it." Constance ignored Unique's request, as she grabbed her by the hips and pulled her closer, kissing her delicately on the lips. Unique pushed her away and replied, "I said cut it out!" Constance chuckled and responded, "Cool. I will cut it out. But please tell me, did you think about the way I ate your pussy? I know I did, and I wouldn't mind doing it again." Unique exclaimed, "We can never do that again!"

"Do what?" Destiny asked, as she walked up on Constance and Unique. Destiny's eyes got big and her mouth dropped open when she looked at Constance's attire. "This is a joke, right?" Destiny asked. Constance responded, "No. This is who I am now. Either you bitches can accept it or leave it. The choice is yours." Destiny exclaimed, "How can we accept this?! You were a girl just the other day. Are you on your period or not feeling well, honey? Because I just don't get this shit!" Constance replied, "It's neither, Destiny. I told you, this is who I am." Destiny asked, "How does your fiancé feel about this?" Constance responded, "I have no fiancé. I called the shit off to become who I am right now. I have been this way for years." Destiny replied, "Something isn't right with this picture, but if you say this is who you want to be, then I will accept it. But know that I don't like it one bit. Does Radiance know about this strange shit you got going on?" Constance replied, "There is nothing strange about my sexuality. I will tell you once and I will not repeat myself again. Either you accept me for who I am or don't accept me at all. And, the answer to your question is, no, Destiny, Radiance has not seen my new look. I will tell her the same thing that I just told you. Take me for who I am or bounce."

Charisma appeared in the crowd and exclaimed, "Hello, ladies! It's nice seeing you all again. Are you guys all right? Who is your new friend? Hello, my name is Charisma. It's a pleasure to meet you. What would your name be?" Constance chuckled and replied, "My name would be Constance. It's so nice to meet you again." Charisma's mouth dropped open and she exclaimed, "I didn't recognize you at all!" Constance, you look a little different from the last time I saw you." Constance laughed and responded, "Yes, I know. This is the new me now and please don't ask why. I would rather not get into it. Just know that this is my own choice and nobody forced it upon me. This is just who I am from here on out." Charisma replied, "Okay, I understand," while thinking to herself, *this bitch has truly lost her mind. What happened to the nice girl that I met only a few days ago?*

The girls stopped what they were doing when they noticed a pearl white limousine pulling up not too far away from where they were standing. Destiny exclaimed, "Who the hell is that pulling up in that limousine?!" Not long after Destiny commented, she noticed Radiance coming out with a long, flowing dress with a split on the side of her leg. Destiny shook her head along with Unique. "Where is she going?" Charisma asked out loud, while turning around looking at Constance. "I don't know where she thinks she is going," Constance responded to Charisma, "and what's up with the dress? She looks like she is ready to walk the runway or something." Radiance got closer and yelled out, "Hey, divas! Thanks for making it out to hear my emergency." All of the ladies looked over at Radiance and they all asked, "So what's the emergency?" Radiance was distracted by Constance's appearance. She exclaimed, "Why the hell are you dressed up like a dude? Did I miss the memo or something? This shit isn't funny at all, C. I need an explanation for this foolishness you got going on right now." Constance replied, "Bitch, please! There is nothing foolish about my attire, so why don't you just tell us all why you have us out here in the middle of the inner harbor? What is the big emergency?" Radiance responded while holding out her hand, "I'm getting married and I wanted to share my news with you all. I hardly know Stephen but we both agreed that we believe that it is fate that brought us together. So let's walk over to the limousine and go to any place that our hearts desire and celebrate. My fiancé told me to enjoy myself and that me and my friends can do whatever we like and he will pay for it all. My man is a millionaire. I hit the goddamn jackpot!"

Charisma looked at Radiance and said, "That is a mighty fine ring, Radiance. But honey, what are you doing? You don't know this man by far and marriage is serious." Radiance rolled her eyes and responded, "I know that. I care for him and he is the one for me. It was love at first sight." Destiny exclaimed, "The hell with love! The nigga is rich! You can grow to love him." Unique replied, "I'm with Destiny on that one. Just do it!" Constance interrupted and said, "Don't do this shit! That nigga don't want you for real, Radiance. He is just trying to play you like a toy. You're shiny and new right now, but when the newness runs off he will just toss your ass to the side and get the newest shiny toy. This shit is just an illusion. Don't fall for the old smoke and mirrors trick. I know you're a little smarter than that." Radiance got angry and responded, "I love this man, Charisma and thanks, Destiny and Unique, for supporting my decision. As for you, Constance, who died and made your fat confused ass a relationship counselor? Could it be that maybe your ass is jealous of me? The only time you're happy is when it involves your own shit going the way that you want it! But I've got a news flash for your ass, bitch! It isn't always about you. Stop being selfish for once and embrace me instead of bringing my joy down." Constance walked over to Radiance, got in her face and replied, "I'm going to act like you didn't just say those things to me. If you were any other bitch, I would have your ass laid the fuck out on the ground right now as we speak. But, I love you like a sister so I'm going to let that shit slide!" Radiance exclaimed, "I meant every word of it, so if you're feeling like a frog, Constance, leap then! I'm not scared of your ass, so there you have it. React if you wish!" Charisma ran and stood in between Radiance and Constance, because she could feel the tension between them. Charisma said, "Now girls, play nice. Let's just go to the limousine and enjoy the rest of the night. This is a celebration right?" Constance responded, "Man, fuck that! This bitch must have lost her mind. She is living in fairytale land. Open up your big, hazel, beautiful eyes, princess, because life is no fairytale. On that note, I'm out. I have better things to do than spend my time here with you and all of your bullshit! And besides, it's taking everything in me not to floor your ass at this very moment." Constance looked down at her watch and bopped off. The other ladies remained speechless and watched. Radiance responded, "Well, now that she is gone, let's get this party started. I'm getting married, so everyone get happy."

Constance picked up her cell phone and called Eric. He answered, "What's good, Constance? Did you change your mind or something?" Constance responded, "Hell no! I'm ready for this shit! I was just hitting you up to let you know that I was on my way." Eric laughed on the other end and exclaimed, "Okay, then! Let's go and get this dirty money. I will see you in a few minutes."

Charles looked at himself in the mirror, dressed in all black. He said, "I'm all suited up for war. Forgive me Father because I have sinned, but with your help I know the devil won't win." Charles grabbed his gun and headed out the door.

Stephen was sitting outside near the pool, when the phone rang. When he picked up the phone, it was Lamont on the other end. Stephen yelled, "You got my fucking money, Lamont?!" "No, boss man, but I will after this last run tonight. I have to meet up with Charles to get it in about an hour. I will have it to you shortly after that." Stephen exclaimed, "You damn *site* better have my money before shit gets ugly!"

Constance was standing at Joe's sub shop and noticed Eric in a beat Buick. She walked over to him and got in the car. Eric greeted Constance with a handshake and said, "Listen, Constance, we are meeting someone at Druid Hill Park. They're getting this kilo of coke. We have to make a smooth transaction. Get this money and move as quickly as possible. All that you need to do is look out for anything that looks suspicious. Can you handle that? This is light shit. I want you to start off with simple shit before we start doing big boy shit." Constance replied, "This sounds simple enough. It's going to be like taking candy from a baby." Eric laughed and responded, "If that's the case, let's get it." They pulled off and headed toward the park.

Charles was already at the park, posted up waiting for Eric to arrive for the fake drug transaction. When Eric arrived, he noticed a blue car parked and a male sitting inside. He looked over at Constance and said, "There goes our man. Let's get this over with." Eric pulled up beside the car, got out, and headed towards the car. When Eric arrived at the car, he noticed that the man appeared to be homeless and terrified he yelled out, "Oh shit, Constance! I think we are being set up! Get in the driver's seat and let's ride out!" Constance had the music in the car playing. She turned down the music and yelled out, "What did you just say, Eric?"

"Get in the driver's seat and let's go!" Eric ran towards the car, only for a car to pull up next to him. It was Charles dressed in all black. He pulled out a gun and pointed it in Eric's direction. Constance yelled out, "Oh shit!" and went into the glove department and grabbed the gun.

She cracked the window down and began shooting at the car. "Oh shit!" Charles yelled out, as he turned around and started shooting at the car. Eric started running towards the car when he noticed Charles wasn't paying attention. Eric finally got in the car after hearing one last fire. He then responded, "Good looking out, Constance. Pull off." Eric was surprised when he didn't get a response. He shook Constance and when he pulled her towards him, he noticed that she was shot in her neck and she was dead. "Damn!" Eric yelled out, as he reached for the gun that was in Constance's hand. He started looking for the sharpshooter that just took his friend's life. At first he noticed nothing, but when he turned to the other side, he noticed that a gun was pointing in his face. The next thing he heard was, "Lights out, nigga." The masked man pulled back the trigger and ended Eric's life.

Charles walked back over towards the other car looking for the homeless man he paid to sit in the car, and noticed he was nowhere to be found. He went back to Eric's car, went in his pockets, and took his money and jewelry. He went over to Constance and went in her pockets, taking her money. He noticed her cell phone, so he grabbed it and the kilo of coke, and ran to his car. He pulled off quickly. There was no way he was going to risk getting caught. Charles called Lamont as soon as the coast was clear. Lamont picked up the phone and Charles replied, "The job is completed." Lamont commented, "Job well done. Meet me at the breakfast spot in one hour." Charles responded, "Sure thing, big homey."

Charles hung up the phone and started removing his all-black clothing, revealing his white tee-shirt underneath. He pulled up next to the river about five miles away from the murder scene and took off his pants, showing his sweat pants underneath. He put all of his items in a bag and threw it in the river. The guilt of killing more than one person consumed Charles's soul. He took Constance's phone and noticed that there was no password on the phone. He read the last text message from Radiance and responded to it, "Your friend was just killed." Charles pressed the send button and waited for it to go through. Then he threw it in the river, headed back towards his car, and pulled off to go meet Lamont.

Radiance laughed as she had the limousine driver drop her friends off after a fun-filled night in Canton. She found herself thinking about Constance and felt that an apology was due on her end. "I will call her in the morning to say that I'm sorry," Radiance whispered, as she waved goodbye to Destiny and Unique. "Next stop is to your house, Charisma!" Radiance exclaimed. "And just picture this, having your house back to yourself with no houseguest!" Charisma laughed and replied, "Well, for your information, I didn't mind my houseguest. She was all right with me." Radiance smiled and said, "I'm glad to hear that." Charisma looked over at Radiance and asked, "About this marriage thing...are you sure that this is what you want to do?" Radiance responded, "I have never been so sure of anything in my life. I believe in love at first sight. He is the one for me, Charisma. For once, my heart and mind agree."

Stephen heard his phone chirp and went to look at it. He noticed that it was a text for Radiance stating that her friend was dead. "What the hell is this," Stephen asked himself, "and how will I tell Radiance such a thing? Maybe it is a sick joke," Stephen whispered. His phone rang and he picked up. It was Lamont. "Hey, boss man, I have your money and I can bring it to you right now." Stephen responded, "Well, bring it here and make it quick. My fiancée will be arriving home shortly."

"No problem, boss. Consider it done. I will be there in about forty-five minutes."

"Make it quicker than that. Time is of the essence!" Stephen hung up and lit a cigar with a smirk on his face.

Radiance and Charisma continued laughing until the limousine stopped and they were interrupted by the driver as he said, "Madame, you are home."

"Thank you, sir," Charisma replied, as she reached over to Radiance and gave her a hug. "I love you, girl," Charisma said, as she exited the door and started walking to her apartment. She yelled out, "Call me, lady!"

Charles pulled up to the breakfast spot and decided to call Charisma. The phone rang a few times as Charisma entered her apartment. She heard her phone ring and raced towards it. "Hello," Charisma answered, out of breath. Charles laughed on the other end. "Why are you breathing so heavy? You sound like you just ran a marathon!" Charisma started blushing and replied, "I had to run to the phone. I just got in from hanging out with my girlfriends. How are you doing?" Charles responded, "I'm good. Just finishing up with work and I wanted to check with you to see if it was all right to come past and lay with you. I want to have some pillow talk with you about our future." Charisma laughed on the other end and said, "It is a bit late for pillow talk, but I could use the company, so come on over." Charles responded, "Thank you so much. I will see you in a few moments. Stay up for me or just unlock your door." Charisma said, "The door will be unlocked for you. See you soon." Charles replied, "See you soon," as he hung up the phone. When he hung up, he saw Lamont heading in his direction. He had two briefcases and he got in the car and handed Charles one of them. "A deal is a deal, partner. You are officially out the game. I'm a man of my word, so take this. Did you manage to get the coke, too?" Charles responded, "Yes, here it is," as he reached in the back seat and handed it to Lamont. Lamont smiled and responded, "I don't even need to check it. I know it's all here. You're one of my best workers and I'm happy and sad to see you go, but a deal is a deal. You're out of the game, but hit me up if you ever reconsider. *But*, take my advice and get out of the game. Go get a girl and have some kids or something, homey! I'm out. Be easy." Lamont got out of Charles's car and went back to his own. He pulled off and headed towards Stephen's house.

Unique arrived home with thoughts of Constance on her mind. She was concerned about her mental state with all that she had encountered. Unique thought that it would be a great idea to lay low from her friends for a little while until she was able to get herself together. Unique whispered, "Maybe a trip to see my dad would do me some good. Just for a few days. His wife is in Egypt for a month. I think I will book a trip to go and see him."

Destiny went inside her apartment and glanced back at the note from Mr. Officer. "I have to find him!" she exclaimed, as his image came to her mind. "I will find him again if it's the last thing that I do. It's linked to my destiny."

Jermaine was in his room packing. He would be leaving for basketball camp in less than a week and he wanted to make sure everything was squared away before he left to pursue his dream.

Ambiance grabbed her luggage at the baggage claim and yelled out, "Atlanta, you are not ready for me!" She attempted to call Virtue and got no response. She whispered, "Don't worry, dear heart, I will find you while I'm in this city." She put her shades on her eyes and waved down the taxi that was closest to her.

Walter and Miguel got out of the taxi and saw the sign in front of them that read, "Welcome to California." Miguel tapped Walter on the head and said, "Well, we're off to a fresh start in California. Get ready for an adventure that will never end. With you and I, this is our new beginning." Walter looked over at Miguel and responded, "Yeah, new beginnings." Walter thought about Radiance and felt that she abandoned him and no longer loved him. He thought to himself, *I'm never talking to her again. From now on, it's just me and Miguel.*

Lamont pulled up in front of Stephen's mansion and called his cell phone. Stephen responded, while sitting at the pool sipping on a glass of wine, "Are you here?" Lamont replied, "Yes, boss man, I'm out front."

"Perfect, don't move. I'm on my way." Stephen walked inside the house and headed to the hallway and down the stairs toward the door. When Stephen arrived at the door, Lamont was already waiting with a briefcase in his hand. "Here you go, boss!" Lamont exclaimed. "Here is the money and I have the kilo of coke in the car. I will make the run to New York in the morning. I will take my cut of the money and bring the rest back to you." Stephen responded, "Make sure you bring me my goddamn money promptly!" He then nodded at Lamont and said, "Have a good evening." The limousine driver pulled right up. The driver got out of the car and went to open the door for Radiance. Stephen started smiling brightly as she walked towards the stairs. He was thinking to himself, *How will I tell her about the sick text that I got on my phone without making her worried or upset?*

As Lamont headed back to his car, he paused and was mesmerized by Radiance's beauty. She even looked familiar to him. He went in his car after he saw his boss mugging him, but Lamont knew that he had to have her, even though she was a forbidden fruit. "Damn! She is beautiful!" Lamont whispered, as he watched her from the rearview mirror and pulled off. "I got to have her."

Radiance walked towards Stephen and greeted him with a tender kiss on the cheek. She exclaimed, "Who was that who just left here so late?!" Stephen smiled at Radiance and replied, "Oh, that's just an old friend stopping past to bring me my briefcase that I forgot over his house last week. I tell you, if my head wasn't attached to my body, I would lose that too. But enough of that, baby. Please come inside and relax. I have to talk to you about something." Radiance said, "Okay," as she sat down and turned on the television to catch the last glimpse of the news. "Talk to me, baby. What do you want to talk about?" Stephen sat next to her and pulled out his cell phone. He entered his password, handed the phone to Radiance, and told her to read the latest text message. Radiance took the cell phone from Stephen and replied, "Okay, I will take a look at the text message, but I don't see where this is leading." Radiance looked at the screen and saw Constance's number and a text message saying, "Your friend is dead." Radiance turned around and yelled out while laughing, "There truly are some sick people in the world. Who sends messages like this?" She looked at Stephen and replied, "That's just my girlfriend Constance playing around. We had an argument earlier and this is her way of getting me to call her back. I will just call her back. She is so crazy. Hold on, baby, just sit back and watch this."

Radiance called Constance's cell phone and it went straight to voice-mail. Stephen asked, "Did she respond?" Radiance exclaimed, "No, she didn't! She must be on the other line. Let me try again." Radiance called for a second time and then a third. All calls went straight to voicemail. "Her phone is just on the charger. I will call her in the morning." Stephen looked over at Radiance and asked was she sure. Radiance replied, "Of course I'm sure, baby. Let's not talk about this anymore. I want you to just stay on that couch just the way you are so that I can make love to you properly. I have wanted to do this all day." Stephen giggled and responded, "I like the way that sounds. Bring your sexy ass over here."

Radiance stood up and unfastened her dress, allowing it to hit the floor. She walked over to Stephen with nothing but her boy shorts and heels on. She sat on his lap and started nibbling on his ear and rubbing his hair. Stephen started licking Radiance's breast like ripe fruit and the passion started to fill the air, as they fondled each other. Suddenly, a news flash came up on the screen that said, "YOUNG WOMAN FOUND DEAD IN DRUID HILL PARK. Victim has been identified as Constance Franks. Authorities are calling this case a double homicide, because a young man by the name of Eric Dickerson has been identified as dead on arrival. Authorities are trying to find the victims' murderer. If you have any information on this, please call your local police department...more news to come on this story. Stay posted."

Radiance's heart fell to the pit of her stomach when she saw Eric's and Constance's faces plastered on the television screen. She fell to the floor and began screaming and crying out loud. She cried, "Dear God, no! Please tell me that this isn't so! Please don't take my friends away from me. What sick bastard would be capable of doing such a cruel thing?" Stephen tried to hold Radiance, only to get pushed away and yelled at. "LEAVE ME ALONE," Radiance yelled from the top of her lungs. "Someone is going to pay for this!" Radiance started thinking about the dumb argument that she had with Constance earlier and she started having flashbacks of all of the good times they shared together.

She then thought about Eric and how he was there for her in her time of need when nobody else was there. He had become a good friend in only a short period of time. "I'm going to seek revenge on whoever did this, if it's the last thing I do!" Radiance yelled out loudly. She was full of rage and had never felt such anger and frustration in all her life. She declared war on the person who had caused her so much pain in such a little bit of time.

To Be Continued...

◇◇◇

DIAMONDZ IN A ROUGH: LIFE'S NO FAIRYTALE

Darkness has taken over me. Completely nothing, but complete sadness lies within. Nothing to look forward to. It's hell on earth. Everyone is a villain in this fairytale. No one is to be trusted. No longer does anyone possess light. Everyone is a suspect. My heart is dark and my emotions are cold. I feel like everyone is out to steal my soul. Everything seems like a mystery, but deep down inside, a ray of light still wants to surface. I find myself wanting to protect the ones that are close to me. I already lost many friends during this journey. Within a short period of time, I have gathered many enemies, I have been through many challenges, and faced much suffering, but still I shine like a diamond in a rough.